FIREBOUND

Fireborn Series Book Four

Vanessa Ricci-Thode

Thodestool Fiction

Publisher: Vanessa Ricci-Thode
Editors: Kristopher Mielke, Chelle Parker
Cover Designed by GetCovers

Library and Archives Canada Cataloguing in Publication

Print ISBN 978-1-7388450-6-4
Ebook ISBN 978-1-7388450-7-1

www.thodestool.ca

This is a first edition of *Firebound*.

For all the queer kids who just needed someone to understand and accept.

And in fond memory of Denise Penney and Brian Thode.
Fuck cancer.

AUTHOR'S NOTE

Hello reader! This is the fourth book of the Fireborn series. If you're skipping the previous books or it's been a while, below is a spoiler-filled synopsis to get you caught up or to act as a refresher! But this book follows *Fireborn*, book 3, more closely than the others, and I recommend not skipping that one. Also note that Canadian spelling is being used throughout the book.

Previously in the Fireborn Series

Dragon Whisperer

Dionelle Joasera was born immune to fire. After moving to her new husband's farm, she catches the attention of the ruling nobles in the city. Forced into the position of dragon whisperer by the cruel Lord Draxli and Lady Karth Dunham, Dionelle is torn between keeping the peace in her kingdom and keeping her husband, Reiser's, desire to keep her safe from controlling her. Tension mounts between the newlyweds as Dionelle grows to love her job and the dragons she works with, exacerbated by her sister's jealous rage.

Then Dionelle fails to come home from her final apprenticing lesson. Discovering her mentor has been murdered, Reiser is pulled into the mystery of her disappearance and the snare of politics surrounding Pasdale's corrupt ruling nobles.

Reiser has no choice but to work with the dragons to find his wife, going against the Dunhams' wishes as they try to write Dionelle off for dead so they can select a new dragon whisperer. The dragons, however, will not be lied to—particularly the black dragoness who leads the local blaze and has grown fond of Dionelle. Enlisting Dionelle's best friend, a dragon scholar named Ondias, and finding allyship from two court wizards, Zev and Nandara, Reiser discovers that Dionelle's sister has manipulated a powerful wizard into murdering her mentor and banishing Dionelle to the fire realm. Dionelle's unique pyromantic nature is due to being part fire demon, allowing her to survive the fire realm. Taken by fire demons, Dionelle is trapped in their realm behind a wall of deceit exploiting the troubles in her life.

Meanwhile, the presence of a human in the fire realm is throwing all of the elements off balance, and the world is slowly tearing itself apart with wild weather swings and dangerous earthquakes.

In a desperate bid to save Dionelle and the world, Reiser becomes the first human to visit the dragon city—a towering structure of diamond and obsidian suspended over a valley—where he is enchanted to be fireproof and sent to the fire realm. He discovers Dionelle is alive and well—and pregnant with his child. He uses the tenuous bond the pair forged before their separation to bring her home again. The elements stabilize, and Dionelle and Ondias are treated with a trip to the dragon city when Reiser is brought back there to remove the dragons' enchantment.

The story ends with the Dunhams removed from power: Draxli is exiled and Karth is executed. Dionelle's sister is imprisoned in a distant sanitorium. The king's cousin, Lady Zyx, is installed as the new ruler of Pasdale and peace returns to the land.

Trueflame

Neesha Joasera, Dionelle's nearly adult daughter, is determined to be as unlike her mother as possible, despite also being part fire demon. She's a talented pyromancer intent on gaining entrance to the Wizards Guild and shunning every attempt to bridle her with marriage. An unplanned pregnancy throws a wrench in her plans, leaving her with an impossible deadline to pass her Guild exams before motherhood sidelines her.

And still her parents are desperately trying to get her married, with their most recent attempts concentrated on a recently widowed farmer named Stone.

Neesha bristles against the new attempts to control her life, even as she alienates herself from her family. But Dionelle needs Neesha to tame her wild ways because Draxli Dunham has allied himself with a powerful aquamancer named Loch and a handful of traitor dragons, and he is coming to reclaim Pasdale and satisfy his vendetta against the Joasera family.

Terrified, Neesha works with Dionelle and the dragons to mount a defence against Draxli's attack. Neesha is permitted temporary entrance into the Guild in order to use her magic to defend Pasdale. She uses her power and the help of demons to open a portal to the fire realm and wield trueflame against the flood Loch has made for Draxli. She vaporizes the waters, saving Pasdale.

But her allies quickly learn that Draxli's attack on Pasdale was a distraction—his real target has been the dragon city. They race to defend it, but do not get there in time, staging only the beginning of a defence before the waters wash away one of the support columns and the dragon city falls.

In the depths of mourning, Neesha convinces her mother and the other wizards that the only way to win is for her to go to the fire realm so they can capitalize on the destabilized elements and use any demons and trueflame she can send back. The plan works, but Neesha is unable to control the fire demons, who run wild while Neesha goes into labour in the dragon chamber of the Wizards Guild. Her daughter, who she names Mita, is fireborn like Neesha and Dionelle.

Now that Neesha's risks no longer endanger Mita directly, she uses the fire realm again to rush to Pasdale, commanding dragons, demons, and trueflame until she and the black dragoness finally push back Draxli's forces and end him for good. But Neesha's spirit is lost to the flame. She is preserved in a magical coma in the remnants of the dragon city, while Dionelle has gone silent in her mourning.

Fireborn

Mita Joasera, aka Spark, lives with her grandparents, Reiser and Dionelle, as well as her uncle and cousin. Spark is the most powerful fireborn yet, able to pull fire out of the air. Spark's family is outcast for supporting the dragon population slowly being enslaved to drive industry. As tensions mount, Nandara, who is mentoring Spark just as she did Neesha, suddenly leaves Pasdale. And just in time, because vicious aquamancer Loch, now Pasdale's magistrate, sends a blaze of enslaved dragons to their homestead. Spark's home is destroyed and her family murdered while she watches helplessly. Dionelle forces Spark to run.

Dionelle's longtime friend, the black dragoness, scoops Spark from the foothills and carries her away from the danger while the loss of her family replays in her mind. Spark and her dog, Shadow, make the long journey with the dragoness to the dragon city, which is still recovering from Loch's attack.

In the valley beneath this city lies a small human settlement filled with dragon supporters. Here, Spark connects with Ondias, and finds Nandara and her family have taken refuge here. But Nandara is distant, and Ondias is no longer the bright, cheery companion from the stories Spark has heard of her.

Lonely Spark meets Stone, who reveals that Neesha is not dead, as Spark was led to believe. The magic of the dragon city sustains Neesha's still-living body. Spark is horrified and enraged by the revelation.

Slowly, Spark befriends the black dragoness, who she calls Abyss. Spark also dusts off the village's old forge to become the resident blacksmith. She eventually befriends some of the other teens in the village, including Stone's daughter, Ember, and Nandara's grandson, Jatt. Spark resumes mentorship with Nandara and learns more about dragons from Ondias. All the while, proximity to Ember sets Spark's pulse racing; a deep crush on the older girl flourishes alongside their friendship.

Spark learns that Nanny Di survived and is now the magistrate's prisoner. Driven by desperation, Spark begins experimenting with the dangerous magic that cost Neesha: demon possession. Spark builds all manner of tools and weapons to help the village and the dragons, including a sling to make it easier for Abyss to carry her in flight, with the hope of eventually freeing her grandmother. While testing the sling, Spark and Abyss narrowly escape the magistrate's mysterious ice dragons.

Spark crafts armour using demon magic and the hide of a long-dead dragon, a banned practice. When Spark learns that the ice dragons are on their way back, she plots with Abyss. But Abyss is captured and the Dragoness Superior is killed by the ice dragons. The wild dragons and their human allies are in disarray.

Spark bundles up the cumbersome gear and disappears on foot. Desperate, she intends to walk to Abyss, if that's what it takes. But several dragons with human riders in slings come to her aid. Jatt and Nandara are among them. Led by Abyss's mate, who carries Spark in a sling, they set off to rescue Abyss.

The battle is intense, but even with Spark's many gadgets, they can't free Abyss. Spark not only summons a fire demon to attack her enemies, she draws power straight from the fire realm by opening a dangerous portal, washing herself, Abyss, and the ice dragons with fire.

One of the ice dragons is killed and the others injured, while Abyss is freed.

Despite success, a budding romance with Ember, and building a new family among her friends and allies in the dragon city, Spark aches to revive her mother and free her grandmother.

Firebound content warnings: abuse and torture (implied), bones (human), burns, death by fire, demon possession, imprisonment, PTSD, the dog lives

Heat level: medium

PROLOGUE

It was the perfect day to go flying—bright and clear with strong thermals—and Void Behind the Stars struggled to hold her patience as the small human spidered across her shoulders, checking the new handholds on the dragon-riding contraption laboriously strapped to her body. She supposed Spark wasn't actually small as far as humans went, but didn't know how else to think of her when she easily fit in Void Behind the Stars's hand.

The carrier's rigging grew more elaborate with the girl's desperation. She'd already checked the handholds once today and likely a dozen times before meeting with Void Behind the Stars. It always felt excessive, like no amount of checking could be enough. They'd come to the unspoken agreement that the accident over the winter, caused by a lack of caution, would remain unspoken. It was certainly the worst humiliation Void Behind the Stars had suffered, left in the nursery afterward through her recovery like some misbegotten hatchling, able to do little more than lie among the eggs, including her own two, and the comforting fires keeping them warm.

Spark growled. "This just isn't working."

Void Behind the Stars turned her attention away from the dazzling light display of sunshine off the city to watch Spark fiddle with the tiny apparatus on the end of the tether meant to keep the human from falling to her doom. The contraption appeared to work perfectly. Unlike her last attempt—a simple hook that had cast her out into the skies the first time

Void Behind the Stars had changed course during flight—the tether was securely attached to the handholds.

"It's too slow." Spark got the contraption detached and tossed it, a long arc to the grass below. She rubbed her hands over her face. "I might as well not leave the sling at all."

While Void Behind the Stars was not used to the sensation of being crawled on, she conceded that it would be a clear benefit for Spark to have freedom of movement during a battle.

The other dragons believed she was debasing herself by submitting to the girl's machinations. (Fools, the whole lot of them.) There were other dragons, four blazes in total, with close relationships to humans, as Void Behind the Stars had with the fireborn Joasera women. These dragons and humans fought together as one, with similar rigging that enhanced their battle prowess. A wizard's sharp eyes and sharper spells proved invaluable in battle. Void Behind the Stars and her mate, Merciless Winter Sky, worked seamlessly together, rarely leaving the other exposed, but they had been outnumbered as of late.

It would, of course, be lovely if it didn't matter whether the girl had sharp eyes and sharp spells. If there was no impending threat, no stolen dragon eggs, no imprisoned family and friends. Long years defined by many troubles left most dragons with little time to fly for pleasure—for the enjoyment of a cold wind over their scales and a warm lift under their wings, of the wisp of clouds and the hard light of the sun.

It was worse now. Loch knew with certainty that Spark was alive and a threat. And worst of all, she had embarrassed him.

The Superiors agreed that an attack by Loch was inevitable, likely before winter, when the snows closed the passes and froze the water he loved to menace them with. So every last dragon in the valley not busy caring for young was out scouting or hunting. Void Behind the Stars and Merciless Winter Sky got a small measure of reprieve by being favoured by the fireborn girl. Their success developing dragon armour earlier in the year meant Void Behind the Stars and her mate had more time to remain in the valley to assist her.

And when they did leave, they did as much scavenging as scouting or hunting, clawing through abandoned human settlements searching for scraps of metal for Spark to build new weapons and more rigging. Void

Behind the Stars ferried Spark in the supply wagon to trade for metal every time a new caravan came to the plains in the south.

About a moon cycle ago, the girl had tentatively asked Void Behind the Stars whether the sparkling red mountains surrounding them had ore that might be suitable to her needs. Void Behind the Stars had held her anger then, and wished someone who knew the depth of the girl's offence had been around to see it.

"These mountains are sacred," she had said gravely.

Spark had not brought it up again.

Though with distance and time, Void Behind the Stars conceded that ore from these mountains would make the most dazzling weaponry. Cursed and blasphemous weaponry, but dazzling all the same.

It was bad enough wearing the skin of her dear friend, the former Dragoness Superior Obliterating Icefield, as armour. Even worse that she was helping the Superiors convince others to donate their flesh after they returned to the starbursts in the sky upon their deaths.

"Would it be okay..." Spark began and hesitated, standing on Void Behind the Stars's shoulder near the base of her neck. "Would it be okay if I stand on your head?"

Void Behind the Stars once again begged for an understanding witness to her patience. She did not immediately flick the insolent little beast off her shoulder. In fact, she didn't respond at all. Void Behind the Stars had already abandoned all sense of dignity by agreeing to the carrier, and so she continued staring at the city arching overhead, its supports spanning the valley to suspend it in the sky, casting pinpricks of light across the drab human residences and the glittering mountains alike.

"Thank you, Mistress," Spark whispered.

While Spark was still terrible at anticipating when she was about to ask something unbearably rude, she was at least getting better at realizing when she'd done so.

While the girl's clambering about Void Behind the Stars's back tickled and itched, her journey up Void Behind the Stars's neck to the spot between her vast horns—more than twice the girl's height—was particularly disconcerting. Spark stood there for only a moment before Void Behind the Stars looked up, inadvertently tilting her head to one side as if that would give her a better view.

Spark shrieked as she fell away, arms pinwheeling to catch onto something.

Void Behind the Stars easily caught her and set her back on one shoulder. Spark muttered her thanks and continued her inspection, a little spider-puppy crawling around and dangling off Void Behind the Stars's side, up and down the handholds, hanging her entire weight off of each one and swinging to truly test their stability.

Like most humans, Spark had such clever little hands to go with her sharp spells and sharp eyes. And it was a true failing of so many of the other dragons to not see that about humans. To not envision the opportunities found in cooperation. They saw humanity's capacity for art, of course, but there were less frivolous reasons to keep the species around.

Many of Spark's tools were foolish, but some of them had already saved dragon lives.

Spark walked the length of Void Behind the Stars's back and turned around, muttering to herself, asking questions she didn't expect Void Behind the Stars to answer. Calculations for expanding the rigging, it sounded like. She nattered frequently—nearly constantly—and the grief driving it was what stayed Void Behind the Stars's frustration with the girl.

Void Behind the Stars knew what Spark had lost. What they'd both lost.

Void Behind the Stars's gaze shifted to the glimmering diamond support column in the west where Neesha dreamed and didn't age, sustained by magic Void Behind the Stars was still learning.

Dionelle hadn't spoken in so many years, and Spark was used to working in silences filled only by her own voice. Void Behind the Stars wondered, not for the first time, what the family would have looked like whole. What banter and arguments and brilliance had the world lost?

It was hard not to dwell on what three fireborn women working together could have accomplished and all the good they could have done. It would have been simple for them to assist the dragons in storming Pasdale and liberating their kin. To rescue the stolen eggs, like the one Void Behind the Stars missed so acutely. Of course, Dionelle was as much Loch's prisoner as Void Behind the Stars's egg.

Spark must have asked something she'd evidently expected an answer to, because she repeated herself.

"Abyss? How much can you carry? Easily, I mean?"

Void Behind the Stars turned her head to face the girl where she stood between her wings.

"Void Behind the Stars," the dragon corrected.

Spark stopped whatever mental calculations she'd been doing and stood up, blinking a lot and staring.

"I'm sorry, what?"

"That is my dragon name. You asked for it once."

"Oh." Spark continued to blink at her. "Would you like me to call you that instead?"

"Abyss is acceptable. A nickname."

Spark gave an amused snort, walking toward Void Behind the Stars's front. "Would you tell Ondias that?"

"Ondias has not asked."

Spark looked at her so fast she nearly slipped. "Wait, gossip queen and control freak Ondias, greatest dragon scholar of all time, has never asked you your name?"

"Scholars believe our names are sacred, not to be shared."

"Are they?" Spark's eyes widened the way they had after she'd asked about mining the Red Mountains.

"No. Humans never ask."

Spark narrowed her eyes. "You could just tell her."

"Then what secrets would we keep?"

Spark laughed and harmlessly tossed a playful fireball at Void Behind the Stars's face before undoing the buckles and clasps on the rigging, freeing Void Behind the Stars from her duty for the moment, though preparations never truly ceased.

Battle would find them soon.

CHAPTER ONE

A dragon roared overhead, rattling the stone house, and Spark dropped the spearhead she'd been working on. It clattered to the floor while her limbs all went cold and janky, urging her to run fast enough to keep up with her heart rate. She staggered toward the door, gaze darting everywhere and nowhere while memories of the battle in Pasdale and Pappy's screams echoed in her mind. Her dog, Shadow, yipped at her before leaning against her legs. She squeezed her eyes shut and breathed a deep ragged breath. Then another.

The racket had only been a greeting to the returning scouting party.

A year in the dragon city and even *the dog*—the very same one who had made Abyss and Spark walk through the forest for two days because he was too afraid to be picked up for them to fly—didn't get rattled by the noise anymore. Why couldn't Spark get used to it?

Even learning to tell the different sorts of cacophony apart didn't make it any easier to ignore, especially not when any cry from the dragons could be a battle cry.

Need to be ready.

Spark picked up the spearhead and set it next to her tools spread across the worktable. She sighed.

Out the window, the red mountains glittered like rubies in the morning light. And while Spark hadn't meant for it, the window had a clear view of the western diamond support column where it came down out of the sky to meet the ridge, casting prisms of light around the valley. It was too far away to actually see Neesha trapped inside that column, but Spark knew she was there.

Shadow nudged her leg and whined. He was a shaggy, pointy-eared, black and white fireswift shepherd with nothing to herd. Maybe she should barter for some chickens for him to manage?

"Right, yes. Time to stop woolgathering and get to work. Can't help her if I don't find some answers."

Shadow, of course, had no notion that Spark even had a mother; he just wanted outside to do his business and go steal scraps from the apprentice's mess tent, like Spark didn't feed him at all. Poor aggrieved creature who had never been fed a single meal in his life.

To be fair to Shadow, the apprentices always had bacon. They were always coming and going from the valley, off on whatever missions their trades sent them on, and coming back with new supplies, usually meat of some kind. Usually bacon.

Spark closed the door behind the dog and sighed. She stuck her hands into the cold coals to ignite them—not so much to work with the fire but for a source of warmth she didn't have to think about maintaining. The days were warm enough, but mornings now held a chill as they barrelled toward autumn and Spark's seventeenth birthday. She'd still had a proper family on her sixteenth. Sometimes remembering that day brought her comfort, but today it only made the emptiness ache.

The emptiness also echoed. It felt like every move Spark made in her new not-quite-house rattled off the walls. Of course, the only soft thing she had was her bed, in her room tucked away in one corner between the kitchen and the forge. The rooms she currently lived in stretched along one side of the house while the not-quite-complete studio stretched along another, all of it made out of the magnificent ruby-hued stone of the mountains.

The studio was for Jatt and Ember, and would have big bright windows, airy and roomy so they would both have a space to work their crafts, instead of being crammed into corners with storage cupboards encroaching like they had been in the little shack she'd first called home.

The idea was that she would eventually finish the second floor, which would hold bedrooms with space for Neesha and Nanny and maybe a friend or two—though she tried not to think too much about that or her head started to spin. And then she could give up her room on the main floor and have some more space. But right now, there were only stairs to get up there and a south-facing wall.

The best part about moving her home and forge to the edge of town like this was that she got far fewer nosy visitors poking around and could use magic the way she liked without having to worry about judgement. Of course, there were plenty of rumours after she'd saved Abyss, but only a handful of people knew the extent of her powers.

Or at least as much as she knew herself.

Nandara was off at the Guild right now—and due back within the week—to talk with the heads of the order and the Grand Chancellor to get a better idea of how Spark could gain more control over the talents she knew about and maybe discover some hidden ones.

More than anything, Spark hoped Nandara came back with something that would help Neesha. Or Nanny Di. Though helping one would certainly help the other. Nanny might have some ideas, given what Spark and Nandara had learned, on how to help Neesha. And if they helped Neesha first, two powerful fireborn women would absolutely be able to rescue the third.

Spark's hand drifted to lie flat over her chest where her grandmother's pendant hung beneath her clothes. She sighed and picked up the spearhead again. She tried to draw a curtain of warmth across the lonely echoes by summoning memories of the farmhouse she'd grown up in, full of family.

Sometimes it worked.

Today, the clatter of metal resounded more loudly than it should have, so that Spark wondered if maybe her next big trade should be for so many piles of fabric to hang from every corner and drape the room to insulate against the noise. Ember would love it.

Spark sighed again and took hold of the metal, focusing on it, the magic rushing hot through her bones and out her hands to turn it into slag she could reshape, first clumsily by banging with her palms and then refining with her hammer. The pyromancy cooled the temperature of the room, not quite uncomfortably, and that was fine. The fullness of the morning air had promised another hot day, one of the last before the winter winds came howling down out of the craggy peaks.

But she had a season before she really had to worry about snow.

Spark finished the spearhead and set it aside with the growing pile, which she still needed to temper for it to be of any use against a dragon.

She glanced out all three windows, worried she'd somehow find an angry dragon there. They knew what she was doing, and that it was to help protect them. It didn't make the spot between her shoulder blades itch less with the need to draw the curtains.

Instead, she picked out another scrap of metal and went through the process all over again.

The itch didn't go away, so a knock on the door startled her so badly that she nearly incinerated the new spearhead with a surge of pyromancy.

Ondias pushed her way into the room without bothering to wait for Spark to answer the knock, and Spark suppressed the urge to sigh. She really needed to get locks on the doors.

"Thought I'd find you here," Ondias said, like she'd solved some kind of riddle, hands on her plump hips, muddy hazel eyes set in a permanent scowl and her greying red hair pulled back into a practical braid.

"Where else would I be?"

"Exactly. Don't you want some fresh air? When was the last time you studied?"

"Studied for what?"

If Ondias brought up any nonsense about taking her Guild exams *now*, Spark would light her on fire. She really wished it was Ondias who had gone to the Guild instead of Nandara. Spark's mentor had a way of tempering Ondias and smoothing things over whenever Spark inevitably got into an argument with her.

"A wizard of your power should always be studying." Ondias gave her a withering look. "Have you learned anything new since the battle?"

Ondias knew full well that Spark hadn't. And Ondias knew why. It was simply too dangerous for Spark to work with demon possession and fire portals. Gods, she wanted to. Didn't want to look at another spear or piece of armour or spend another second alone in this giant unfinished house.

But she needed information, or she'd end up ensconced in diamond right alongside her mother. And Ondias had spent the majority of the last year insisting every move Spark made would result in just that.

"You have something in mind?" Spark tried to keep her tone neutral, still working on the new spearhead in the hope Ondias would take the hint.

"I've been going through old records, and Nandara is bringing me copies of more, about your grandmother and what little we understand of what happened to your mother—the accounts of how it all affected the dragons. I want you to work with me on that. With the black dragoness in conjunction with the other dragons. It's clear their power changed, that more than their voices were weakened when we lost your mother."

"Is this about that weird white egg Abyss has?"

"In part, yes. Those eggs will hatch soon enough and I think we should understand more before they do."

"Is there something wrong?"

Ondias let out a long, weary breath. "Things have been wrong since the day Draxli's forces brought down this city."

Spark held her breath to keep from snapping and waited for Ondias to get to the less obvious answer.

"There's no way it's a coincidence that the dragon closest to your family has a fireborn-coloured egg after we lose your fireborn mother to..." Ondias gestured vaguely. "...Wherever."

Spark patted the spear into approximate shape and then stopped, looking right at Ondias. "I want to wake her up. Nandara agrees it's the best way to get a lot of the answers we're looking for. That's the only thing I plan on studying until one or both of my remaining family members are in this house where they belong."

Ondias cast a reflexive glance around and then fixed Spark with the same pitying look she always did when Spark talked about rebuilding her family.

"You've got a family here already." It was probably the gentlest thing Ondias had said since Spark had first arrived in the valley.

"Yes, but also no. It's not really the same—you know that."

Spark bit down and stilled before her traitor mouth set off yet another argument, but this time both of them startled when the front door clattered open and Ember called from down the hall.

"Honestly, Spark, you have got to—oh." She drew up short when she came in and saw Spark and Ondias facing off across the anvil.

Shadow came prancing in behind her.

"Um."

Ondias gave them both a brittle smile. "When Nandara gets back, we're going to get to work," she said to Spark, and then let herself out.

"Sorry?" Ember took a tentative step farther into the room.

"Don't be. You got rid of her and she wasn't interested in saying anything helpful."

"Ah, yes. I'm sure she's got to head off and go be the queen of dumptown some more."

Ember's brown eyes glittered as a laugh burbled out of Spark.

"It's not so much a dump these days," Spark said.

"Well, that's more on you than anyone. Maybe *you* should be queen of dumptown."

"Okay, but only if we rename it."

"Why hasn't this place got a name?"

Spark shrugged. "You're the one who's always lived here."

"But your Nan started the place."

Spark nodded but didn't really want to keep the banter going in that particular direction. Nanny should have given the place a name.

"I wonder what the dragons call this place," Spark said.

"Oh, you should ask Abyss and then we can rename dumptown! Ondias will love that."

Spark chuckled. She pulled the remaining heat out of her lumpy not-quite spearhead and set it aside. Ember came closer and laid her hand over Spark's, even her light brown skin so much darker than Spark's bone white. Spark's breath stilled, a tingle running down her body.

She lifted her gaze slowly to meet Ember's. The other girl was tall, but not quite as tall as Spark, and she had a similarly strong build from helping on her father's farm, though her body was also round with generous curves in a way that Spark's was not. Ember's dark eyes watched her intensely, making Spark's heartbeat drum away at her chest.

Ember took a step around the side of the anvil and leaned in closer. Spark felt a rush of warmth that made Spark's pyromancy feel like a chill as she leaned to meet Ember, the lightest touch of their bodies electrifying the room even before their lips met.

They parted slowly, Spark keeping her eyes closed a beat to savour it, feeling melty and like maybe things would be okay. But when she opened her eyes, Ember gave her a curious look.

"Spark, have I done something wrong?"

Spark stood up straighter. Blinked. "What? You chased Ondias off, so really I'm in your debt for just about all eternity."

Ember gave her a playful look, but her expression settled in a pout. She absently traced a finger over the back of Spark's hand, but the usual sparkle faded from her gaze.

"No, I mean with us," Ember said. "Did I do something wrong? It's like you're behind a wall, and I know you're there, but there's no door. I can't access you."

"I'm just busy. You've been busy too. Harvest and all that. I wish I could help, but..."

"You're building your dream home, I know."

Spark opened her mouth to point out it was *their* dream home, but something in Ember's tone raised an alarm, so she only blinked some more. Ember was doing that thing where she never quite said what she meant. Something about the house bothered her? Spark didn't know what to do with that. Or what exactly the problem might be. The old forge had gotten too crowded; even the new workshop was too busy. Too many other people, and not enough space for her and Ember and Jatt to just be... whatever it was they were.

Jatt and Ember had been the ones complaining about the cramped space in Spark's old home, and they'd been enthusiastic when she'd started talking about a bigger space that could be theirs. But Jatt was always with his mentor, always some reason he never came out to the new place. He said it was because he had so much to catch up on now that his broken arm had healed.

Neither of them offered much help. Spark didn't know what they could do, since she mostly used magic to raise the place. She'd used terramancy to create a solid, level foundation and low walls from the dark grey bedrock, and the rest of the structure had been cobbled together using pyromancy to fuse ruby-coloured blocks.

Was it because the studio wasn't finished yet? She was close, but she needed to get at least one bedroom upstairs finished. It wouldn't be ideal for Neesha and Nanny to share, but better than nothing—and better than the two of them having to find space to sleep in Ondias's increasingly heaping trash heap.

"Why don't we get your table out of the old place and set it up in here for now?" Spark suggested. "It's still more space than before, and I'll have the studio done before winter, I promise."

"Mmm. Maybe." Ember wasn't even looking at her.

Spark opened her mouth to plead with Ember to say what she meant and ask for what she wanted, but a crash from above rattled the entire building. Spark's mind went entirely blank as the fire flared in the forge and she was flooded with visions of Loch's dragons toppling the last proper home she'd had.

The sounds followed, the way Pappy had gone silent.

And then Ember's warm hands gripped her shoulders, and she stood safely back in her forge.

Ember held her gaze and then nodded toward one of the windows. There was nothing to see. Blacker than the deepest depths of night. Only a void where a view of the valley should be.

"Oh." Spark shook herself. "It must be Abyss with a new delivery of stones for upstairs."

"Right." Ember's tone was flat.

Spark desperately wished she knew what, exactly, Ember was upset about. "Do you want to come up and say hi? You can ask her about renaming dumptown."

The ghost of a smile flickered at the corners of Ember's mouth, but she shook her head, patted Shadow behind the ears, and headed to the front door.

She stopped in the front hall and turned to Spark. "Some things are worth taking risks for. But you need to decide which things are worth which risks."

Spark was caught between begging to know what in all the stars in the sky Ember was talking about and pointing out that Spark's life had become one unending risk ever since Loch had tried to wipe out her entire family. And before her brain could pick either or something entirely different, Ember left.

Spark looked at the dog. She wished he could speak. Maybe he'd have answers.

"What are you doing back so early?"

Shadow barked and pawed at the door.

"Yes, fine, but maybe try to talk some sense into Ember while you're at it."

Dog adequately released, Spark dashed up the stairs, pushing aside the tarp at the top to find that Abyss had, indeed, dumped the travel wagon's load of red stone across what was currently the roof but would soon be the floor of a bedroom. Abyss stood next to the house, looming over it, with her head lowered enough to be level with where Spark stood.

Spark gave the dragoness a proper greeting, something she tried to do whenever Abyss helped her. In return, Abyss nodded her head in the vaguest semblance of a bow.

"And how might I repay such a debt?" Spark asked.

"City." Abyss gestured with her head to the dazzling great structure.

"Now?"

Abyss shook her head.

"I'm here whenever you need me." It wasn't like she had anywhere to go or much of anything she wanted to do.

"Sundown."

"Yes, all right. I'll meet you back up here."

Abyss nodded once and launched herself into the sky, Spark bracing herself against the wing gale.

Spark looked around at the pile of red stone and sagged. It was so much work that very few people could help her with. Ondias was an elemental wizard and could probably help with the fusing, or at least use some terramancy to move the blocks into place while Spark did the fusing. It could go so much quicker. But Ondias would rather make useless demands.

Spark hefted one of the blocks and stopped, torn between getting the upstairs started and finishing the studio. It had been like this all summer, so that she felt like she was half-assing everything. But when it came down to it, Jatt and Ember had everything they needed, even if they didn't have as much of it as they wanted nearer to Spark. Neesha and Nanny had nothing.

Decided, she set the stone at the southwest corner, glanced to the pillar that held her mother, and got to work erecting the west-facing wall. It would give her a bit of practice before she headed up to help Abyss rebuild the dragon city.

CHAPTER TWO

S park worked on the upstairs wall most of the morning, until the heat baking off the stone was too much. She retreated to the forge to finish her pile of spearheads and tried noodling around a bit with designs for different types of launchers, things big enough the dragons could use. But finding a design that wouldn't be too much bulk for a dragon in battle proved tricky.

More armour was probably the best bet.

But the growing list of projects needing Spark's attention only made her more anxious when there were so few completed. So little ready to defend or attack or help Neesha or save Nanny.

She ate a quick dinner and was back on the current roof/future floor trying to finish up the wall before sundown. Maybe it would prompt Abyss to drop off another wagon full of stone again tomorrow. She was certain she'd feel a lot better about everything if she could cross anything at all off of her mental to-do list.

Just as she headed to the pile for another stone, a sudden gust of wind announced Abyss's arrival. Spark braced herself as the dragoness landed next to the house.

"I've got more spearheads ready!" Spark grabbed up the sack she'd put them in and stood at the edge of the roof.

"Fire robes."

"Oh, sure, just a sec."

Spark hurried down into the house to change, wondering at what she'd need the fire protection for, what Abyss had in mind. It wasn't just their usual chore of adding more stone to the city above, raising the central globe into a spiralling tower. Spark didn't need a firecloak for that anymore than she did for the simple fusing she'd been doing up on the roof.

She rushed back up to grab the bag of spearheads before Abyss scooped Spark in her claws and shot into the sky. The crush of wind pressed Spark tight against Abyss's hand and stole her breath. The rush of cold air tickled through her short frizzy hair. Spark grinned. Abyss circled the valley, spiralling higher, and Spark's concerns dropped away like the ground until there was only flight. The clouds grew closer, the village a cluster of dots surrounded by glittering light.

Instead of continuing up into the city, Abyss headed north to one of the tallest and most imposing peaks in the range, its craggy summit always lost in snow. Spark had been up here for the first time only recently. It was one of many places in the valley inaccessible to humans, one sacred to the dragons, where they brought their dead for sky burial.

Spark hated what they came up here for now.

Abyss landed on the long plateau that occasionally served as burial ground, empty but for ice and gravel right now. Going carefully while still holding Spark, she edged between two spires of rock into a gap that looked like nothing until just the right angle revealed the gaping mouth of a deep foreboding cave.

Spark had no idea how deep the cave went or what else was in it, as Abyss stopped at what Spark thought of as the first landing. Or maybe it was a shelf? The cave clearly went deeper, but it was a relief to go no farther.

The landing held a pile of weapons and gadgetry Spark didn't have much confidence in—long coils of tempered leather straps and slings, and carefully folded piles of dragon armour. Out of necessity, she'd designed smaller slings that strapped to the dragons' arms. Those took up less space, used fewer resources, and made it easier to communicate with the dragons. Made it easier to climb out of the sling for better positioning if battle required it.

Spark had grand plans of larger slings to hold many riders and their supplies for longer distances, along with ladder-like rigging to make it easier to get around. The only thing keeping her from trying a prototype was not having a solid way to keep from falling off the dragon. That and time.

The design of the dragon armour was still the same. Had to be. There wasn't as much of it as they needed, not even close, and it hurt Spark's heart to look at the lovely white armour made from the hide of the former Dragoness Superior. Spark had been staggered when Abyss brought that one for her, but of course the Superior had had an inkling of what Spark and Abyss were conspiring to do and had volunteered herself to their use before her untimely death.

Spark tried not to think about it, tried not to feel guilt over it. She didn't like to admit when Ondias was right, but she had pushed too hard, gone in without thinking, and brought the ice dragons down on all of them with disastrous effect.

Though the ice dragons had been close anyway. It was hard to say if the extra time it might have taken for them to attack without Spark helping things along would have been enough to make a difference.

None of it really mattered. It was done. But there were probably lessons she needed to learn.

Needed to stop feeling miserable first.

So she emptied the bag of spearheads with the others and quickly went back to Abyss, who flew off. Spark expected to go up to the top of the dragon city to help with the rebuilding efforts, but instead Abyss went into one of the entrance tunnels down into the main chamber of the city.

She had just set Spark down to walk when one of the Dragoness Superiors—the grey and indigo one who had caused all the problems when Spark first arrived in the city—bounded over, hissing and snarling. Spark's body electrified and she staggered away as Abyss turned to meet the attack.

There was nothing physical this time, both dragonesses stopping a barely respectable distance from each other, postures rigid, snapping and snarling and growling at each other. Then the Superior spat a sudden fireball in Spark's direction, easily diverted even in the scrambled state of mind she was in, before the Superior turned away, disappearing deeper into the heart of the city.

Spark stood motionless, holding her breath while her pulse thrummed.

Abyss turned, heading down a different branch of the massive base of the city, toward what Spark recognized as the section where the dragon eggs were kept. She walked like nothing had happened, and Spark wasn't sure what to do.

"Um." The word escaped in an exhale.

Abyss stopped and looked back the way the Superior had gone, but there was no one else around. She leaned her head down, close to Spark. "She doesn't like how I interact with humans. She believes I should accept my circumstance and give up on my egg. I will burn first."

Spark blinked rapidly, trying to understand, trying to think of what to say. But Abyss turned and walked calmly. Spark had no choice but to follow.

With another dragon's fresh clutch hatched just a month ago, Abyss's eggs were the biggest ones still there. Spark hadn't seen the recent baby dragons—they'd been swiftly removed to one of the clan towers lining the valley to be raised until they weren't quite so helpless, then the entire family would return to their original mountains in distant lands.

Spark wasn't sure what Abyss and Zephyr would do once their hatchlings were old enough. Their home was in the mountains near Pasdale and might never be safe to live in.

Of course, Abyss was the head of her circle and climbing the hierarchy quickly. It already granted her the privilege of being in the city more than most dragons.

The mountain range itself could not indefinitely support a great number of dragons, and most of them only saw the city a few times in their lives, usually for major festivals, like when they'd filled the sky over the winter for that meteor shower.

Spark hoped Abyss stayed as long as she did. Which looked like it would be forever. Spark couldn't go back to Pasdale any sooner than Abyss could, and there wasn't anywhere else she wanted to be. Maybe once she cured her mother and freed Nanny, they would want to go south to where her uncles lived.

It was a lot of maybes.

When they reached Abyss's massive boulder-like eggs—one pure white like a chicken egg and the other jet black with a bright blue streak—Abyss startled her again by picking her up and setting her down on top of the white one. Spark was further startled by the reminder of how this egg had Spark's exact colouring.

Spark stood where Abyss had left her, the two of them staring at each other.

"Sit," Abyss finally said.

Spark sat. "So, why am I up here? Don't you want me to help with the repairs?"

Abyss shook her head. "Too dark."

Abyss applied the dragon venom, something she vomited up and coated the eggs with. A secret Spark probably wasn't supposed to know, but it seemed like Abyss kept few things from her anymore.

"Okay... so did you just want the company?" Spark kept the annoyance out of her voice, but she really could be at home building walls and trying to make her home a space someone other than her alone could enjoy.

Abyss continued until she was done coating the eggs, Spark watching silently all the while, until she fixed her dizzyingly black gaze on Spark.

"Speak," Abyss said.

Spark blinked at her for far longer than was polite. "What, you mean to the eggs? Why?"

Abyss waited.

"Speak, like, you want me to tell you about my day? It's the same as every day, just like being in Pasdale, but lonelier. I make things and I sleep."

Abyss kept waiting.

"I'm not sure what else—"

A rustling sound came from directly beneath her and she went rigid.

"Did it just move? Oh, shit, is it hatching?"

Abyss shook her head. "Soon."

"What, like tonight? Should I really be here for that?"

"Weeks. Months?" Abyss tilted her head in a way that could have been interpreted as a shrug.

"But... it moved." The sound came again, and Spark was tempted to slide down off the egg and scramble away. But Abyss had brought her here with intention.

"Wait, you want me to talk to the eggs? Can the babies inside hear me?"

Abyss nodded.

"If I talk to them, will they hatch able to speak? Ondias says you pick up languages with astounding speed. Is that what you want?"

"Yes. And more."

"So, the weird connection we have. The way you all stopped talking when whatever happened to my mother?"

"You came and I rediscovered my voice," Abyss said.

"Yeah. Is that weird?"

Abyss tilted her head, her eyes glittering.

"Ondias thinks we should find out more about that," Spark said "You already have an idea, don't you."

"We have suspicions."

"If I talk to your babies and they hatch speaking as much as you used to, would that confirm some suspicions?"

Abyss grinned. It was always such an awful thing to see, full of gleaming teeth half as long as Spark was tall.

"Would it prove you right? You trying to gloat or jump ahead another circle?"

Abyss puffed some fire into Spark's face, but it was a playful gesture that suggested she wasn't wrong.

"Oh, but if this one is close to hatching…" Spark glanced at the other egg and back to Abyss, who had gone utterly still. "Oh no. So they're all close. All three."

Abyss's silence was all the answer Spark needed.

"Should I really spend time up here talking to eggs when I could be figuring out how to save the other one?"

"We need Nandara."

Spark sighed. A lot rested on whether or not Nandara came back from the Guild with any answers. Retrieving Abyss's stolen egg, rescuing Nanny—none of it would be easy. It wasn't possible without Spark learning to control some terrifyingly dangerous magic. She would have to use the same sorts of skills—demon possession and wielding trueflame—that had done whatever to Neesha.

"All right." Spark leaned her elbows on her knees. "I hope she's back soon. For now, I can talk to your eggs."

Spark had already spoken of her loneliness, and it was easier to talk to Abyss about it, who didn't judge because she cared little about most human affairs. So Spark kept going, letting some of her grief pour out of her—how much she missed Nanny, how much they both did. How the silence of her big stupid new house haunted her, and that she just wanted her friends around but Jatt was being weird and Ember was angry about gods only knew what.

Abyss listened, eyes glittering, occasionally nuzzling Spark when she needed comforting.

No more sounds or movement came from the eggs, and Spark wondered whether the babies were sleeping or listening intently. Either way, she spoke until it got late and Abyss plucked her down off the egg, bringing her down to the valley floor and the sad little life she had.

Shadow waited for her at the door. She fed him, fed herself, and stood in the forge trying to decide what to do next. She wanted to finish the house, but if Abyss's eggs were near hatching, Spark suspected she needed to be ready for a fight. So she dragged herself to the workbench and got back at it.

CHAPTER THREE

S park blearily made a notation in her notebook and then trudged over to her pile of scrap to see if she had anything to make a workable prototype. She'd been up far too late last night trying to figure out a quick release for the tether on her harness that could lead to an easier system of getting around on a dragon in flight.

She'd hoped to get some extra sleep this morning, but there'd been a fresh blaze of dragons arriving at dawn and all the noisy fanfare that involved. And then, of course, Shadow had insisted on being let out, and once Spark was out of bed, that was the end of it. With thoughts of Nanny and going back to Pasdale weighing so heavily on her right now, Spark couldn't hear much of any kind of dragon noise without being flooded by memories of the night the wrong sorts of dragons had come for her family.

Muttering at her pile of junk and realizing nothing was quite right, Spark snatched up a random piece and brought it to the anvil. She'd probably have to melt the piece down entirely and make a mould to get what she really needed, but she wanted to see if she could tinker it into the right shape first.

She'd tried hooks already, but there was no shape she could come up with that would both easily attach to the loops and not just swivel and send her flying to her death.

"There's got to be a way to…" She looked at her drawing again, then back to the anvil, moving pieces around. "Oh, wait, what if I—"

A gentle knock at the door shattered her concentration. She bit back the foul oath trying to escape her lips, especially since Ondias never knocked with so much restraint. Maybe it was someone she actually wanted to talk to.

Spark unlatched the door and stopped short, breaking out into a grin. "Nandara! You're back! Was that you the dragons were making all that racket about this morning?"

Spark wanted to fling her arms around her mentor and mention the eggs and all the work they had ahead of them, but Nandara wasn't alone. Ondias was just behind her, looking troubled, and Jatt was even farther back, looking annoyed.

"Hello, Spark." Nandara grinned, her brilliant green eyes sparkling as she swept her blonde and faded-white hair off her forehead. "Abyss came to collect me from the southern trading post herself and decided everyone needed to know I was back. She was quite pleased to see me."

"What's going on?" Spark asked, trying to meet Jatt's gaze.

Nandara glanced back at the other two and her expression went solemn.

"We have something to talk to you about," Ondias said. "Something we've put off long enough."

Nandara's expression suggested she didn't agree but was probably tired of arguing.

"Um, okay." Spark backed up and let them all in.

Ondias glared at the work on the table but at least kept her thoughts to herself. She leaned against the worktable while Nandara settled into the only chair. Spark stood a bit helplessly next to the anvil, while Jatt paced silently with his long arms crossed and dark mop of hair hanging into his green eyes.

"I'm not sure there's an easy way to say this, and I wish your grandparents had mentioned it to you at all," Nandara said. "But after what happened with Neesha, Dionelle didn't want to push things—"

"Bleeding-heart fool," Ondias muttered, a touch of good nature to it.

"—so this has been a little less official than normal. We didn't even run it past the temple, you understand, but—"

"Oh, for star's sake, just tell them," Ondias snapped.

Nandara gave Ondias a sharp look. Jatt abruptly stopped pacing and cast Spark a worried glance.

"Spark, when you were just a wee thing," Nandara continued, "but Pasdale had soured against your family, your grandparents wanted to be sure you'd be secure once they were gone." She took a deep breath, watching Ondias.

Spark's insides felt heavy at the mention of her absent grandparents. She wanted to object—Nanny wasn't really gone, not like Pappy, and Spark would get her back, probably soon—but Nandara went on.

"I got Sharanda involved back when she still lived in Pasdale."

Ondias paced, Nandara watching her while she spoke to Spark.

"We agreed—and I hope you understand the final decision rests with the two of you—"

"You and Jatt are betrothed," Ondias said, not caring about whatever story Nandara was crafting or the threatening look she'd been giving her. Nandara's expression darkened.

And then what Ondias had said clicked into place.

Spark's skin went hot and her insides went cold, and then they switched, and for good measure she was pretty sure she was drowning in the open air. She didn't think she'd ever be able to close her mouth again. Was screaming an appropriate reaction?

She turned what she assumed was an unhinged look on Jatt, who was blinking a lot but didn't seem nearly as horrified as she felt. He snapped his mouth shut and tilted his head to the side, like when he was trying to figure out how to make a painting work when it was almost right but not quite.

Oh no. No no no...

Nandara full on glared at Ondias.

"We just wanted you to know," Nandara said. "It's not a done thing—these never are, and Neesha certainly rejected all her suitors to the end—but it's there if you want it. You're both old enough to make that sort of decision."

Ondias shook her head on her way to the door, and Spark still couldn't quite breathe.

"Gran, what does that mean?" Jatt asked, speaking at last. "Spark and I have to get married?"

Nandara's smile was a fragile thing. "You don't *have* to, no. We'd like it if you did."

Spark was shaking. Hoped her head was shaking enough to stand out. This could absolutely not be happening.

"I know neither of you has been prepped for this, that with the mingle of cultures here in the valley, this sort of thing has fallen out of favour and isn't talked about a whole lot. But think it over, talk about it a bit now. Let me know if you have any questions."

Nandara got up, following Ondias out the door.

"No! I—" Spark saw the look on Jatt's face and snapped her mouth shut.

Once the women left, Jatt sagged into the chair his grandmother had vacated.

"Well, this is weird," he said.

"We can't."

He flinched and folded his arms, hunching in on himself.

"You don't want a wife anymore than I want a husband!"

His expression darkened. "Yes, they're trying to force us into boxes we don't belong in, label us in ways that are wrong. Gran still thinks it's a phase that I'm not interested in anyone, but Spark, just think about it. We either both have to settle somewhere that doesn't care about marriage the way our families do—"

"I'm staying here, and no one here cares."

"Okay, fine, but I don't know where my art will take me. I don't want them forcing me to marry some woman who will expect children."

They both shuddered at the same time.

"See?" He stood again. "You understand. It can work. It would be, I don't know, a sham, I guess. You can still have Ember; I don't care. No other husband they force on you would do that. Don't you see?"

Spark saw, all right, and she wanted to vomit. She wanted to incinerate Jatt where he stood, and then Ondias and Nandara for good measure. She wanted to march straight into Pasdale to slap Nanny as much as to save her.

"But they didn't even get it approved," she said. "We don't have to do this."

Jatt sagged. A tinge of warning itched between her shoulder blades.

"Look, I've got a lot going on—Abyss brought me up to the city a few days ago and her eggs are... I don't know, alive? They're going to hatch soon. I only have weeks to figure out how we're going to save the egg and get Nanny back. Can we talk about this after that? Nanny will be here, and we can get more of a sense of what she intended with it all. It's... a lot to think about."

Spark couldn't stop shaking and hoped she kept some of the panic out of her expression. Jatt was actually considering this. How could he? After being such close friends for the better part of a year, how could he not see what a terrible idea it was? Had their entire friendship been a mistake?

Spark's body finally decided to settle on going cold, like she was full of ice.

Neesha had rejected all attempts at betrothal, and Spark wondered if she'd felt the same rage and despair.

"It's a lot," Jatt said. "I was really not expecting this when Gran said I had to come with her to talk to you. I thought it was about whatever you've shut yourself away in here to work on."

"This is Ondias's doing. It's got to be. Why would your gran care? Why would she make all the excuses and give us every out like that if she cared? You've got your art, and you're doing fine. I've got the blacksmithing, and it can get me work anywhere I go—not that I'm going anywhere. I don't need taking care of!"

"It's really not that bad, is it?"

Spark stopped and held her breath at his tone. It wasn't the betrothal he thought she was rejecting, but him.

"It's... I really need to think about it more, okay? Later. I've got a lot... shut away here."

She'd tried to aim that last bit as a joke, but Jatt nodded solemnly. "Yeah, you're... busy."

Ugh, he's just like Ember.

Spark set to pacing while she spoke.

"Look, this was a surprise for both of us, and even if we decide on anything, that'll be much, much later. Honestly, I need to get back to work. A few weeks at most, okay? And I'll help Abyss and get Nanny out of Pasdale, and we can all sit down and talk about this, okay?"

His eyes widened. "You're not actually going to Pasdale, are you?"

"How else am I supposed to save Nanny?"

"Someone else..."

She skewered him with a hard look. "There's no one else—Loch's seen to that. Either the dragons go by themselves and take on all the risk, or I go with them."

"But you're not ready!"

"You're right, I'm not, so I certainly hope your gran has come back from the Guild with the answers I need. I've got a lot of work to do if I'm going to be ready in time. So you can stick around and help me with it, but I've got to prepare."

"This is a bad idea."

"On that we agree. But what else am I supposed to do? I've lost everything, Jatt. *Everything*." She gestured around wildly at the empty, half-finished house. "This is my chance to get some of it back."

He tapped his hands against his knees, staring into the space between them. He went still, stabbed at the air in a shrug with his bony shoulders and got up.

"Just be careful, all right? And think about it—the dangers of what you're working on and the dumb new thing they've thrown at us, okay?"

Spark just managed to snatch back an angry retort about how it was *all* she thought about. That she didn't have a choice but to think about the dangers, not with her mother's near-corpse presiding over everything little thing she did. And this colossal distraction was the absolute last thing she needed.

But it wasn't Jatt she was angry at—it was the situation. If she was going to aim her frustration at any single person, it would remain Ondias. And who knew? If Spark could rescue Nanny, if Ondias had her best friend around, maybe it would smooth away the worst of the woman's hard edges.

Jatt had reached the door and Spark joined him.

"You really can stay," she said. "I do miss your company."

He shrugged again. "I'll see you around."

Spark watched him go and let out a long breath once the door was closed. She dragged herself back to the work station, putting everything to do with the betrothal nonsense out of her mind.

Spark set down her tools and stretched. She hated how an entire day's work hadn't amounted to anything useful, hated even more that it had been like this for weeks. Something *had* to give. There weren't many hours of daylight left, but she felt compelled to fill them somehow. There had to be something useful she could do.

She pushed out the door into the cool evening air and wandered, trying to clear her head. She stopped abruptly when River's shouting voice echoed from between buildings. She was near the market and immediately changed direction, eventually ending up near the apprentice mess hall.

Shadow bounded over to her from where he'd been foraging through the scraps behind the kitchen, getting in her path to press his side against her legs.

"Hey, boy, you find anything good?" Spark scratched behind his ears and patted his butt. He leaned harder against her.

A chorus of laughter went up from inside the tent. Shadow barked and pranced around. One person's laughter stood out, and Spark was through the door before her brain registered where her feet were taking her.

Ember wasn't the only one in there she wanted to see, even if Ember and Jatt sat on opposite sides of the tent. Most of the others didn't even notice her come in, though a couple went silent and Jatt stood up suddenly. Did they all know? Had he told them? Was it gossip flung wide?

That was possibly the only thing Spark missed about Pasdale. Her family was ostracized, but the gossip was nothing like this.

Jatt was next to her before Ember was even out of her seat. "Everything okay? I'm just finishing dinner. Why don't you join me?"

Spark glanced at his seat, at all the faces around and the strained look on Ember's face.

"I need to talk to you. Both of you. Not here."

Spark motioned for Ember to join, and she did, clutching her mug of wine like a shield.

"Both of us?" Jatt gave Ember a look.

"What if we go back to the old place?" Spark said. "It's got nowhere to sit but it's quiet. Private."

Ember swallowed a huge gulp of wine. Jatt stared at Spark for a beat, sighed, and swiped the last crust of his bread off his plate. He nodded for her to lead the way.

Her old forge wasn't far—nothing really was, in the village proper—and Spark got them there quickly and pushed inside. The place felt weird and empty, like they were trespassing somehow. Spark sat on the old worktable,

Jatt leaned against the old forge, and Ember stood uncertainly near the door.

The air was heavy. None of them really looked at each other.

"Did you tell her?" Spark asked Jatt, gesturing to Ember.

"He did. Would have rather heard from you."

Spark glanced at Ember. "I'm sorry. I'm just distracted. This is a lot."

Ember crossed her arms and paced in a tight line in front of the door.

"You were right about Ondias," Jatt said. "Most people have figured out you and Ember are more than just friends, and Ondias doesn't miss gossip for long."

"*That's* why she threw this betrothal on us?" Spark said, exchanging a quick glance with Ember. She looked panicked, like she wanted to bolt from the room.

"She's such a toad," Ember spat.

"Her life is miserable, so she's got to make it everyone else's problem," Spark said.

"She's so hung up on appearances," Jatt said. "On what the cultural norms in Pasdale are, what a perfect life looks like according to a bunch of backwater bumpkins. And since she can't have it for herself, she's trying to force it on everyone else."

"What's her excuse for being so miserable to my mother, though?" Spark said.

"Oh, that one's easy," Ember said. "It's because your Ma wasn't married when you were born. It's not as big a deal as it used to be, but Ondias is old-fashioned. Your granddad was too."

A million questions bloomed in Spark's mind. She ran her hands over her face and tamped the questions down. These were distractions and she needed to focus on her friends.

"Ondias can go suck rotten eggs," she said. "We can worry about this whole thing later. I learned just a little while ago that Abyss's eggs are going to hatch soon."

Ember stopped her tight pacing and faced Spark. "That's good, isn't it?"

"It's good for two of them."

"There's a third in Pasdale," Jatt said. "Stars above, Spark, are you still thinking about going back there to save that egg?"

"I have to try. Even if every dragon in this valley went with Abyss, the risks are pretty high. They could get killed or taken. But just me on my own isn't enough to help them, and I still haven't figured out how to build anything that more of us could use to help them."

Ember came closer and took Spark's hand. "I'm sorry, Spark. I know you're not going to stop trying, but this is maybe a matter for the dragons on their own."

"But they're not doing anything. It's Abyss on her own. And she can't even leave, because she's got to be here for the other two."

Ember looked pained. "I know. This sucks. But it really looks like there's nothing anyone can do."

"I don't know for sure. Nandara was supposed to bring back information." She looked desperately to Jatt. "Did she tell you anything?"

Jatt shook his head. "She dragged me over to your place and then slept all day."

"Maybe there's still something I can do," Spark said. "Maybe she learned something that will help?"

"All you've got right now are maybes," Ember said gently. "What were you two working on that might help?"

"I don't know. Using demons to give us an edge?"

Ember seemed curious, but Jatt interrupted. "Spark, I know you want to help, but you know what happened when your mom unleashed demons in Pasdale."

"Right, I'd need a lot of help." She took a deep breath. "Do you think anyone here would come with me? Or could I get Guild wizards to meet me in Pasdale? They helped Neesha."

Jatt stood up and laid a hand on her shoulder. "Spark, please. Everything you're suggesting will take far longer than you've got. I don't want to tell you to let it go, because you won't. Abyss is your friend, and telling you not to help her would be cruel, but... I just don't think there's anything anyone can do."

Spark swallowed hard, glanced around, and suddenly didn't want to be in this space anymore. She wanted to run until she collapsed—not that running away had helped one bit the last time.

"Why don't you take the night off?" Ember said. "You've been working nonstop, and there's nothing you can do right now. Talk to Nandara tomorrow. Maybe then you can come up with something?"

"I can't just let it go. It's not just about Abyss and her egg. Nanny's there too. And I don't know, maybe if I got her out first, she could help me with the egg and the rest of it. But I'm so tired of feeling alone, and I just want her back."

Jatt and Ember shared a glance.

"If they were going to do anything else to your Nan, they'd have done it by now. She's not in more danger if you wait a bit longer to go get her," Ember said.

Spark leaned her head back and looked up at the ceiling.

"And do you really want to sacrifice the gains you've made here just to get one member of your family back?" Jatt asked.

She squeezed her eyes shut and took a deep breath, letting it out slowly. The whole problem took shape in her mind, and she wasn't sure how to deal with it. She didn't think she could make them understand what she was going through, but she gave it a shot anyway.

"You both have family—here, in fact! You have access to generational wisdom that I don't. And yes, Stone and Nandara have both been invaluable mentors to me. But they're not family; they're not Nanny. I *need* someone. It doesn't have to be at the expense of what I've got here."

Ember squeezed her hand.

Spark swallowed again, the air in the room suddenly seeming too thick. She was beginning to understand what Ember and Jatt wanted of her, what they were trying to build. And as much as she wanted them to be family, it wasn't the same. The sense of belonging and shared history was different. That was what she needed right now.

And she didn't want to put them in a place of suffering if something happened to her. The situation was bad. She didn't think she could get out of taking the sorts of risks that had doomed her mother. No one else really saw that. Even if Spark could somehow abandon Nanny and Abyss's egg, Loch's dragons would still come for everything she loved and try to finish what they'd started when they toppled the dragon city all those years ago.

She didn't like it, but Abyss's impending hatchlings gave her focus. It was time to go back to Pasdale.

CHAPTER FOUR

S park sat in the shadow cast by the corner of the southern wall and the nearly finished western wall, sheltering from the midday sun and eating the sandwich she'd cobbled together from scraps and leftovers in her pantry. She really needed to do some more bartering for supplies, though that meant doing work that wasn't either finishing the house or coming up with something that would help Abyss and save Nanny.

She still hadn't heard from Nandara and hadn't been able to find her. Both she and Riz weren't home when Spark went there earlier. Ondias wasn't home either, and Spark tried not to let her mind wander to conspiracies about the two women avoiding her. But the village was *tiny*. How could anyone just *disappear* in a place like this?

Sure, just drop that awful betrothal on me and vanish.

When she finished eating, she'd try Nandara again. If she still couldn't find her, she'd brave the market and find Stone, who kept an eye on the gossip almost as well as Jatt did.

Jatt might have been a better choice for finding his gran, but Spark didn't care to interrupt his studies, not when he and Ember were both sore about her neglecting them. And he was extra sore that she wasn't jumping at the chance to be his wife.

Spark shuddered. She didn't much like the idea of being *anyone*'s wife. Maybe Ember's, but that sort of thing was forbidden back home. Not that it was really home for any of them. But there weren't any unions like that here in the valley either, and she didn't know why. It didn't seem like much of anything was forbidden here. It wasn't necessarily lawless, though since

Ondias had set herself up as queen of the place, what counted as acceptable tended to skew toward Pasdale's norms.

Spark sighed. Her brain hadn't had the chance to go down all these terrible rabbit holes when she'd been busy with work.

She stuffed the last of her sandwich in her mouth, intent on getting a few more blocks fused into the wall before going to find Nandara, and nearly choked on her meal as a fierce dragoncry rose up to the south. It was met by the dragons in the city, the noise of it crumpling her as she tried to surround her head with the rest of her body to block out the sound.

Spark's entire body tensed against the noise, her spine feeling like ice while the rest of her body ran hot as flame. She gasped in a breath and managed to exhale slowly, then sucked in another, slower this time, and her shoulders relaxed. The noise moved off to the edge of the valley.

She hadn't heard dragoncries like this since the Superior had been killed in the spring.

"Shit, shit, shit..." Spark scrambled from the rooftop, pulled on her fireproof clothes, and picked up the axe that she'd tempered to break dragon skin.

When she opened the front door, Shadow bolted in past her and cowered under the table. Spark went out into the field surrounding the house, the noise making her eyes water. A massive blaze of dragons headed south. She couldn't spot Abyss from here; she wasn't sure if she'd even joined them.

Spark waited, every part of her buzzing. The more she listened, the more she realized it wasn't a battle cry. She didn't recognize it at all.

At last, the blaze streamed back in, a few of them circling a trio of new dragons. The trio and their escort landed briefly in the field south of the settlement before they all funnelled up into the city.

"What the...?"

Spark put the axe back inside and jogged to the field where Ondias hosted dragons when she spoke with them. There were no dragons present at all, but three humans Spark didn't know were there with Ondias.

"Ah, here she is." Ondias turned toward Spark's approach. "I suspected the noise would draw you out."

"What's happening?" Spark asked. "Who are they?"

"Riders from south of Golden Hill. This is Barlo, Eltir, and Raia. I've already told them about you."

Spark gave the riders a sidelong glance. They were a dishevelled bunch, with the look of storybook bandits to them, the way they all seemed to have blades attached to every convenient surface of their clothing. But a lot of those blades were poor quality, nicked or dented or warped, so that Spark wanted to gather them all in her forge and make things right. Their leathers were worn, their clothing patched and stained.

While they smelled like people who'd spent an awful lot of time in the wilderness, it wasn't necessarily a bad smell—dust in sunlight, damp tree bark—so they had some supplies, including soap.

The riders clustered with Eltir in front. Though the shortest, he was probably the leader, with a wispy build, black and grey hair cropped close, a cool taupe skin tone, and warm amber-brown eyes that crinkled at the edges with his careless grin. The other man, Barlo, was taller, though not as tall as the woman, Raia. She was as tall as Spark and twice as thick, her hair shaved away entirely to reveal warm terracotta skin and deep brown eyes that also crinkled in the corners. Barlo was somewhere between her and Eltir in height, and burly so that his russet skin put Spark in mind of a potato, with black hair in braids gathered at the back of his head. His eyes were dark brown and watchful.

"What are they doing here? What was that noise?" Spark asked, too rattled for pleasantries.

"We've changed protocol for newcomers," Ondias said. "I vet the humans, the dragons vet their own, and then we reconvene to see if anyone's getting incinerated."

Eltir shifted uneasily. "Incinerated?"

"Well, maybe not. It's to avoid a fight like we had when the black dragoness unexpectedly arrived with Spark last year. I try to vet everyone in advance. It's been awhile since anyone has shown up unannounced."

The three newcomers were perceptive enough to look abashed.

"Sorry, mum. We didn't know."

Ondias gave Barlo a hard look. "You claim to be close enough to those dragons that they're your friends and not your possessions, but didn't know that this valley is not open to visitors and hasn't been for quite some time?"

"We don't get much news out in the wilds. These ones haven't been back here since before the city fell," he said, looking up to where the city was far from fallen these days. Not back to its former glory, but still an awesome sight to behold.

A whole year and Spark still wasn't tired of watching it glitter. And still intimidated by how it must weigh as much as an entire mountain range just suspended up there above her head.

"We heard about a battle against Loch's ice dragons," Raia said. Her eyes danced. "We've lost so many comrades to his treachery. It gave us hope to hear someone had successfully fought back. Took us this long just to track down the truth. It didn't come with instructions, I hope you understand."

Ondias rubbed her hands over her face.

"Wait, you're dragon riders? And there's more of you?" Spark came closer, giving them all a more thorough look.

"There's pockets of dragon and human allies all over the place," Ondias said.

Spark gave her a look. There'd been others like her out there all this time, and Ondias had never mentioned it. She felt foolish for assuming she'd been the only one, but it really seemed like the sort of thing someone in a place like this would have told her about. And now she was angry about it. Spark could have learned from them, could have been in contact for months, swapping tips.

"So she's one of the fireborn?" Barlo asked, glancing in Spark's direction.

"Only one we've got active at the moment, yes," Ondias said.

"I'm working on it," Spark said. "I need help to rescue my grandmother from Loch's dungeons in Pasdale."

Raia winced. "Loch's a tricky one. We've lost so many to him—some killed, others taken."

"He took Nanny and killed the rest of my family," Spark said, a hard edge to her voice. She shouldn't be angry with these people—she probably needed them as allies, especially when Ondias was only interested in getting Spark to do useless nonsense like getting married.

"Yes, well, Loch has plenty of spies, and plenty of dragons he's broken." Ondias gave the three newcomers a hard look. "You're going to have to convince me we should trust you."

"Not sure what else we can do but give you our word," Barlo said. "Maybe you'll take the word of our dragons when they come back. They *are* coming back, yes?"

"That will depend on what my colleagues in the city find. If your dragons have been broken in any way, they'll be sent away for healing and retraining. You won't get out of here alive." Ondias rubbed her face again. "And if you are who you say you are, I'm going to need you to help me reach others, because I thought I'd gotten the message out there that this valley is closed."

"There are certainly others," Raia said. "I suspect they'll gather here. Seems a natural rallying point."

"Rallying against what?" Spark's eyes widened.

"Loch might be focused on this valley, but the king in Golden Hill has his eye on the whole of the world, and he's adopting Loch's methods."

"All the more reason to start fighting back properly." Spark glared at Ondias.

"Winning a battle of this magnitude takes some real preparation."

"But you've had a victory over the ice dragons already." Raia sounded uncertain.

"At cost and with difficulty, using extremely dangerous magic that only Spark can perform and not with any great reliability yet—and it remains to be seen if it's even possible to use that kind of magic safely and reliably."

"What I can do is only useful against the ice dragons," Spark said. "They've got captive dragons to contend with."

The armour was their real advantage, though if Spark could just free Nanny and wake up Neesha, three fireborn working together might really make a difference. But these newcomers didn't need to know any of that, especially when Ondias clearly didn't trust them yet.

More noise erupted from the city, and a host of dragons spiralled out, one of them heading toward the field. This was dragon whisperer business, and Ondias could have it. A crowd had gathered on the edges a safe distance away. Nandara was among them, so Spark abandoned the group.

When Spark was close enough, Nandara asked, "Spark, what's going on? Who are they?"

She filled Nandara in hastily, watching as a dragon dropped down into the field to address Ondias. The three newcomers weren't immediately incinerated, and in fact they were standing quietly to the side, mostly being ignored.

"Good sign?" Spark asked.

"Probably. I look forward to hearing more of what they have to say."

"In the meantime, you can tell me what you learned at the Guild. You *did* learn things, right?"

Nandara smiled, the crow's feet around her eyes crinkling. "A bit. I've been discussing it with Ondias and the Superiors, trying to better understand. I still don't know if we can achieve any of your goals, but I think I'm at least close to some answers."

"Are you busy now?"

"Now? Are you in some kind of rush?"

Spark's stomach clenched. It was always a rush; there was never enough time.

"Not yet," Spark said. "But battle's coming and nothing I've tried since you left has worked. I really need to learn to control one of the bigger pyromancy techniques."

"We left off with demon possession. Is that where you'd like to start?"

"I don't know. I don't really have much of a plan. Do you have any idea how we can save Nanny and the egg?"

Nandara tapped a finger against her lips, staring unseeing into the field. "I might be able to help with that, but I'll need some time to go over my notes and incorporate what I discussed with the Superiors."

"Will you meet me back at my place?"

Nandara studied the group dispersing in the field. "Let me grab something to eat and some supplies. We'll need to get Abyss and head somewhere isolated."

Spark remembered the pain of their last attempt at dealing with demon possession, but Nandara had new information. Spark nodded grimly and headed home to prepare.

CHAPTER FIVE

Spark stood outside the northern mountain's cave, which she'd started to think of as the armoury. Abyss loomed next to her, angled so she could quickly come between Nandara and Spark if necessary. Nandara still seemed confident, probably because they were starting with a demon Spark was in control of.

This part wasn't so bad, and with a nod from Nandara, Spark pulled fire out of the air and summoned a demon. The fire flared on its arrival, the vaguely humanoid shape flickering as it grew closer, like a body made of flame, the heat of its power washing over her like a warm summer breeze. It was a fresh demon, not one that felt familiar, like a voice she didn't recognize.

"It's new." Spark glanced at Nandara, who nodded.

"Good. They'll recognize you, and also that you're related to Dionelle and Neesha."

"Is that a good thing or a bad thing?"

"At the moment, it's just a thing." Nandara shook her head helplessly. "We're learning this as we go."

There was certainly danger there, in demons too familiar. They'd become focused on the Joasera women and were full of trickery.

Spark took a deep breath and invited the demon in. The euphoric wash of heat tried to drown her, but she fought it off.

"Are you all right?" Nandara asked.

"I've got it."

"All right. Just keep your composure." Nandara wove her hands in the air, pulling from the little fire Spark maintained, and spoke in the demon's language. Spark recognized it as a summoning.

There was a pull Spark felt in her bones as the demon resisted. Spark wanted to push it out, but Nandara needed to be able to do this entirely on her own if they were to be successful. But the pull got harder, and Spark felt the tearing, like she was being ripped out of herself. She hissed through her teeth and braced against it.

Nandara paused her spellwork, going silent and keeping the magic and the demon suspended.

"It's all right, Spark. You're safe." Her voice was gentle but strained with the effort of holding everything steady.

The pressure decreased. With a shaky breath, Spark felt centred again.

"Focus on you," Nandara said. "Keep the demon at bay. Put a mental wall between the two of you. Remember who you are and where you belong."

"Will that help?"

"It could. This is all unprecedented magic we're trying. But holding yourself separate won't make anything worse."

Spark focused. Who was she, exactly? Alone. But that wasn't going to help now, was it? And the wall between her and the demon was probably more helpful anyway. She envisioned that she was a house and the demon was on the porch. The door opened, but the demon wasn't allowed inside.

Eyes closed, Spark said, "I think I've got it."

Spark shouldn't have been surprised that the mental self-house she'd imagined was the old farmhouse where she grew up. A place that didn't exist anymore. She felt the bittersweet longing for a place she couldn't return to, and with it, the door opened wider. The demon took a step closer.

Spark thought of Nanny—Nanny as she used to be, with her freely given smiles and frequent hugs, her aura of warmth and safety. The door slammed on the demon.

Nandara did the summoning again, and Spark felt a push-pull sensation, like a strong gust of wind. It didn't hurt, wasn't taking anything from her.

"I think it's working," she whispered.

Nandara's expression didn't change, her focus entirely on her task. And then Spark felt like she'd been pushed over without moving, and the demon was next to her, both of them two separate beings again.

"It worked! Nandara, you did it!"

Nandara smiled, but looked tired. Spark rushed over and hugged her, held her shoulders to make sure she was okay.

"Should we stop for tonight?" Spark asked.

"No, I can do that a couple more times."

"Do we try again with me in control?"

"You want to jump ahead, don't you?"

"If you think you can manage the banishing safely..."

"In theory, it should be exactly the same."

"In practice?"

Nandara's smile was tight and grim. "This *is* the practice. No Guild members have studied anything like this."

Spark let out a long breath.

"I will keep you safe," Abyss said.

Nandara took a steadying breath, and Spark called another demon out of the fire, this one as lacking in familiarity as the first, so she sent the first one back to its realm.

Spark let the new demon in, waited until Nandara signalled she was ready, and then let the demon's heat wash over her, push her under.

But something was wrong. As her heart rate hammered in her ears, Spark realized she had no control at all.

Where the heat of the demon had once been inviting and euphoric, it was now hot and suffocating, like she was experiencing fire the way other people did. And then even more heat rose up through her body as the demon readied an attack. A cold spike drove through Spark as she tried to claw it back.

Don't let it hurt Nandara...

But Nandara was already speaking the words of the summoning, and Spark felt that pull again. She focused on herself as a house, safe with Nanny's love and care. But the house was bright with fire.

Like the night her family had died.

The demon was out the door, but Spark couldn't stay in the house.

There was another tearing sensation, far worse than the last time. Spark opened her mouth to scream but no sound came out. And then the heat and pain were gone, and she felt cold and empty and far more alone than she ever had.

The demon stood next to her, but she felt no relief.

She tried to turn to Nandara, but her body wouldn't go. Nandara was talking to her—she could hear the voice, but the words didn't make any sense. Spark kept trying to speak, but no sound came out.

Nandara's voice pitched into panic, and she stood in front of Spark, took her shoulders in a grip Spark was barely aware of. Nandara stared her in the face, still talking, her eyes wide.

Spark still couldn't speak. She could barely think.

Nandara backed away out of her line of sight.

Spark filled with heat again. The house inside her was still on fire, and the warmth was enticing. The world outside grew black as night.

Abyss's rumbling voice broke through. "You must fight it."

Fight what?

Spark blinked and found Abyss's face in front of her, with no sign of Nandara.

Right, Abyss was keeping Nandara safe from the demon. The demon! That's what Spark needed to fight. Maybe this was something they should have spoken about more. But again, this was theory that had no practice.

Spark needed to get the demon out of her house.

She couldn't close her eyes, but she focused internally. She didn't have any control of her body, but Abyss would keep the demon from throwing her off the mountain or any such foolishness.

She tried to shut out everything else. The demon couldn't actually hurt her as long as Abyss was there, so that gave her all the time she needed to regain control. Maybe it would get bored? But she couldn't count on that. Not when they'd kept Nanny in the fire realm for months. So she made space in her mind for herself again. She shut out the noise and the chaos and did her best to ignore how nice that heat felt, filling her.

She remembered why she was doing this. To save Nanny. And Abyss's egg. Maybe even find out what had happened to Neesha.

Back in her mind-house, she managed to conjure Nanny again—the comfort of her smile and the warmth of her presence a stark contrast to the overwhelming burn of the demon. That gained her one entire room in the house, and the fire receded. Spark thought of her and Nanny alone in the kitchen, and with that frantic effort, she managed to slam the door on the demon.

That startled it enough for Spark to speak.

"Nandara, get it!"

The demon almost broke through, the kitchen door in Spark's mind alight with flame, but she kept that little corner of herself. She felt the pull again—in her bones and her thoughts. She fought against it, held herself in the little mind-kitchen she'd built. But the pain dug into her. She needed that demon all the way out.

She focused harder on her memories of Nanny, who had always been so gentle, but who Spark also knew could be fierce. She remembered how Nanny had fought against Loch's dragons. How it had been the two of them against ten. In her mind, she and Nanny were fierce again, and though pyromancy would do nothing against a fire demon, she used what felt like aeromancy, cool and wild and rushing.

She held herself in the little space she'd built and gusted the demon to the door and finally onto the porch.

And at last she returned to herself. She was lying on cold stone, and the demon was beyond her, already disappearing back into its realm.

Nandara knelt over her, cautious like she was about to run at the first sign of trouble. Her mouth was moving. Spark blinked.

"—hear me?"

Spark tried to confirm that she could hear Nandara, but a wordless grunt came out.

"What was your great-grandmother's name? The one you grew up with."

Spark could think only of Nanny. Had she ever had family other than Nanny? Nandara's face grew more pinched, her body tensing.

"...Sharice?"

Nandara crumpled into sobs next to her. Spark struggled to sit up, wincing as everything about her, right down to her thoughts, felt wobbly.

"It... worked?" Spark asked.

"Nothing about any of this was a success!" Nandara's voice was clipped and hard.

"I'm still in myself. I mean, it could have been worse."

"It was a near thing. Too near." Nandara looked up, and Spark followed her gaze to where Abyss leaned above them, her eyes narrowed and head tilted.

"I would like a tiny moment to celebrate the tiny victory of un-possessing myself," Spark said, rubbing her forehead. "Abyss helped, of course. Gave me something to focus on. I think I can learn to keep myself separate so you can pull the demon out."

"No, absolutely not." Nandara clasped her arms around herself and shook her head.

Spark recoiled. Her chest tightened and her limbs buzzed, and she flexed her hands.

Nandara sighed and her expression softened. "I suppose... with time and practice, you could learn. But this was entirely too close. Abyss's quick reflexes are the only reason I'm still alive."

"Oh no." Spark sat up straighter. "Nandara, did I hurt you?"

"The demon tried. I know there was nothing you could have done."

A cold pit hardened in Spark's stomach. A demon could use her power, make her do anything it wanted, and they always wanted trouble—longed to burn anything they could. It was why they'd had Abyss with them, since she was impervious to the demon's most destructive whims.

They'd tried to prepare, but it didn't make her feel any better.

Spark thought for a moment. "Demon possessions can be ended successfully. I've read how to do it. Sometimes they get bored and go on their own, even."

"That will not happen with you and fire demons. They kept Dionelle in their realm for months."

"Yes, and she'd probably still be there if Pappy hadn't gone for her. But still, if an air demon possessed you, I could banish it. You'd be fine. Well, scared and tired, but fine. Why is this different?"

"I think you would also be fine if we were working with air demons. Or any other element. But you are part of the fire, Spark. Grand Chancellor Dira was certain that if you could isolate your internal essence from the demon, we'd be successful."

"I think so too. That's what I meant."

"And I'm telling you that it's entirely too dangerous to try again."

Spark leaned her head back, staring into the late-day sky, deep blue and perfectly clear. Nandara kept herself in check, but her fear had been obvious since the moment Spark lost control. Spark suspected she was still terrified. Possibly more afraid than Spark was herself.

She couldn't risk Nandara like this again.

"Mistress, do you have insights?" Nandara asked.

Abyss snorted and picked the both of them up, leaving the mountaintop. It felt like giving up, like failure. Spark wanted to lie on the ground and cry.

Abyss left them outside Nandara's home rather than Spark's, which was odd. Though Spark had been taking her lessons at Nandara's lately. Did Abyss think they would do more today?

Spark could hardly stand, still feeling wobbly and watery. Nandara looked drawn out and ashen. But she did invite Spark in even before Abyss had flown off.

Spark shook her head. "I think I need to go home and lie down."

"You don't look well." Nandara frowned. "Jatt will be back soon. He can walk you home."

"If I wait, I'll fall asleep on your doorstep. I'll be fine—it's not far."

Disappointment painted Nandara's features. Spark tried to keep her expression steady as she waved goodbye and headed home, her footsteps heavy with the effort of holding firm so Nandara wouldn't try to stop her. Having someone accompany her home, or even napping at Nandara's, was probably a good idea. But Spark knew why Nandara made the offer. Why she wanted it to be Jatt to bring Spark home.

And maybe stay there with her a bit.

The stupid betrothal was the last thing she wanted to think about, nevermind talk about. She had no energy left to be diplomatic about it. All hells, she was in a dire enough mood to tear it all down. If she couldn't free Nanny or save Abyss's egg or help Neesha, then what was the point of any of it?

But maybe there was another way. Maybe she should focus on helping Neesha instead of Nanny? She wasn't sure what kind of magic that needed and would have to ask Nandara if she learned anything else at the Guild. But later.

Spark could learn to keep the demons from taking her, but she would need another fireborn to help her figure it out safely. She wasn't sure if she should keep working with demons or try to practice something new.

But she couldn't let the failures keep stacking up.

CHAPTER SIX

Spark grated open her eyes, groggy and disoriented, but nothing like when she'd first collapsed into bed. Part of her wanted to give into the despair of failure. Instead, she blundered out of bed, grabbing a drink and breaking off a chunk of cheese, then let Shadow out to do whatever it was he did all day. She watched him vanish into the low light—the sun having recently set—and went into the forge.

Normally her safe haven, it only made her limbs jangly and her stomach roil. If she made one more useless weapon instead of actually *doing something*, she would melt it all to slag.

Enough wasting time.

She had to focus on magic, so she flipped open some of her notes from past lessons with Nandara. With a clearer mind, she tried to see where things had gone so wrong on the mountaintop and where she could improve. It would have been helpful if Abyss had given them a bit of time and maybe some input to figure out more of that.

Or maybe she'd seen it was futile and left them to figure that out on their own.

Spark sighed, lit a fire, and called a demon. She recognized its essence. Her stomach tightened, and she called another. It shouldn't have made her so weary, but it did. At least the second one was new to her, and she sent the first away.

"This is a bad idea, isn't it."

The demon, if it understood her, didn't move, held by the magic and waiting for her command. She wanted to send it back and crawl into bed, wishing more than she ever had that anyone at all in her family was here with her, like an adult to make decisions. But if she wanted that, she needed to do this.

She let the demon in. The heat washed over her, trying to drown her.

She immediately cast the demon out onto her mental porch and left it there, trying to figure out how she could strengthen her mental defences. Maybe she could stop the demons from taking over at all, and she wouldn't have to worry about Nandara endangering herself.

"All right, now what." She sat at her workbench and stared at her notes. "You got any ideas?" she asked her porch.

The demon seemed annoyed, fire flaring around the doorframe, but also curious, as its attention remained on her rather than on any attempts to escape. Spark hoped the demons didn't talk to each other. If they did, even a fresh one could be a risk. Would anyone even know?

Her focus on the pages broke, and she had the strong urge to look around. Likely the demon getting bored and looking for mischief.

"You want mischief, maybe I'll take you up the mountain and make you stare at my mother until I get bored. Would that be enough for you bastards to tell me where she is?"

Spark stopped and considered what she'd actually said. She had only been talking to pass the time and fill the silence, but maybe it wasn't such a bad idea. If they let a demon possess Neesha, would she wake up? Could they figure out how to get the demon out of her safely? If she was in there and could hear, Spark could talk her through it.

"Now that's something I'll have to talk to Abyss—"

Ember burst through the front door, calling for her.

Spark stifled a scream and barely held onto the demon. She stuffed the demon back into its realm as Ember came in, her eyes wide and face streaked with tears.

"Oh, gods," Ember said, "you're working with demons again? After what happened?"

Spark didn't even need to ask how Ember could have possibly learned of that already, or from who. Nothing about the speed of gossip surprised her anymore, though it did make her profoundly weary.

"I think I can give myself better odds with it," Spark said.

"You'll never convince Nandara to do that again. You'd have better luck convincing Ondias."

"Maybe I will, if it comes to it. Maybe there's another way." Ember's eyes were red and puffy, like she'd been crying for a while. Spark came closer and took her shoulders. "What's going on?"

Ember turned away and paced the room. "It's River! He's gone!"

"Gone where?"

"I don't know. He didn't show up for dinner yesterday. Pa spent all today looking for him, but one of the apprentices said she saw him head into the forest, to the south. Ondias got a dragon to scout, but he's not in the valley anymore. And then Pa was in River's room tonight, going through his things—and Spark, it's awful! There were a lot less things, and then Pa found a note. He's gone!"

Spark blinked and tried to think of what to say, not wanting to show the deep sense of relief she felt knowing that River was gone. That she'd never have to dodge his cruelty again.

"Where did he go?" It was all she could think to ask.

"He's probably not far yet, but he was headed for the southern trading camp. He said he couldn't stand it here anymore, that he was going to make his fortune or some nonsense."

Spark knew she should say something comforting, but River didn't have a shred of decency in his body, and she'd never understood why Ember couldn't see it. She couldn't offer words of comfort because they would be lies.

"My only brother is gone forever, possibly dead in the wilderness, and you've got nothing to say?" Ember had stopped pacing to stare, her tone rising.

Spark knew she was about to say the wrong thing—these days it didn't seem like there was a right thing to say to Ember. She forged ahead anyway. "I'm sorry you're upset, but you know I hated him. He hated me! He hated *everyone*. Including you. Let him go be miserable somewhere else and we can have some peace."

"Spark, that's terrible!"

"Do you want me to lie to you and tell you I'm sorry he's gone?"

"You're such a paragon of honesty, are you? But you can't even be bothered to tell me what's going on with that betrothal!"

Spark threw her arms in the air and turned away. "That's because there's nothing to tell! I'm never going to marry Jatt."

"Well, he sure seems to think otherwise."

"Then he's a fool," Spark replied, turning back to see Ember with her arms crossed, fresh tears on her cheeks. "I've agreed to nothing, and I never will."

"You haven't said that to him. If you're so certain, why haven't you shut the whole thing down already?"

"Because Jatt doesn't want to hear what I have to say, and I don't have the energy to make him listen."

"So you've very clearly told him no? How can he possibly misunderstand that?"

Spark sighed and rubbed her face. "Ember, I'm sorry that you're having a rough time over your brother. I wish I could be more present for you—I know this is a weird time. But I adjusted to losing people I genuinely liked, people who were kind to me and everyone around us. You will adjust to this. Hopefully I'll be able to support you with that soon, but right now I have nothing left to give. All of my focus is on rescuing Nanny and Abyss's egg."

Ember crossed her arms, lips trembling. "Yes, you've made it abundantly clear where your priorities lie for quite some time."

"Ember, do you really expect me to value your family above my own? When your brother has never been kind to me for a single second in his entire life? Please, think about what you're saying. This is ridiculous."

A fresh torrent of tears streamed down Ember's cheeks. Then she stormed off, muttering something about dying alone.

Before slamming the door as she left, she shouted, "Jatt can have you!"

Spark let out a long breath and returned to her worktable. She wished she had more time to devote to her friends, to give Ember the comfort she needed—to have the energy to figure out what that even was. Both Ember and Jatt were upset by how they'd been cast aside while Spark tried to save what was left of her family. She wished they understood, wished she could get it over with sooner before she lost them both.

But she had to take the chance—she had to get Nanny back. And for that, she needed to be ready. So she called another fire demon and got back to work.

CHAPTER SEVEN

With a new demon cast out on her mental porch, Spark spooned the last of her porridge into her mouth, wondering if she should leave the demon there all day just to see what would happen. Everything she came up with seemed ridiculous. But nothing had worked yet. As soon as she had her breakfast dishes cleaned up, she would talk to Nandara again. She needed to know everything her mentor had learned.

She'd just opened the cupboard to put her bowl away when someone knocked on the door. Had Nandara come to see her?

Spark expelled and banished the demon, then dashed to the door and threw it open, blinking as her brain caught up to the fact that the person standing there was very much not Nandara. Not anyone she was used to seeing. She continued blinking at the wide smiling face of the newly arrived dragon rider until her brain finally snagged on the woman's name.

"Raia? Hi! Can I help you with something?"

"Ondias says yer a blacksmith."

"Is this about your blades?" Spark noted that Raia was not outfitted in all the sharp pointy bits Spark had first seen her in. She looked cleaner and more relaxed, and this close, Spark noticed the fine lines on her face that put her around Stone's age.

"Aye."

Spark beamed. "Come in and let me take a look."

Raia set a clanky bundle on the worktable and unfolded the sackcloth to reveal an entire raggedy arsenal.

"We understand ye barter. We've not much to barter with."

"Information," Spark said immediately.

Raia tilted her head.

"Honestly, I'd do this for free just because I can't stand to see weapons in such disrepair. But also, I've never met other dragon riders. Tell me what it's like while I work."

Spark set to it immediately, using a mix of traditional methods and pyromancy so she could both impress her (hopefully) new friend and get through the work quickly. She needed to get over to Nandara's and figure out a new plan.

But Raia managed to make hanging out in alpine forests all day sound like the most fascinating thing in the world. It didn't sound much different than Spark's journey with Abyss from Pasdale, but Raia had her wanting to wander out into the trees. And Raia and her crew looked the part of bandits because they occasionally played the part, using the dragons to steal from nobles when they were in dire need.

"And you work in tandem with the dragons for this?" Spark asked.

"Oh, aye. We learned the sorts of people they don't like and they're happy to help. Usually there's a fat horse or ox in it for 'em too."

"Your dragons don't talk, do they?"

"Nay, none of them do."

Spark's face must have betrayed something because Raia stood suddenly and came to stand next to the anvil where Spark worked.

"You got dragons that talk, then?" Raia asked.

"Just Abyss."

"She's the great black one. And she talks to ye? Gods, I thought Eltir was having a laugh when he said his used to speak to him when they first met."

Spark looked up. "He's known his dragon that long?"

"Aye. He was apprenticing to be a dragon whisperer—that's how he found out about your kin being fireborn. What's that mean, anyway?"

"We're part fire demon—me, my mamma, and Nanny."

Raia stared. Cleared her throat. "Well, that's not anything I ever expected to hear. And I suppose that's why yer dragon talks?"

"Ondias thinks so. Abyss didn't start talking again until a few months ago, after I'd been living here a while."

"Abyss? That her name?"

"Near enough. I had to guess at first, because she wasn't talking at the time. She told me her actual name not too long ago."

"Well, this has been illuminating. Think you can find out my dragon's name? I just call him Dragon."

Spark laughed.

"What, it's true!" Raia said. "Eltir calls his Ice. And it seems right enough—she's about the same blue as those old glaciers get. I dunno, didn't seem right to give mine another name when he already had one."

"Abyss says I've given her a nickname. I can ask if she'll tell you your dragons' names if you want."

"I feel like maybe this transaction is still a little one-sided."

"Tell me about air battle while I finish up. I've been rubbish at it, but sounds like you know what you're doing. I've just been lucky so far."

Raia started relaying one of their misadventures in stealing from terrible nobles, about hopping from one dragon to another when they met particularly dangerous resistance near Pasdale from slave dragons.

"Wait, are you telling me you just... climb around on your dragons?" Spark set down the blade she was working on and stared at Raia. "You're not harnessed in or anything?"

"Oh, we've got the little riding carriers that sound like what you've been using, but we don't *stay* in them."

Spark gasped and her eyes widened. "Aren't you afraid of falling?"

"The dragons catch us."

Spark tilted her head. "Every time?"

"Not always." Raia bit her lip. "We used to have an aeromancer in our group who kept us up till a dragon came back around." She clenched her jaw and stared at the space between them. "Little over a season ago, Loch took him. And his dragon."

"Right, you mentioned. I'm sorry."

Raia gave her an appreciative glance but continued staring into the middle distance. "He was my brother. His dragon—he called him Shell—was Dragon's brother. We dunno what Loch's done with 'em. Dunno if they're still alive."

Spark's chest tightened and she put her hand on Raia's shoulder. "I'm going to get my grandmother back. And figure out how to wake up my mother. And then the three of us are going to stop him. Maybe we'll find your brother."

Raia considered her for a moment, a smile touching her face. "We was right to come here. Even if we don't stay. I know there's a lot here I don't understand, and I think you've got a lot ahead of you before you really can do anything, but we'll help you. When the time comes, we'll fight Loch with you."

Spark sighed. "Don't go too far. We expect he'll attack us again before winter."

Raia rubbed her face and nodded. "Well, I best let you get back to work, then."

"I'm almost done." Spark smiled at her and got to the last of the weapons.

"It's a wonder we managed as long as we did with such shoddy hardware." Raia ran her fingertips along one of the new blades. "Course, the dragons do most of the heavy lifting. And my brother, he rarely used a blade if he didn't have to."

Raia's gaze went inward, and her smile turned brittle. Spark knew the pain in her voice as she continued.

"He's a good head taller than me, even. We had the same dad, but I swear to all the gods, Croves's ma had to be a bear. He has these arms like tree trunks and had his skull-crackers he liked in a fight. One neat little club, reinforced, and then this big ol' warhammer. I swear it was longer than Eltir is tall!"

"I've never really thought of hammers as weapons." Spark looked down at her hammer and a flicker of memory—flattening her thumb when she was a wee thing just learning—revealed the truth of Raia's words.

"Oh, aye, anything's a weapon if you swing it hard enough." Raia laughed. "And Croves knocked so many fancy nobles in their fancy armour right off those dragons they had. Like he was flingin' mice around! Our last successful job, we got right into the estate of one of Loch's cronies and took half his coffers. Croves did most of the work on his own with that hammer."

Spark looked away as Raia's expression darkened, keeping her focus on the hilt she was working.

"None of it mattered once we got too close to Loch himself. Hammer doesn't do nothin' against a flood. Neither does all the magic any of us have."

Spark pressed her lips together and nodded solemnly, still not meeting the woman's eye. She bundled up the blades, shiny and like new again, and handed them back. Raia clutched them and sighed.

"Sometimes I wish I hadn't escaped," Raia said. "Sometimes I feel like I abandoned him. Or like if they'd taken me instead of him, he'd have been able to save me. But there's nothing the three of us can do."

"I know." Spark swallowed the lump in her throat. "Sometimes, especially early on, I wished I'd died along with the rest of them. Or that Loch had taken me instead of Nanny. But he's keeping Nanny alive, and I don't think he'd have done the same for me. I have a chance, if I can get better control of my magic. I don't know if I can do much to help you on my own. But I think me and Mamma and Nanny together will be more than Loch can handle. And I mean to make him pay for what he did to my family."

Eltir and Barlo were playing cards in the grass just outside Spark's door, waiting for Raia, and they followed as Spark brought Raia out to the workshop across the field where the whetstone was. Eltir and Barlo helped sharpen the weapons. Spark told them a bit of what she'd been doing, showed them her launchers, and tried to explain how she tempered the blades.

"Well, that's a right handy trick," Eltir said. "Croves was our wizard. Well, Barlo's a healer, but—"

"I ain't a very good one." Barlo shrugged.

"You can mend broken bones," Raia said. "That's not nothin'."

Spark let them talk, trying not to let the weight of the misery Loch spread press her down. She showed them Abyss's rigging. Eltir let out a low whistle.

"It's huge," Raia said, running her hand along part of a strap. She gripped one of the handholds and looked at Spark. "You don't need these. You're sure enough on your feet, and those strong blacksmith hands of yours... We can show you."

"What, show me how to climb around a dragon?" Spark's mouth fell open before she grinned.

"People call us dragon riders, but it's more dragon-walking."

Spark tried to envision it. But thoughts of all the work she had to do crept in. And there was no guarantee this would be useful, or that she could be good enough at it for it to matter any time soon. But everything else she'd tried was a dead end.

What was one more day? Nandara had seemed like she needed more time to prepare anyway.

"Let me see if Abyss will agree to it."

Raia first convinced Dragon—who was a lovely teal with ribbons of forest green—to let her show Spark the ropes (or scales). They spent the rest of the morning climbing along his back, Raia showing Spark how to use his spikes for handholds, and both of them occasionally falling off—Spark falling off rather more frequently—and needing to be caught by a patient Ice, who was on hand to observe.

"You're lucky with Abyss, if she'll let ye do this," Raia said as Ice deposited Spark next to her. "It's easier to get used to the technique on the males—their spikes are smaller and closer together—but the females are so much bigger. If you stick to their spines as much as you can, falling doesn't have to mean falling *off*."

They broke for lunch and then Ice tolerated Spark climbing around with Eltir. Barlo's dragon, a scarlet male with black tips who he called Flame, had come to watch on as well. After the second time Flame set Spark back on Ice's shoulder, Abyss and Zephyr came down from the city. Zephyr circled overhead, while Abyss watched silently beside Ice.

"Let's race," Eltir said, a spark in his eyes. "See who can get to the other side of her wings first."

Spark shrugged and they each stood on either side of the ridges that made up Ice's spine. Eltir counted it down, and they both dashed off. Raia was right that it was far easier on Ice than it had been on Dragon. That didn't mean that Spark was any good at it. She did a lot of tripping and stumbling, and nearly fell off despite the extra width of the dragoness.

Eltir got to the other side of Ice's wings ages ahead of Spark.

"Once you get your footing, then you go from dragon to dragon," Raia called from Dragon's back. He extended his wings like he would if he was gliding, and Raia raced across the top of one and hopped off to land on Ice's back.

Spark stared. "And you do all this while they're actually flying?"

"Let's try it," Abyss said, leaning her head closer.

Raia and Eltir stared wide-eyed at her. Barlo gasped.

"The day's wonders never cease," Raia said.

Abyss plucked Spark from Ice's back and dropped Spark onto her shoulder. Spark jogged from Abyss's shoulder to the base of her tail and back again.

"Hold on." Abyss gave her only a moment to wedge herself between two spikes before taking off into the air, crying out. The other three dragons shrieked from behind her, chasing after Abyss. This call Spark recognized as what she thought of as their play call.

Smaller and faster, Dragon and Flame zipped by and circled overhead. Raia jumped from Dragon's shoulder to Flame's wing as both dragons passed by. Spark glanced down and couldn't quite bring herself to leave her semi-secure spot. She watched on, utterly transfixed, as Raia raced down Flame's back while he pitched into a loop. Barlo scuttled over Flame's shoulder to his underside as it became his over-side, but Raia was quick and stayed ahead of the loop, until she reached the tip of his tail, where she grabbed the spikes and swung herself out to drop onto Abyss's back.

She stood next to Spark near the base of Abyss's neck, her body swaying as she shifted her balance to accommodate how Abyss moved while she flew.

Raia called out, "Sorry, Mistress! I should have asked first if you minded an extra passenger."

Abyss shook, just a little twitch. It was enough to send Raia, laughing gleefully, sailing out into the clear skies and nearly dislodge Spark from her place. Spark turned in time to see Zephyr snatch Raia—who was still laughing—and drop her back onto Dragon.

"Try," Abyss said.

Zephyr dove under them to circle where Flame was. The settlement was a tiny blot far below, the glittering city just above them. Spark took a deep breath. It wouldn't be the first time she'd fallen from a dragon. She stood.

wobbled, and inched along, getting a feel for how Abyss moved, how the wind pushed and pulled her.

Dragon drew closer and Raia cheered Spark on.

Spark went slowly but kept watching the others. Eltir jumped from Ice to Dragon and met Raia on the middle of his back. They pretended to spar until Raia grabbed his shoulders and pitched him off Dragon, cackling all the while. Eltir landed on Flame, and Ice swooped past a moment later, snatching him up as she went.

Spark would have to figure out how to improve her balance on the ground before she had any hope of being good at this. But when she reached Abyss's wings, she turned and sprinted toward her shoulders.

Crosswinds took her by surprise and she tumbled, bouncing off one of Abyss's spikes and rolling down her back. Spark scrabbled, fingers brushing a ridge before she sailed out into the open sky.

The wind was fierce, whipping around her, tugging at her clothes, and pinwheeling her as she fell. She saw the shimmer of the city, searing blue skies, the green valley floor, glittering red rock—they all swirled past, and Spark had to squeeze her eyes shut against the chaotic riot of colour. All while she held her breath against a scream and tensed her body, waiting.

Someone will catch me, someone will catch me, someone...

Abyss spiralled back around and caught Spark in her claws. Spark's heartbeat slammed in her ears, and she panted. Raia called for Spark to come over to Dragon. Spark didn't think she could move just yet, but Abyss helped her along, picking her up and dropping her next to Raia.

"Let's do something that looks harder than it is." She whistled to Dragon, and he changed course to glide about ten feet up from Abyss.

The memory of jumping from Zephyr to save Abyss from the ice dragons overtook Spark's thoughts, and she shuddered. She could almost feel the tenderness in her ribs again, and the hot rage coursing through her. She took a steadying breath against it.

"I've done this once before." Spark's voice was small. She took another breath to steel herself. "Let's see if I can do a better job of it this time."

At least she didn't have broken ribs to worry about.

She edged around Dragon's side, clinging to his spikes, until she had a good view of Abyss's wings. Then she leapt. She hit her mark but didn't have anything to grab onto—no spikes on the wings—and lost her footing.

The wind took her. She slid, not graceful in the least as she raked her hands along the wing membrane. And then Spark slid out into the sky, where Zephyr waited to catch her.

They tried it twice more until Spark, nowhere near approaching graceful, landed on the wing and managed to scramble to Abyss's body and find something to hold onto.

Spark couldn't believe the stunts the other three pulled with ease. She wondered at exactly what they'd been able to do when they'd had Raia's brother and his aeromancy to buoy them.

The sun had sunk near the horizon by the time the dragons left the humans on the ground outside the big workshop. Spark was startled by how much time had passed. The other three laughed and joked with each other while Spark watched Abyss disappear into the city.

"Well, that was the best money I've ever spent on weapon repairs," Eltir said, a chuckle in his voice. "We need to find more places that will trade like this."

"Take me up again to practice more and I'll temper all your gear for you."

Raia laughed and clapped her on the back. "That's the spirit, eh! We'll make a dragon walker out of you yet."

"We're going with our three to hunt and scout out on the plains for a few days," Eltir said. "We'll find you when we're back."

Spark felt light, like a dandelion fluff on the breeze, as she practically skipped back to her house.

"Spark!" Nandara called, catching up to her just outside her door.

Spark grinned until she saw the pinched expression on her mentor's face. "Is everything all right?"

"What exactly was that? You're lucky Ondias is having dinner with Lina right now. She's been waiting for you to land for hours."

"A lecture?" Spark sighed.

"And right enough. What were you thinking?"

Spark paused. "Were you looking for me? I thought you needed more time?"

"There's that—you've got magic to study. But the danger!"

"The dragons kept us safe."

Nandara gave her a dubious look. "You haven't got time to waste on those kinds of antics. With strangers!"

"I spent half the day talking to them before we practiced anything. And Abyss was with me. She's no stranger!" Spark snapped her mouth shut and stared at her mentor. She'd been so supportive until now. What had changed? "Nandara, you've got to see how useful something like that would be if I can get to be any good at it."

Nandara sighed. "I forget sometimes how young you are. You need to focus."

"But nothing we're doing is working. I wanted to try something new."

Nandara made a placating gesture, and stared the way Raia and the others had gone.

"Yes, all right," Nandara said. "But please, take greater care. Stick to your lessons."

"Do you have something new?"

"That's something we've got to work out together. Which I can't do if you're flying through the air all day."

Spark didn't like the way her chest tightened. Had she really done something wrong by giving Nandara time to rest and go through more of her notes? She didn't answer Nandara, but would pay closer attention to what her mentor wanted. And maybe schedule their magic lessons? But there was promise in dragon-walking, and she wanted to explore it further. Because even if she'd barely admit it to herself, it had been fun. Terrifying, but exhilarating.

But should she really be enjoying herself, even if it had potential? She couldn't afford a distraction if she wanted to figure out how to save Nanny.

CHAPTER EIGHT

Void Behind the Stars stood on the burial plateau not far from the entrance to the Vault, watching the human struggle with demon possession. It was both easier and harder for her. She could call and control them, work their magic to do stunning things, using them in ways and with ease that no other human had. As long as she remained in control. But once she lost control, as with her mother, regaining it was nearly impossible.

Banishing demons from other humans was typically simple for a skilled wizard. Banishing a fire demon from a fireborn hadn't yet been accomplished with full success.

Void Behind the Stars had been able to assist Spark last time, and it seemed worth exploring whether Spark could regain her capabilities on her own.

"All right, I'm imagining it back out on the porch," Spark said. "I have no idea what to do now. How do you do it when you've got a demon?"

"They don't take control."

Spark stared up at her. "Really? A demon-possessed dragon has never been under its control?"

"When we combine, it is more like wizards harnessing each other's power."

"But what about me? I'm linked to them as well."

"Your power is different from the power of dragons." Void Behind the Stars tilted her head. "Is that how you affect me? Through fire, like a demon?"

Spark stood straighter. "Could it be that simple?"

Void Behind the Stars snorted.

"Maybe not simple, though that seems pretty obvious now that you've said it. I've been using way more demon magic the last couple of days and you've spoken more than I've ever heard from you. How would that work, though? I'm not possessing you."

"The fire bond is different. Perhaps your humanity alters it, connecting us through fire in other ways."

"So the answer lies in those other ways. And how? It doesn't make sense."

"I will talk to my Superiors. You are stalling."

Spark huffed. "It's not stalling if we're solving our other problem. If we understand the connection, maybe it will make it easier for Nandara to pull a demon out of me."

Void Behind the Stars narrowed her eyes and reminded herself that Spark was still a child.

"Fine. I'll let it off the porch. Are you sure?" Spark asked.

Void Behind the Stars waited.

Focusing once more on the training, Spark's gaze unfocused and her expression went slack. Her body twitched, her fingers bunching like claws, and the fire in her eyes took on a familiar sheen.

She turned her startling gaze on Void Behind the Stars for barely a glance before looking away, taking a step toward the edge of the mountain.

Void Behind the Stars snatched her up, cupping her in a hand. The demon thrashed Spark's body against the restraint, trying to break between Void Behind the Stars's fingers, but she tightened her grip.

Spark felt the demon's rage like a burst of heat. It must have been enough distraction, because a moment later she blinked, her expression normal once again. Then girl and demon separated, and Spark instantly banished the demon and collapsed against Void Behind the Stars's palm.

"Better," Void Behind the Stars said. She hadn't expected Spark to succeed so quickly. It was a long way from where she needed to be, clearly having capitalized on the demon's distraction, but she'd pushed the demon out without assistance this time.

The girl's exhaustion was a concern, though. It would need to be addressed.

"Enough for now," Void Behind the Stars announced. "I have duties."

Ondias had complained to her that morning how Spark was foolishly resisting a pairing the boy Jatt was enthusiastic about. Void Behind the Stars did not understand humans' coupling rituals, though she tended to agree with Neesha and Spark that the choice should be theirs, not others'.

Spark had been despairing, seeming to believe she could not have a union with the other girl, Ember. Perhaps she required a reminder that there were other options.

Merciless Winter Sky was monitoring their eggs today so that Void Behind the Stars could assist Emerald Starlight and Cedar Jewel with their young. She brought Spark to one of the dazzling emerald clan towers. Much like the dragon city itself, this one had a long winding entrance and a large, tiered space deep inside where Emerald Starlight and Cedar Jewel waited with their five hatchlings.

Three of the hatchlings napped on one of the lower tiers, while two wrestled in the main room as the two dragonesses looked on. Emerald Starlight's three young took entirely after her with their silvery green markings, one of them almost entirely green of varying shades, despite all five hatchlings having the same sire—Consuming Fire, who still lived near Pasdale with his mate, Towering Spires, though he was due back to assist with hunting any day now. Cedar Jewel was bold green with scarlet spines and her two hatchlings had a mix of her markings and his. One was burnt orange with scarlet spines and the other a marbling of emerald and orange.

Cedar Jewel greeted her and commented that she was early. "But why the human?"

"She is useful, and needs to learn our ways," Void Behind the Stars answered, both of them speaking in the dragon tongue.

Emerald Starlight nuzzled her nose into Cedar Jewel's neck.

Void Behind the Stars felt a flicker of satisfaction as Spark's eyes went wide. The girl clearly brimmed with questions. Thankfully she did not appear interested in testing Void Behind the Stars's patience today by giving voice to any of those questions.

"We shall be swift," Emerald Starlight said.

"Do not rush—they are in good hands."

The two dragonesses took their leave, Spark watching them with her head tilted. Void Behind the Stars hadn't told her why they were there, though she hoped it was obvious. It was expected that impending dragon parents help new ones so that the former could learn some child rearing and the latter would have support. It was especially difficult these days, with all of them crammed in on top of each other in the city like this—hiding.

Void Behind the Stars longed for Spark to successfully harness trueflame and demons so that they could lay siege on Pasdale and reduce Loch to cinders. When she was feeling at her worst, she would recall how Neesha had helped her do that very thing to Draxli.

She would have her home back. They all would.

And maybe, if the stars were willing, they could take back what was theirs in time to save her third egg.

In the meantime, she would watch over Cedar Jewel and Emerald Starlight's hatchlings so that the two mothers could hunt. It was increasingly difficult to keep from depleting the range's resources entirely, and they had to cast farther and farther from the city.

The orangey-scarlet hatchling broke from the play fighting to lunge at Spark.

"Snack!" he burbled.

Spark didn't even have time to scream before Void Behind the Stars deflected the hatchling with her tail, nudging him back over with his sister and hissing a warning to leave the human alone. He glared at Void Behind the Stars, looked around her at Spark, and made a snapping gesture in her direction.

"Humans are not for eating," Void Behind the Stars said, switching to a language Spark could understand, even if the hatchling continued to speak dragonish.

"Hungry!"

"Humans are friends, not snacks."

"Friends?"

Void Behind the Stars beckoned Spark over.

"Should I really be here if they haven't been told not to eat me?" Spark said.

"They learn."

"Are their mothers friends of yours?"

Void Behind the Stars nodded and gave Spark a nudge to close the distance. The hatchling—who was roughly the size of Spark's first workshop—leaned down to look at her. He pressed his snout into Spark's side.

"Too many bones!" he declared. "No snack."

"Yes, too many bones," Void Behind the Stars said.

"Really?" Spark glared at Void Behind the Stars. "You convinced them not to eat me because I haven't got enough meat?"

"They are young. They'll learn better reasons. Show them."

And so Spark made fireballs for the hatchlings to chase and play with, and she stroked their chins and noses until they got used to her soft touch and small hands.

"When do they learn how to tell good people from bad ones?" Spark asked.

"When do any of us?"

Spark sighed, nodding glumly, and then went back to tossing fireballs around for the hatchlings.

The other three woke up and the first two went to nap. Void Behind the Stars once again went through the lesson that Spark was not a snack, while Spark did her best to stay away from the snappy hatchlings.

"They're like hungry bottomless pits," Spark said.

"The situation is not ideal."

"Because there's so many of you in one place?"

Void Behind the Stars growled. "Small blazes spread wide is the standard for this reason. They will have to leave soon or their growth will be impeded."

"Are they big enough to leave safely?"

Void Behind the Stars turned to watch the hatchlings. She could not safely answer the girl's question.

They were overcrowding this valley and the surrounding range precisely because it was the only place their hatchlings—or any of them, really—were safe.

Emerald Starlight returned not long afterward with the corpses of several elk and one bear clutched in her talons. All five hatchlings sprang on the carcasses, finishing them even before Void Behind the Stars had completed her farewells to her friend and gathering up Spark—who had watched the hatchlings eat in something Void Behind the Stars interpreted as fascinated horror.

The hatchlings had left not a scrap of fur or trace of blood, and they turned expectant looks on Emerald Starlight, barely satiated.

"Unsustainable," Void Behind the Stars grumbled as she took Spark up to the dragon city.

Void Behind the Stars dropped into the main hall that served as home to the Superiors.

Void Behind the Stars had hoped to catch them in a rare moment of quiet to discuss her new hypothesis on the fire bond and how Spark's magic affected her, but there was quite a lot of hissing and snapping, and even some stamped feet going on, all indistinct at this distance. The seven Superiors formed a semicircle with the new Dragoness Superior at the centre—she was formidable, with rich gold colouring veined with silver and a deep black much like Void Behind the Stars's own markings. She stood tall and silent, scowling over the proceedings, while the other six argued with the three newcomers Spark had practiced flying with—Lava Flow, Boundless Glacial Lake and Imposing Shores—clustered in the centre.

As she listened, catching only snatches of phrase here and there, the picture came together, and Void Behind the Stars's annoyance at the living conditions Loch forced upon them erupted into fury once more.

"Is everything all right?" Spark whispered, the strangeness of her voice carrying through the glittering halls.

"Possible exile," Void Behind the Stars said, keeping her voice low. Majestic Sunrise, the Dragoness Superior, had already flicked a glance of acknowledgement their way.

"Have they done something wrong?"

Void Behind the Stars scowled. "Too much human intervention."

"What? But... how are they different from you?"

Void Behind the Stars tilted her head. How indeed.

"Oh no. Should we intervene?"

There were a few other dragons around, but none of them were the heads of a circle like Void Behind the Stars was, and her rank on the dragon council that occasionally advised the Superiors granted her a few privileges and no small measure of influence. She approached, standing where Majestic Sunrise could easily see her, and waited to be acknowledged. Unfortunately, Ocean Deep, with her grey and indigo markings, was the first to notice, and she snapped her jaws at Void Behind the Stars.

"You will maintain comportment," Majestic Sunrise growled. The room went silent.

Spark kept behind Void Behind the Stars, where she could observe but not easily be observed. This was likely not the ideal moment to bring an outsider into their midst, even if they all generally tolerated this particular outsider. No dragon was quite so fond of her as Void Behind the Stars was.

"You have input on this matter?" Majestic Sunrise asked.

Void Behind the Stars bowed formally. "I wish to understand the matter fully before deciding if my opinion is warranted."

"She's just going to side with these human-aligned filth," Ocean Deep snarled.

"Void Behind the Stars is our expert on dragon-human relations not because she sides with human causes blindly, but because she understands the humans well enough to know when they are worthy of our attention and when we would be wasting our time." Majestic Sunrise glared at Ocean Deep. "I shall not tolerate further interruption."

Ocean Deep snarled, smoke rising from between her bared teeth.

Ignoring her, Majestic Sunrise summed up the problem for Void Behind the Stars: the trio of dragons had forsaken their original blazes and gone rogue, marauding with the humans. Some on the council believed that they had abandoned their duty to the betterment of dragonkind in doing so.

"Blazes are regularly reformed," Void Behind the Stars said. "And my understanding is that the marauding they have done is against Loch and his extended forces, or those aligned with Golden Hill, who have become our bitter enemies. I daresay they're doing more to better our kind than those of us hiding in this valley."

Ocean Deep snarled again.

Majestic Sunrise gave Void Behind the Stars a withering look. "Yes, we are all aware of what your preferences are in regards to taking action. But carelessness is the reason that I am Dragoness Superior now, when Obliterating Icefield should have had decades left in her reign."

Void Behind the Stars bowed her head.

"We have concerns that they are too involved with humans and are forgetting who they are," Majestic Sunrise said.

Void Behind the Stars stepped aside to leave Spark more visible. Some of the dragons who hadn't noticed her yet shuffled. Some grumbled quietly. No one outright objected.

"I have brought a human into the midst of our proceedings, as I have done in the past. And she brings up a good point. Why am I any different from these three? If you exile them for their actions, should you not exile me as well?"

"A fine consideration," Ocean Deep snapped.

"Your humans have been indispensable in the safety of our kind," Majestic Sunrise said. "While your methods are still to be condemned, the human's discovery of how to make armour for us has saved many lives. She has worked directly to assist in rebuilding the city."

"So it is less about my worth and more about the worth of the humans I associate with?" Void Behind the Stars asked.

"The human also doesn't pull you from your duties," Majestic Sunrise said. "We understand she assists you."

Spark stood respectfully silent, though her wide eyes certainly betrayed her anxiety as her gaze took in the assembled dragons. Void Behind the Stars took a moment to translate the conversation for her.

"What duties have these three failed to perform?" Spark asked.

Void Behind the Stars waited, knowing Spark would see.

"What, like helping with the hunt?" she asked. "I know you used to do more, when humans were actually honouring their treaties with you. Could they perform their duties now that they're here? Surely they can hunt. Or whatever else you want them to do."

"They have offered." Void Behind the Stars looked at Majestic Sunrise and switched to dragonish. "And there's no reason their humans cannot help them, or at the very least not hinder them. But they are clever, and I have seen how they work together. They have been showing Spark and I how to work more closely."

Spark looked around at the dragons. "Should I really be here? Isn't this interfering?"

Majestic Sunrise drew nearer, parting the crowd like a talon through moss. She lay with her chin on the floor and her deep gaze on Spark.

"We... came to talk about the fire bond between my family and your kind," Spark said hesitantly, glancing up at Void Behind the Stars. "Isn't this—" she gestured around "—a matter for dragons alone?"

"Mistress Superior would like to know why you think allowances should be extended," Void Behind the Stars said. "And should we extend them to all who have been absent?"

Void Behind the Stars couldn't parse all of the emotions that ran through Spark's expression before she drew a neutral veil across it. This conversation was, in many ways, beyond her. Likely they should have had Ondias present for such discussions. But Ondias had grown more conservative over the years, and Void Behind the Stars feared that bold risks like the ones she and Spark had been taking were what they required to survive the months ahead.

"These are unusual times," Spark said carefully. "I believe that we all need to cling to what alliances we have. Abyss—" Spark covered the nickname with a cough. "Void Behind the Stars befriending me has benefited all of your kind and helped keep those of us in the valley safer. Until the threat from Loch is over, I think we should all take what help we can get, if it's coming from trusted parties."

Spark glanced up at her.

"We help each other in different ways, just as Void Behind the Stars and I were recently helping care for the new hatchlings. It's mutually beneficial and makes it easier for all of us. If these three can hunt and patrol, and maybe fight if we need it, I don't think they should be turned away."

Majestic Sunrise narrowed her eyes.

"That's what I think." Spark crossed her arms and stared down at the floor. "And there's no reason you can't re-evaluate later any decisions you come to now."

Majestic Sunrise glanced up at Void Behind the Stars.

"Could these humans be taking advantage?" Void Behind the Stars asked Spark.

"I think only those three dragons can say for sure. Do you think I take advantage of you?"

Void Behind the Stars snorted an annoyed fireball at Spark. Spark shunted it to either side of her and stood with her hands on her hips.

"I think we're friends, don't you?" Spark said. "And I thought maybe we were unique, you and my family, but maybe we're not? And I don't think it's bad if there are others, because we've accomplished some pretty great things."

She looked back to Majestic Sunrise, who stood and went back to her place presiding over the conversation.

"We are still vulnerable," Void Behind the Stars said.

"But that's what being friends is. Aren't you vulnerable between each other? Weren't those two dragonesses taking a risk leaving their young with you? You'd never hurt them, but you've been betrayed by your kind. Those ice dragons are the most recent, but I doubt they were the first. There's a bigger risk here because humans don't understand your ways as much as we could, but Ondias's work over her lifetime has done a lot to change that."

Spark shrugged and fell silent, looking small and sad.

Void Behind the Stars bowed to the council. "I agree with the human. I believe we should explore how the relationship can benefit us as a whole, and that these three be given the opportunity to prove themselves and the worth of their humans before decisions to cast them aside are made."

Ocean Deep growled, smoke trailing from the corners of her mouth. There was more grumbling from the assembled council.

"We have faced enough loss from outside," Void Behind the Stars said. "I do not believe we should cause it from within."

"Thank you for your input," Majestic Sunrise said.

With the dismissal, Void Behind the Stars bowed to the Superiors and then held out her hand, collecting Spark and leaving again. The politics of the council were wearying, and while the new dragons and their humans didn't pose a threat in Void Behind the Stars's mind, they had been allowed to become a distraction by naysayers like Ocean Deep.

Void Behind the Stars had not had the opportunity to speak about the fire bond between her and the Joasera women. There was much to learn there, but it would have to wait. Void Behind the Stars returned Spark to her studies and experimentation so she could take up the vigil over her eggs.

CHAPTER NINE

S park sat in her kitchen at the rickety old table she'd scavenged, and nibbled on a slice of bread, trying to summon the energy to get back to work. She'd been exhausted in new and interesting ways since Abyss had brought her home. As she contemplated going to bed early and trying again tomorrow, Nandara came in, Shadow trotting in with her.

"I've got some news for you," Nandara said, "if you've got a few minutes."

Spark sat up, grateful for something to do that wasn't a danger she was unprepared for, but Jatt slunk in behind Nandara.

Spark tensed. "Sure. I'm not quite ready to get back to the demon work."

Nandara sighed. "Ondias mentioned you and Abyss were still trying that."

"We're getting close."

Nandara sat in the other chair, and Jatt leaned against the wall. Spark was reminded again of how the place wasn't quite fit for the company she wished she had more regularly.

"I've been working with a contact in Pasdale," Nandara said. "Someone who can help you once you get there. I think it will make it easier for you to succeed with smaller numbers. A small, quick stealth attack to free Dionelle and recover the stolen dragon eggs."

"You don't think we should attack in force?" Spark leaned forward, her elbows on the table.

"You've said yourself that we're not ready for that. We can't wait to recover the eggs, but there's no reason we can't give ourselves more time to prepare for a large-scale battle."

"It gives you more focus too," Jatt said. "Less to worry about all at once."

"My contact can get you to the dragon eggs and into the palace where Loch is holding Di. You can go to her first and then strike both positions simultaneously. Those three dragon riders will help—and their dragons, of course. I understand you swayed the Superiors on that matter."

Spark sat back. "I did? It worked? Abyss seemed disappointed when we left."

"The Superiors have already picked which dragons will go with you." Nandara shrugged. "You can think about who you'd like to come with you on the human side."

Spark bit her lip. In a lot of ways, she didn't want anyone else to come with her, in case something went wrong.

"I'll think about it," Spark said. "It'd be nice if you were there, in case I need to be stupid with demons. You didn't get it to work, but we're close enough that it might next time."

Nandara pressed her lips into a thin line.

"That's still risky." Nandara fished around in her bag and left a stack of papers and a book on the table between them. "I've got everything I could find on your mother's work with fire portals, including analysis from dragons and speculations from the heads of the Guild to try to fill in the blanks. It doesn't make sense to most of us, but you might be able to make some advances with it. Neesha was the only human to have opened one previously. It's dangerous, but not as dangerous as demons."

"And once I open a fire portal, I can summon trueflame, can't I? That would take care of those ice dragons for good."

"It certainly would. I'm convinced that's what you did in the spring, and I'm convinced you can do it again. Intentionally this time. With control. As soon as you've got it, you can leave for Pasdale. Ondias has already begun preparations, so there won't be much delay once you figure out the magic."

Spark picked up the scroll on top of the pile and gave it a glance. "Guess I've got some homework for tonight." A block of text stood out while she skimmed. "Wait, I can use fire portals to travel, too, can't I?"

"In theory. You really shouldn't. Getting trapped in the fire realm is a real risk, and we've got no one to come for you if demon trickery keeps you there."

Her grandfather had been enchanted by the dragons to go for Nanny when she'd been trapped in the fire realm. Spark was pretty sure dragons could pass through the realm as well. Someone could come for her—it would just be a tremendous risk. But taking a fire portal to Pasdale would improve her chances of getting to Abyss's egg in time.

"All of the magic we've been working with lately has been last-resort stuff," Spark said. "And we are getting to our last resort. One of these has to work or we're doomed."

Nandara reached across the table and squeezed Spark's hand. "Remember this burden isn't yours alone. This whole village and all the dragons are supporting you."

"I know. I still feel alone in this, though. I need Nanny here."

Nandara's smile turned sad. "We'll do what we can to make that happen." Nandara glanced at Jatt. "Speaking of which, I know you've been busy, but have you put any more consideration into the betrothal?"

Jatt pushed away from the wall and stood up straight, his expression eager.

Spark pulled her hand back and leaned away. "I haven't had time to even think much of food."

Nandara's mouth tightened, and she nodded slowly. "Well, I'll leave it for the two of you."

Spark gathered up the books as Nandara left. She turned to Jatt as soon as the door was closed. "You're welcome to stay—you always are—but I have work to do, and I don't want to talk about the betrothal."

She headed into her workshop and he followed.

"It's not a bad idea, Spark. Is there really that much to consider? How is it really going to change our lives that much? I'd live here with you, once this place is done, which is what we've been talking about anyway. Ember would still be here. Nothing would change but a stupid tattoo on our wrists."

"I don't want to." Spark tensed and dropped her stack on the worktable harder than she'd meant to. "That should be enough. If nothing's going to change, then what's the point? Now I've got work to do. You can help me or you can go."

Jatt sagged and came closer to the table, looking over what she'd been reading. "It's dangerous."

"It's been dangerous since the winter. Doing nothing is more dangerous."

"Spark, I didn't come here to fight with you."

"Then why did you come?" She glared at him.

"I want to help you. So does Gran. But we want you to be safe when you do it. There's still lots of time to get to the dragon eggs."

"I can't take that chance."

"You should take as few chances as possible. What do you think happens to us—to the whole village—if you die in Pasdale or get trapped in the fire realm? You're exhausted and distracted. Forget about the dragon riders and maybe get some sleep."

"I get plenty of sleep."

Jatt gave her an oblique look.

"I do! I look this tired because I've been fighting demons for two days straight."

"And it's clearly taking a toll on you. You need more rest. You need to wait until you're ready before you move on Pasdale."

"I'll do what I need to. If you're just going to lecture me, then you might as well follow your gran. I've got too much to do for this."

"But Spark—"

"Out!" She whirled on him, pointing at the door. The embers in the forge ignited into a furious blaze.

Jatt recoiled like she'd slammed him with a fireball. Then he stiffened and stormed out the door. Shadow barked and jumped to his feet, trotting to the door to sniff it and then bark some more.

Spark sank to the floor with her back against a table leg and sobbed. Shadow crept up to her, nosing her shoulder until she wrapped her arm around him. He settled in at her side with his head in her lap.

For all Nandara's talk of support, Spark had never felt so alone.

There were all these wizards around her with so many decades of experience, with knowledge of spells she could only guess at, who knew what her mother and grandmother had been capable of—and still it was all on Spark to save them. Not one of them was taking the lead. All their wisdom, and it was down to only her. Because she was the only fireborn.

She had to change that. Had to. She couldn't keep doing this by herself.

Spark cried until her face ached and her bottom hurt from sitting on the floor for so long. Then she washed up and gathered up the books, taking them to her room so she could sit in bed, somewhere comfortable and with Shadow still snuggling her, and read up on fire portals and what Neesha had done.

If no one was going to help, she had to use the solitude to figure out how to save them all.

CHAPTER TEN

Spark stood outside the armoury with Abyss again, dressed in her fireproof garb. Tired and weary but a little less alone. There were no humans who could help her the way she needed, but at least there was Abyss.

Spark pulled a fire out of the air, suppressing a yawn. She should have slept in, maybe should have waited another day. But she had to try. She'd read through everything the night before and thought she knew what she needed to do. Nandara was right that the notes did make a bit of sense to her.

Neesha had used fear and anger and a desire to protect her loved ones to open fire portals and channel trueflame from the fire realm. She hadn't really had control of it, and it had ultimately been her undoing. Spark couldn't afford the risk. She needed control.

Abyss lay with her chin on the ground, shrewdly watching everything Spark did, ready to pounce in an emergency.

There was less likely to be an emergency with this. Either Spark would open a fire portal or she wouldn't. There was the off chance she'd open one and trueflame would burst out unbidden, but that wouldn't do much harm where they were. While Spark needed control, she first needed to open one at all, just to know how to do it. Then she could refine it to something more easily controlled, something she was conscious of doing.

So she started to call a demon, but halted when the fire shifted quality without a demon emerging. She focused on maintaining that balance, getting right up to the flames and reaching in like she could pull the fire apart with her hands.

And maybe she could.

Spark reached in with both hands, trying to feel the difference—whether it had definitive edges, whether it went deeper.

But there was nothing.

She sighed and thought back to the battle in the spring, when they'd been at risk of losing Abyss, and when Spark herself had been so badly injured. She remembered how angry the burning cold nets had made her, how she'd used her rage to dig into the fire.

The fire in front of her flared brighter, and she squinted against it. She held that ghost of fury and fear, her pulse rushing, and fought to breathe evenly.

The changes to the fire still didn't amount to a portal. She wasn't sure how she knew that, or how she'd know if she was successful. Maybe Abyss could tell her?

"Am I close?" Spark asked.

"No. Keep trying."

Spark grumbled in wordless frustration and the fire flared with her mood. She let her anger and exasperation, the despair and crushing loneliness, wash over her and pour out of her. She pushed the fire wider and resumed the summoning. When the demon came, she caught the difference in the fire—there was a strange boundary, with the normal fire diverting around it.

Ignoring the demon, she plunged her hand into the fire, feeling a buzzing difference and closing her hand around it. She sent the demon away again, but held her hand where it was.

"You have it," Abyss said gently.

Spark's breath hitched. She clenched around the sob forming.

She let the portal close, widened the fire so that it was all around her, and tried again, gripping all that rage and loneliness—consumed by images of Ember's tears, Jatt storming off, Abyss in burning cold restraints, Neesha entombed in diamond, Nanny in a dark cell, and so much silence where Pappy and Bren and Breen should have been. Spark squeezed her eyes shut, tears sizzling off her cheeks. She sent her attention deep into the fire, trying to find that electric buzz, the spot where the fire burned against the wall of reality.

Nothing.

Spark shouted a particularly foul oath, and the fire flared around her. She let it, making it bigger. She'd been pulling a massive blaze to help Abyss when she'd opened that fire portal in the spring, so she did that again, digging into the fire like she tore through dirt to get at the roots of a particularly stubborn weed.

And the fire changed again, a buzz opening up where her attention had been.

A demon burst out of the centre of the fire, coming right for her.

Spark shrieked, startled more than anything. The entire blaze collapsed in on itself, snuffing itself out, leaving her with a charging demon. She hissed the command to *stop*—it crackled in place, immobile. Spark started a new fire and banished the demon back to where it belonged.

"Is that supposed to happen?" she asked, panting.

Abyss tilted her head curiously. "Any fire can contain a demon."

As much as Spark had always known that at an intellectual level, it was something else entirely to live it. And while a demon would have to be particularly quick to overpower her and take possession, she didn't have the energy to deal with that right now.

Spark sighed and cautiously opened the fire wider again, digging. But she was still on edge, still waiting for a demon to pounce.

"Stop holding back," Abyss growled.

"Easy for you to say," Spark muttered.

She immersed herself in the blaze and dug in again, but her concentration was shot. She folded the fire in on itself and lay down on the cool rock, breathing deep until she didn't feel as agitated anymore.

She didn't have time for breaks.

Taking one more long, slow breath and letting it out just as slowly, Spark stood. She pulled up another fire and put her new focus into it, into its depths.

And it shifted again. She tensed against the burst, but there was no demon this time, and she tore at the fire some more.

"You have it," Abyss said again.

Spark closed the portal, snuffed the fire, and took a step back, her heart pounding. She went through another round of slow breathing before starting a new fire. It was a little easier to rip open this time.

"Holy shit! It worked!"

Spark was equal parts stunned and overjoyed as she shut the whole thing down and looked to Abyss for confirmation. Her friend grinned, her eyes glittering. Spark opened one more fire portal, just to be sure.

When she'd finished, she said, "Let's go. I need to show Nandara."

Abyss reached for her, but Spark had another idea.

"Wait! I want to try one thing. I'm going to go in—to the fire realm. Just in and out to see that it works, okay?"

"This is a risk," Abyss said.

"It's all a risk. Count to ten, and if I'm not back, you can come for me."

Abyss stared unmoving, her gaze hard and bright. Then she nodded.

"Count of ten," Abyss said.

Spark pulled up a fire, opened the portal—so easy now!—and widened it. She stared at what she'd done, her pulse gone wild and her body buzzing. But she had to know. If she could travel through this portal, she could get to Pasdale in seconds.

Deep breath. Spark closed her eyes and took a step.

Even through her eyelids, the light was close to blinding. The electricity around her intensified. When she opened her eyes, it was all fire. She stood on what looked like a bed of hot embers.

In the back of her mind, she started to count.

But the place felt so familiar, and shapes moved around her. Were they demons or something else? She'd never heard much about what the actual fire realm was like, not from Pappy or Nanny or from anyone recounting what had happened to Neesha.

There was a presence. No shape to it, just a feeling—a warmth she felt in her soul, something different from the heat baking her skin and washing through her bones.

Trickery.

Nanny's pendant was cold and heavy against her skin—like a warning. She'd been here seven seconds, and that was enough.

Behind her, the way she'd come, the fire brightened in a vague sort of circle. She quickly popped back through.

The real world—the realm where she belonged—seemed dark and drab by comparison. Abyss's gleaming black shape was even more eye-watering than normal, so that Spark had to look down at the rock beneath her feet until she got her bearings again.

"Eight," Abyss said with a touch of reproach in her voice.

"Sorry. Maybe I should have said fifteen? I didn't mean to worry you. It was just so strange, and it took some time to really understand my surroundings. But the trickery was still there. I don't think I should do that alone again."

"Not entirely alone."

Spark smiled. "No, of course not. I'm glad you're here."

That same familiar warmth nudged Spark again, and she gasped, realizing she'd left the portal open. She snapped it shut before anything could get through and cause havoc.

"All right," Spark said. "*Now* down to Nandara and Ondias. We've got lots of daylight left. We need to go."

CHAPTER ELEVEN

Abyss had just set Spark down in the field where Ondias took her meetings with dragons when a blinding flash of light soundlessly erupted from the western diamond column. Spark cried out in alarm. She was echoed by several others throughout the village, shouts going up everywhere.

Was the column compromised? Was the city under attack? Did Loch somehow know what she'd been planning?

The fear that it was some sort of pre-emptive strike got Spark moving. She sprinted toward the village, but Ondias came out of it from one end and Nandara from another, with a bigger crowd gathering in the laneways. Both women were heading toward Spark, and she halted.

The light had subsided, and the column looked okay from a distance, but the dragon city was emptying, a riot of colour and cacophony of sound that made Spark's legs rubbery.

"We must go up," Abyss said from behind her.

Nandara reached her first, and Abyss snatched up the two of them. She stretched out her other hand to collect Ondias and took flight.

Spark didn't have to worry about her rubbery legs anymore, but her wibbly stomach had complaints as Abyss exploded into the afternoon sky. Spark didn't think they'd been in the air for more than a couple of seconds before Abyss deposited all three of them on the mountainside near the column and circled to land.

Spark's rubbery legs had had enough. She sprawled across the rock, Nandara stumbling beside her. But Nandara kept her momentum going, continuing into a run.

"Oh no," she whispered and was gone from Spark's side.

"Oh my stars!" Ondias gasped in a tone Spark hadn't heard since the day Spark first arrived in the valley with bad news.

"Nandara?" a third voice croaked, strained and weak. A voice Spark didn't recognize. "What happened? Where's Mamma? How did I get here?"

Spark staggered to her feet as Nandara reached Neesha, who was on her hands and knees at the base of the column, surrounded by diamond debris. Nandara wrapped her arms around Neesha's shoulders, rubbing her back and speaking softly.

"Hush, dear, you're safe. It's over and you're safe."

Ondias got there next. Abyss landed behind Spark, both of them staying back.

Spark couldn't stop blinking, her whole body abuzz all over again, her breath coming in harsh gasps. After all this time, how could this be possible? Had it really been as simple as getting another fire portal open for Neesha to escape? Spark breathed hard, trying to push down the anger at everyone who said it wouldn't be easy, couldn't be done, and had stopped her from trying for months.

"Why am I here?" Neesha asked. "Where's Mita?"

"Hush, she's safe," Nandara said. "You did it, Nee. You beat Draxli, and you kept us all safe. But the cost was high."

Spark was far enough away to have not been noticed yet, but near enough to see the tears in her mother's eyes.

"Draxli's gone?"

"He is." Nandara kept her tone even.

Spark pressed her hand over her mouth. She hadn't even considered for a moment what this would do to Neesha. She'd had the victory she wanted, but didn't know about the battle that followed, the loss the long years had brought.

This was everything Spark had wanted, everything she'd been working for. And it couldn't be what she needed right now.

Neesha barely paid attention, patting at her body, looking down and around at it. Had she aged? Spark had no idea what she'd looked like when she'd first gone into that column.

"Mistress!" Neesha called out, spotting Abyss. The confusion evaporated, joy taking its place.

The dragoness leaned forward, bowing her head and nudging Neesha's side with her snout. Neesha hugged it, stroking Abyss's nose as Spark herself had done so many times.

"You're all right!" The relief was palpable. "Where's everyone else?"

Abyss very carefully shuffled aside so her thick leg was no longer near Spark, leaving her visible. Standing exposed.

Neesha saw her, confusion overtaking her expression again. Spark stood stiffly and swallowed hard. To have that blue-amber gaze on her was like looking in a mirror. Her throat thickened, growing hot as she blinked back unshed tears.

"You found another fireborn?" Neesha asked, turning to look between Ondias and Nandara on either side of her, Nandara with a hand on Neesha's elbow to steady her. She blinked at them, staring. "Why do you look so... different?"

"I mentioned the cost of your victory," Nandara said gently, gesturing in Spark's direction. "This is Mita."

"No." Spark saw the way her mother's chest heaved. She would have collapsed but for Nandara and Ondias. "How long?" Neesha gasped.

"Mita is nearly seventeen."

Despite Nandara and Ondias, Neesha did collapse, wailing the word "No!" until it cracked under a sob and she fell silent, her body wracked with tears.

Spark got moving, reaching them swiftly and falling to her knees in front of Neesha, taking her hand. It was the same startling white as her own.

"It's okay," she whispered, not sure if she meant it but suspecting it was what her mother needed to hear. "Nanny took care of me."

"Nanny Sharice? She's okay?"

Spark blinked for a moment. "She helped, but mostly it was Nanny Di. She kept me safe and taught me pyromancy, told me about what you did."

"I lost it all. I missed everything. You were a newborn, and now..."

"You're here now. That's what matters."

Ondias took Spark's shoulder and gently pried her away while Nandara helped Neesha to her feet.

"I'm afraid that cost may be higher than you're ready for," Nandara said gently. "It's not just the years, but what filled them."

"But Draxli's gone. You said so." The uncertainty in Neesha's voice dropped a ball of lead into Spark's gut.

"Draxli's gone, yes. But he had followers."

Neesha sagged. "So it was all for nothing."

"Not nothing, no."

"Draxli was coming to kill you," Ondias said. "All three of you. He would have taken down most of Pasdale to achieve it, too. His followers are odious, but without the targeted vendetta."

"Mostly," Spark muttered.

Ondias gave her a pitying look. "Loch has been driven more by jealousy than revenge. It doesn't make him less dangerous."

"What happened?" Neesha's voice had a sharp edge. "What else did I miss?"

Ondias and Nandara shared a look.

"Let's get down to the village, get you inside and something to eat. We've got a lot to talk about," Nandara said. She glanced at Abyss, who scooped up the four of them and glided back down into the valley.

Spark stared ahead at nothing, allowing herself to be ushered inside when they reached Ondias's house. She couldn't understand why they were here when there was barely room for Ondias in this place. Spark hated it in Ondias's house— it always felt claustrophobic, and somehow the piles of things had gotten worse. Few people threw things out in the settlement, because they were so isolated and new supplies were so damned hard to come by, but everyone else repurposed things to use or kept them in storage in sheds or under tarps.

Ondias's entire house was storage. Stacks of crates and furniture and books and scrolls lined every wall and teetered next to living spaces, creating artificial barriers. The parlour seemed to have shrunk, ceding ground to the stack encroaching from the kitchen. It was dusty and musty and warmer than it had any right to be. Darker, too. Like a stuffy cave.

But Ondias got them all seated around the table. It was a squeeze, but it could have been worse. Ondias quickly got tea in front of all of them. Neesha couldn't stop staring at Spark.

Nandara tried to be gentle about things, but Neesha cut her off.

"Just give it to me. It's clearly bad if Mita is here by herself, which she appears to be."

"Loch has Nanny," Spark said. "I'm going with Abyss soon to Pasdale to get her. I was working with fire portals as part of our rescue plan, and I think that's what woke you up."

Nandara gave her a quick look, but Neesha jumped in with questions, wanting to know where everyone else was, going through a cascade of grief learning that Sharice, Reiser, and Breen were gone, that the nephew she'd never known was gone. Spark hadn't been able to deliver that news, sagging in her chair and breathing back tears as Nandara recounted what had happened.

Neesha closed her eyes and leaned back in her chair, silent tears washing over her cheeks as she listened to Nandara and Ondias fill her in.

"My sacrifice didn't do a godsdamn bit of good," Neesha snapped. "I lost half my life to delay the inevitable."

"No, Mamma." Spark took her hand across the table. "I wouldn't be alive if not for what you did. You need to rest, but I'm going to get Nanny, and then there will be three of us. Loch can't stop us."

Neesha gasped back a sob. Spark had been trying to comfort her and didn't understand how she'd made it worse.

"You shouldn't be fighting my battles." Neesha leaned forward, her head on the table, and sobbed harder.

Spark rested her hand on Neesha's shoulder for a moment, then abandoned her tea and went outside. Abyss was there, cautiously crammed into the laneway, and Spark paused, wanting to talk to her but not sure what to say.

But Abyss had plenty of her own to say. "Merciless Winter Sky came and went while you were inside and—"

"Who?" Spark looked up at her, feeling like she'd forgotten how words worked.

"My blue mate." Abyss stretched her neck to gently nudge Spark's side. "The eggs have changed. All of them, not just mine. They are closer to hatching. Much closer."

Spark cursed. "How much time?"

Abyss shook her head. "The Superiors are assessing."

Spark rubbed her hands over her face and stared at nothing, trying to catch a single thought and make it make sense.

Nandara came out the door behind her and put a hand on her shoulder.

"I'm sorry, Spark. I know this is hard right now. But your mother is a tough woman, and we'll see her through this."

"She needs Nanny. We all do."

Nandara sighed.

"Ondias has everything ready to go," Spark urged.

"I don't think you should leave when Neesha is so fragile. She's going to need to talk to you. She's got so much guilt."

"She shouldn't."

"I know, but that's for her to work out. I suspect once she's done grieving what she missed and all she's lost, she's going to get very angry. An angry Neesha, particularly if she clears her head by then, will be the help you need."

Spark shook her head vehemently. "We can't expect her to do more the day she's woken up. Maybe not even the same month. We had a plan that didn't depend on her."

"But waiting for her will be safer."

"We don't have time. Abyss's egg doesn't have time."

"It's a long journey. The more people you have with you, the better."

"I can go by myself. Me and whatever dragons are willing. I got the fire portal to work. I went into the fire realm to test it. I think that's what brought Mamma back." Spark gritted her teeth against the anger trying to build. "I can use fire portals and take the dragons, and we can get Nanny back. Free that egg. Maybe others."

"You can have more support. You just need to wait. I know you think there's no time, but the eggs here in the city are still quiet and—" Nandara glanced to Abyss, who shook her head.

"There's been a change," Abyss said.

"We might have days yet," Nandara said.

"Or we might have hours." Spark looked to Abyss. "This deadline is yours. What do *you* want?"

"We should not delay."

Spark gave Nandara a hard look. "Who is your contact? How do I find them?"

Nandara sighed. "Her name is Unari." Nandara told her how to find the woman. "Please let me talk this over with Ondias and your mother first."

"Ondias is just going to try to stop me. It's what she always does. If I hadn't listened to her, maybe we'd have gotten Neesha back months ago!"

"This isn't all Ondias." Nandara braced her hands on her hips and stared up at the city. "We've all been trying to help you, but to keep you safe as well. You need to learn to trust us. We just want to be certain you're ready before you take on something so huge."

It was so much like what Jatt had said—that she wasn't ready. They were all out to stop her, and she couldn't understand why. All she wanted was help. The right kind of help. Anger buzzed through her body, and she didn't think it was possible to feel more alone, more abandoned.

It was time to go to Pasdale. It was time to rescue Nanny. She couldn't keep going like this for a single day longer.

Spark turned away without a word and stormed off, away from both Nandara and Abyss. Nandara called after her, but neither of them followed. She passed through the market and stopped at Hextir's cook fire. It was lunch time and he was roasting a brace of conies, but Spark couldn't think of food right now.

She stopped next to the fire, glaring into it. Hextir asked her something but she didn't really hear it. Her mind was filled by the call of the blaze and her need to do something. Anything.

She strode over to the fire, dug into it, and opened a portal. Without hesitation, she stepped through.

CHAPTER TWELVE

The fire realm was brighter than she was ready for, though she could distinguish between variations in the shades of brightness—the ground was a glowing ember shade, more orange than the rest of her surroundings, which were yellower with flares of blinding white.

It all roared in her ears, like the rush of a superheated storm raging around her.

It was almost enough to make her turn back and wait for help—to go back for Abyss, to make her think twice about what she was doing.

But that would waste time she didn't have.

If the notes Nandara had given her were accurate, she didn't have to do any travelling in the fire realm. She could open a portal where she stood to anywhere in the world with a fire lit. To several somewheres all at once.

She knew where to find Unari and focused on that, hoping she wasn't going to come out in another cooking fire and smack her head on a cauldron. But the portal she opened came out into a dark room—not only dark in comparison to the blinding light of the fire realm, but dark enough that she tripped on the outer hearth, landing in the middle of the parlour with a scream.

"Who's there?!" a woman's voice called, tired but alarmed.

"Unari?" Spark froze a moment, realizing she hadn't asked any details when Nandara told her how to find the woman. She had no idea if Unari lived alone or if she had a family that could be trusted, and it was a bit too late for that now. "Are you Nandara's friend?"

"Oh my stars. Spark, is that you?" Unari came into the room, a woman about a decade younger than Nandara, with greying black hair, a plump body wrapped up in nightclothes, and deep umber skin, rich and warm.

"You're not that surprised." Spark wasn't sure what she expected, but calm wasn't it. "A girl just fell out of your fire, and you're just a bit annoyed that you've been woken up?" The details caught up to her and Spark frowned. "Wait, it's the middle of the night?"

"I've never traced it on a map to be sure, but I suspect the dragon city is half a world away from here." Unari came closer, inspecting Spark. "Nandara warned me you'd come eventually. Told me to keep a fire going, not that I wouldn't with this kind of weather."

"You know the plan, then?"

"I helped come up with it." She drew her curtains and lit a lantern before ushering Spark into one of the chairs. "Nandara suggested we start with the eggs. From what I've heard, there's four of them. How many dragons have you got?"

Spark swallowed. "It's just me."

"What?" Unari frowned. "That wasn't the plan at all."

"There were complications. I came through a fire portal—I can get Nanny and the eggs back that way too."

Unari pressed her lips together. "If you're sure."

"We're running out of time."

"Yes, all right. So you can do fire portals? Good. We had a contingency for that, and I can send you where you need to be in about an hour."

Spark emerged from the fire realm, this time exiting a fire around one of the eggs being held in the textile mill. According to Unari, it was a storage building in the back designed to look like a regular part of the mill, but its main purpose was holding the eggs.

But Unari had been wrong about the number of eggs—there were six. Five were modestly sized, no bigger than a cart. The last was massive, a gleaming black with marbled blue markings, and was next to the wall, near a window.

Spark rushed over to it and laid her hand on the side.

"I'm going to get you out of here," she whispered. "Your mamma is waiting for you."

Spark glanced around in the dim light, but there was no one around. A quick peek out the window gave her a view of crates and some distant hulking mounds that were probably captive dragons. The room was guarded from the outside, Unari had warned her, and the whole mill compound would have soldiers posted. But there was no reason for Loch's people to expect anyone could come through the fires.

There was a scheduled shift change right now, an extra element of chaos working to Spark's advantage. If she ended up making any noise, it would be a few minutes before she was heard. There was no reason for anyone to poke their head in just to check.

She still had to be quick. Unari had said she'd get ten minutes at best. She couldn't waste any of it.

She opened a fire portal, but just like the one she'd come out of, it was next to the egg. She tried expanding it under, but there was no gap between egg and stone that she could squeeze it through.

Cursing under her breath, she pressed her hand against the egg's smooth surface and walked the perimeter until she got to the wall. The shell was tight against the stone, but the rounded shape left a small gap filled with flame that Spark could squeeze into. It wasn't ideal, but it would have to do.

She opened a new fire portal opposite the wall, big enough for the egg to drop into, and then wriggled into the gap. There was no room for leverage, no hope she could push the egg. Even if it weren't so heavy.

But there was cobblestone beneath her and the egg, and Nandara had taught her to work the earth.

Spark turned and got her hand on one of the stones sticking out from under the egg. She poured the slow, stubborn magic of terramancy into it, getting it to lift a few inches.

The egg didn't budge.

Spark cursed louder this time.

She reached out with her other hand and raised a second stone, but two still weren't giving her the leverage she needed to get the egg rolling.

She tried to focus, but the gaps between the cobblestones made the magic diffuse before it reached any other cobblestones. Under them was gravel.

If Spark had the command over earth that she did over fire, this would be done already.

With effort, she used the gravel to shift the cobblestones closer, managing another stone to wedge under the egg. But the stones directly beneath Spark sank and shifted like wet clay. She was using too much magic with no outcome at all—except making her slowly sink into the ground.

She kept trying, tears sizzling and evaporating off her cheeks in frustration.

When the ground got so soft she feared it would swallow her, she stopped and wriggled out, back around to her fire portal. If she couldn't raise the stones on the other side, maybe she could lower them on this side.

Spark had gotten only a single row of stones to sink a few inches, still not enough to move the egg, when she heard voices outside the door.

"No," Spark gasped. "No, no, no."

The lock rattled and Spark dashed to the far side of the egg, where she couldn't easily be seen.

"I'm sorry. I'll come back for you," she whispered. "Just sleep, stay at ease. There's nothing good out here for you to rush out into anyway. Sleep and wait."

The door opened and a man's voice called instructions to others. "Fire's gettin' low. Get in here with them planks."

Spark closed her eyes. "I'm so sorry," she whispered.

Opening a fire portal, Spark slipped back to the fire realm and returned to Unari's parlour. The fire here wasn't enough to burn away the tears on her cheeks.

Unari tried to comfort her, but the night was growing late, and Spark had to have something to show for her foolish efforts.

"That egg, and how close it is to hatching, is the whole reason I came now. The reason I couldn't wait. And for what?"

"Go for your grandmother. No one at the mill saw you, so there's nothing stopping you from trying again tomorrow night. Or the next. Or for as many as it takes for you to get it right. Go home, practice what you need, and come back. I'll keep the fire going here until Nandara tells me I don't need to. And even then, winter's coming."

Spark clenched her jaw and swiped the last of the tears from her cheeks.

Unari helped bundle Spark into a large hooded cloak over her firecloak, one deep enough that she could hide her face, and the two of them stole into the damp, drizzly night.

Unari managed the kitchens in Loch's palace, so it wasn't uncommon for her to come and go at all hours. When Spark had asked why she couldn't just open a fire portal into the kitchen or something, Unari had explained that no fires were left burning unattended in the palace.

"So he must have some idea of what Mamma could do. Of what I can do."

"He's got a notion, though I don't think he's got specifics."

They went quickly, and Unari let them in through the servant's door, the guards around barely giving them a glance. Unari turned before the kitchen, down more servant corridors and a long, winding flight of stairs lit only by the pocket lantern Unari held. They got to a heavy iron door and stopped.

"This is it—the servant entrance to the dungeons." She told Spark how to find her grandmother's cell, asked her to repeat the directions to be certain she had them, and then asked for the cloak back. "I've got someone on the inside who can wear it back out of here with me so I don't leave on my own and raise suspicions."

Spark blinked. "You two really thought of everything."

Unari smiled. "We spent some time on it. Now go. Be swift and quiet. There's only one guard on patrol down here, but a dozen in the hall beyond."

Unari retreated back up the stairs and, with her pulse pounding in her ears, Spark waited what she hoped was long enough for the woman and her alibi to get clear. The door was locked and Spark didn't have a key, so she melted the lock's mechanism and slowly creaked it open, just enough to squeeze through before closing it again.

When Unari had taken the light, she'd left Spark in darkness, and Spark couldn't risk fire drawing the attention of the guards. She pressed her hand to the wall and walked to her right, going carefully and slowly, especially when there were turns she had to navigate past rather than follow. Footsteps echoed from the way she'd come, and a faint glow brushed the corridor.

Her heart raced, and she urged her own footsteps faster—past one more junction, then left.

The dungeons were strangely quiet. There was another level of them above, where there were other prisoners. But down here in the deepest depths, there was only Nanny.

Loch probably thought this would make it too hard for the dragons to come for her. To an extent, he was right. But he'd never truly understood Spark's power. Sometimes she didn't either.

As she passed by one cell after another, she trailed her hands across their barred doors, and stopped when she reached one with a glossy smooth finish.

The rest had been rough, partially rusted and flaking, or crudely worked by a blacksmith unconcerned with their aesthetic and worried only about function. But these bars were new.

Spark snapped a fire out of the air to give herself some light, and a gasp came from deep inside the cell.

She looked up and a pale, familiar face loomed out of the shadows, eyes wide, head shaking.

"Nanny?"

Nanny Di clasped her hands over her mouth, her eyes shining with tears, still shaking her head.

"I'm going to get you out, won't take a minute."

But Nanny kept shaking her head and started flicking her hands as if to shoo Spark away. There was a fiery storm in her eyes, and her expression was dark.

"I'm not leaving you." Spark's voice was edged in steel. "I already failed Abyss, and I'm not turning back now."

Nanny reached through the bars and pushed Spark farther away.

"No." Spark came right back. Pressing her palm over the lock, she poured fire into the mechanism. "I didn't come all this way to leave you. Nanny, Mamma woke up. She's not doing okay. She needs you. *I* need you."

Nanny stepped away from the bars so suddenly it was like Spark had slapped her.

"I didn't come all this way just to leave you. Not now."

But the fire in the lock wasn't doing anything.

"Rotting moons, is this tempered steel?" But of course it was. Tempered to withstand a dragon, both force and fire.

"Hey! Who's there?"

Spark gasped. Light bobbed down the hall at the nearest junction. There was no time to call up demons to untemper the steel, and she really couldn't turn back, not with the guard between her and the way out. One guard she could fight, but there were others. This one was still shouting. Nanny was sobbing.

Spark waited until his light reached the junction. Just as he came around the corner, she pulled a massive fireball out of the air and heaved it out toward him.

He screamed, mostly in alarm. She'd missed him, but hopefully it would give him something to think about.

She pulled up another fire, this one allowing her to see into Nanny's cell, searching for a way to help the woman, but there was only a bucket and a pile of old straw.

The fire flared with Spark's rage. They hadn't even given Nanny a proper bed, forcing her to sleep on the floor like some barnyard animal.

But old straw would burn, and as the guard's shouting came closer, Spark flung the fire out in two directions—another warning for the guard, but also a small ball of flame into the cell, igniting the straw. Nanny cried out, startled.

"I've got this."

Spark pulled up one more fire in front of her and opened a portal. She dashed through it, squinting through her eyelashes as she closed the portal in the hallway and opened one into the straw-fire in Nanny's cell. Even trying to protect her eyesight from the light, the darkness of the cell was all-consuming, and it took longer for the afterimage of the fire realm to fade enough to see.

Shouts increased in the hallway.

The first guard was at the door, fumbling for keys. Two more ran their way, and Spark spotted the glint of crossbows in the firelight. She flung another fireball at them to give herself some space and turned back to Nanny.

"We have to go. I know the fire realm is awful for you, but it's the only way out."

Nanny froze in place, shaking her head more like a side to side vibration. Spark urged her, but she wouldn't move.

The door clanged open. Spark cried out in alarm, wrapped an arm around Nanny's waist, and heaved them both into the fire.

CHAPTER THIRTEEN

Neesha sat with her cheek pressed in a puddle of tears on Ondias's shitty table, staring at nothing. Silent tears continued to pool under her face as she struggled to put her thoughts in order.

Everything felt insurmountable and pointless. All her efforts had amounted to nothing. Seventeen years and the wheel had come full circle, this time grinding down the child she had sacrificed herself to protect.

There was a lot she needed to get a handle on. Suddenly waking up after all this time seemed to be a byproduct of whatever Mita—Spark? She'd said that's what everyone called her, right?—had been doing, but Neesha waking up had been an accident. A lucky one. It sounded like they needed her, even if none of their plans had accounted for her return.

But half her family was gone. Half her *life* was gone. She'd never again see Nanny Sharice beaming over Neesha's successes. Never goof off with her favourite brother. Never know if she could ever earn her father's forgiveness.

A fresh round of sobbing seized her. She gasped for air.

"Sit up. Have some tea." Nandara put a gentle hand on her back.

Neesha pulled out the rudest words she knew to decline the tea, but her old mentor ignored them.

"You're going to make yourself sick. Sit up and at least take a deep breath if you don't want tea."

Still sniffling and wiping her face with her sleeves, Neesha sat up and took a deep, shuddering breath. She sobbed the air all back out again.

"Well, at least you're sitting up." Nandara smiled and patted her cheek.

Neesha wanted to lie down forever. She went back to staring at nothing, because she couldn't stand seeing how old Nandara was. She was wrinkled and grey and faded—overnight!

How am I supposed to get used to any of this?

Seeing Spark was the worst visual reminder of all that she'd lost. Of how badly she'd failed. Only yesterday, her daughter had been a squishy little bundle. The broad, lanky teen Spark had become was unrecognizable—a complete stranger.

"This is all my fault," Neesha said.

"How so?" Nandara rooted around in Ondias's overstocked cupboards.

"I was reckless! You were right. I didn't listen to you, and I took too many chances."

Nandara sighed and sat down again. "No. These failures belong to all of us. I saw it only too late, when we started repeating the same mistakes with Spark, that we cautioned you where we should have encouraged you. Lectured you where we should have guided." Nandara's wistful expression turned inward before she fixed Neesha with a sad smile. "She's learned so much in such a short time. Just wait until you see it all. We can guide you now, as I've been guiding her. We can teach you the full extent of your power, instead of making you restrain yourself."

Neesha shook her head and stared, tears continuing to smear her face.

Nandara got up and went to the cupboards again. "How about wine, if you don't want tea?"

"That sounds like the best and worst idea." Neesha wiped her face again and looked around. The cluttered piles quietly loomed all around her. "Where is everyone?"

"Spark needed some air, but she's been gone a while. Ondias went to fetch her."

"Gods, that poor kid. Nandara, what do I *do*?"

Nandara pressed her lips together and shook her head. "I don't know. This has been so unexpected. But Spark has been so desperate to revive you since she got here, so desperate to free Dionelle after she found out she hadn't perished with the others."

"I should have been there to protect her." Fresh tears started up again.

"You're here now. Protect her now. She needs you, Neesha. Even if you're strangers and you have no idea what to say."

"I can't even—"

Ondias burst through the door. Neesha had never seen such a foul expression on the woman's face.

"Mita's gone," Ondias said. "Word in the market is she disappeared into a fire. The dragoness is still here."

Nandara gasped. "She's gone to Pasdale alone?"

Neesha sat straight up, suddenly alert. "What the hell has she gone to Pasdale for?"

Ondias started to snap something, but Nandara cut her off and explained the plan they'd come up with for Spark and the dragoness and others to go to Pasdale to save Dionelle and the dragoness's stolen egg.

"She has eggs? And someone stole them? What in the hells?"

Ondias sighed and dragged a hand over her face. Everything about her demeanour seethed impatience and annoyance, igniting Neesha's rage.

It felt good to feel something other than the profound disorientation that had plagued her since she woke up.

"Gods, O, I'm *so* sorry that waking up from some *magical curse* has put a rut in your day, but maybe you noticed the part where I lost *seventeen years* of my life and my kid is off confronting villains you should have put a stop to when I gave you all the chance!"

"I know that mentally you're still the same girl who got herself devoured by flame, but do try to act your age," Ondias snapped. "We did everything we could to stop Loch."

"Oh, did you now? Please, indulge me. What exactly did you try? *Anything* other than waiting around for the Guild to figure it out for you? Is it because you were wasting away in a gaol for years after trying to *stab him in the eye* or *light him on fire?*"

Ondias stood abruptly, her mouth open to shout, but Nandara grabbed her arm and hauled her back into a seat.

"We really should have done something like that," Nandara said.

"Gods, now you sound like Zev!" Ondias snapped, her expression darkening.

"He had it half-arranged when you talked him out of it."

"I'm sorry, what?" Neesha erupted. "There was a plot to take him out—Draxli's special pet, who's done all this harm—and you *stopped* it?"

"We can't just go around killing people because they're dangerous or we don't like them." Ondias gave her a withering look.

"We can—I did! It worked great! It saved the entire city. But for what? So you could let it all go to shit again? Gods, no wonder Spark went off on her own, if this is what she's been up against."

Nandara interrupted the start of another of Ondias's tirades.

Neesha pushed out of her seat and paced the cramped space. "Get that dragoness to take me up to the dragon city. The Superiors can send me to the fire realm and—"

Ondias slammed her hand on the table. "Absolutely not."

"Neesha, no. It's far too risky after what you've been through."

"So Spark—who is a *literal child*—should just sacrifice her own safety?" Neesha snapped. "You're both ridiculous!"

"You really think you're going to be able to resist the call of the fire realm?" Nandara asked.

"The dragoness was supposed to go with Spark. She can come with me, drag me out of there if I get stuck again."

"She's risked enough," Ondias said.

"Spark went to save *her* egg." Neesha gestured angrily toward the door. "She *should* be taking some of the risk."

"*All* of the dragons have been taking more than enough risk, and it's cost us all dearly." Ondias glared and leaned forward on the table. "We need to—"

The fire in Ondias's hearth exploded with light and screaming, startling all three of them. Nandara's magic welled up in the room, electrifying the air, ready to counter any threat.

A heartbeat later, Spark staggered out of the fire, dragging a naked and screaming Dionelle with her.

Neesha gasped. Ondias cursed. Dionelle stumbled out of Spark's grip and fell to the floor, her screams breaking into sobs. Neesha took one look at her skeletal, bruised, and scarred mother in a heap on the floor and had a horrifyingly clear notion of what had filled the last year.

Nandara draped a cloak over Dionelle while Ondias took her face in her hands and whispered gently. But Neesha's attention was on her daughter.

Spark panted, staring in horror at Dionelle, withered and filthy, crumpling in on herself. Neesha's heart seized. She should have been the one going on the rescue mission. She'd set these horrors in motion and then slept for seventeen years, leaving her loved ones to deal with the fallout. And instead of being helpful once she'd woken up, she'd been crying like a witless coward while Spark—her foolish, brave, amazing child—had done the thing she'd insisted she would.

Whatever Spark had planned for Loch, Neesha couldn't wait to help.

CHAPTER FOURTEEN

S park sat in one of the dusty, overstuffed chairs in Ondias's parlour, cradling a half-eaten bowl of soup in her hands, desperate to get the echoes of Nanny screaming out of her mind. It kept replaying in an endless loop—one almost as bad as the memory of Pappy's sudden silence during the attack on their homestead.

But Nanny wasn't screaming anymore, and she'd finally stopped sobbing, after clutching Neesha for what felt like an eternity.

They'd gotten Nanny some clothes, since Spark hadn't been smart enough to bring any for her. She hadn't even thought about how the fire realm would burn everything away. Ondias had gotten Nanny to drink some tea, and had gotten the story out of Spark, before giving the girl the soup and sending her to sit in the parlour.

Now they were all crowded in the kitchen and arguing again in hissed whispers, while a recently summoned Lina fretted over Nanny.

Now that she was out of the dungeon gloom and into the late afternoon light, it became obvious how poorly Nanny was doing. Her skin was sickly pale, her body thin, and her face sunken and hollow. She was covered in a rainbow of bruises old and new, and a latticework of old scars. Her hair was scraggly and dirty and matted. And she smelled *awful*.

In the midst of the hushed argument the other three were having, Spark picked out Ondias snapping, "...She's *your* daughter!" and a moment later, Neesha strode over to crouch in front of Spark with a sad half-smile on her face.

"You did the right thing." Neesha put a hand on Spark's shoulder, meeting her gaze.

Behind her, Ondias growled wordlessly and threw her arms in the air. Nandara bit her lips to hide a twitch of a smile.

Neesha stood and turned around, arms crossed. "You don't get to tell me to mother her when I've known her for all of five minutes, and then get angry about how I choose to do my job. And she *did* do the right thing!" Then Neesha turned on Spark. "Though you should have waited for the dragoness to come with you. She could have gotten the egg while you got Dionelle. Half the time and twice the success."

Spark's stomach roiled. She didn't think she could eat ever again.

"Hey, you're still practically a child, forced to do far more adulting than could ever be considered fair," Neesha said. "You've done well. And you've got us all here now. We'll figure something out, okay?"

Spark shook her head and wouldn't meet her mother's eyes. It didn't feel like she'd done well—it felt like she'd failed. And she'd been too much of a coward to tell Abyss the truth, making Ondias go out and do it once Nanny had some clothes and was sitting quietly.

She was still sitting quietly. Too quietly. She wasn't paying any attention to the chatter around her. Nanny was supposed to fix things, to make them better. Instead, it was unexpected Neesha taking Spark's side, arguing with Ondias so she didn't have to.

Spark's stomach clenched. She curled in on herself.

"Come on, love, let's get you cleaned up," Lina whispered, helping Nanny out of her chair and into the bathroom.

Once she was gone, Spark turned her gaze on Neesha.

"I didn't think at all," Spark said. "I wanted Nanny because I thought she'd have answers. I didn't consider at all what a year in a dungeon would do to her. What a year of Loch's cruelty would do."

"You've been driven by desperation for a year," Neesha said. "You can't be blamed for not thinking of everything."

"We *had* thought of a lot of it, if she'd only spared a few minutes to hear us out," Ondias said.

Neesha rounded on Ondias again. "Oh, because you were going to help her today? You were all so focused on me and slowing down when it sounds like you'd been ready to go full speed ahead—until my waking up threw a wrench in things. Not that it should have thrown a wrench in anything. Spark was right that I'm not in a state to help. Not today. I'm still getting caught up. But she was ready, and you said you'd support her. It's not her fault you halted everything."

Neesha eased the cold soup from Spark's hands and gestured to the door.

Spark stared at her mother. Her *mother*. Standing right here, walking around and so *alive*. And doing exactly what Spark needed most. How was this even possible? Her throat felt hot, but she couldn't look away as they both left Ondias's creaky old house.

Neesha stopped in the laneway, hands on hips and head tilted back so her thick white braid hung passed her backside, staring up at the dragon city. She let out a long exhale, and Spark remembered to let out a breath of her own. Her mother seemed so much smaller now, outside and away from the others, her determination and big personality falling in on itself while she took in the moment.

"The city was rubble on the flooded valley floor the last time I saw it." Neesha's blue-amber eyes glittered, one corner of her mouth tilted up.

"Everyone who saw it before it fell is always sad about it. They know it's beautiful again, but all they see is what it used to be."

Neesha looked at her. "Really? Well, that's foolish. It looks amazing! I didn't think it would ever look even close to this beautiful again. But maybe that's because my brain still thinks it's been something like a week since it fell." She sighed.

"I'm sorry, Mamma. I didn't think about you, either—about what all the lost time would do to you."

"Better to have missed a bit of time than all of it. It's... It's very strange. In my mind, you were a newborn yesterday. And it hurts me in ways I can never explain that I missed your entire life. I have no idea what to do or how to do it, but I know you need someone who does. I think... I need to find a quiet, soft place away from O's nagging to have a good cry in private, and then maybe I can start figuring it out."

Neesha sagged and Spark stepped closer, pulling her mother into a hug.

"You can come with me." Spark's throat tried to close around the words, but she swallowed hard and held her voice steady. "I have my own place. It's... not finished. I wanted space for you and Nanny but didn't get it done in time."

Neesha smiled, her hand on Spark's cheek. "You're a marvel. I can't wait to hear about all you've done and what you can do. Nandara said you can create fire from nothing!"

Spark grinned and pulled a flame into the palm of her hand, holding it out like a rare blossom. Neesha's eyes danced. She cupped it in her own hand, marvelling at it. Then she pursed her lips and glanced back at the door.

"Let's walk," Neesha said. "Show me where you live."

Once they were a good distance from Ondias's house, Neesha craning her head to look back like she expected they would be followed, she slowed her pace.

"I don't know how much they told you, but I wasn't certain who your father was until just now."

Spark stopped entirely and blinked. "What... How did you figure it out *now*?"

"He was an elemental. And possessed by a fire demon when I took him as my lover, but I didn't know that at the time. There'd been another wizard, an aeromancer. And one who wasn't a wizard at all. I expected, given what I was doing with magic while I was pregnant, that you would be at least as powerful as me, that there wouldn't be any diluting of your gifts regardless of who your father was. But that your power is so much beyond mine..." She nodded, then sighed again. "But that means you'll never know him, because the demon possession consumed him before I even knew I was pregnant."

Spark stared, not entirely sure what to do with this information.

Neesha blushed. "Sorry, maybe I shouldn't have dumped that all on you like that."

"Um... I guess it's useful information? I honestly hadn't really considered it much. Pappy said you were the only one who knew, and I thought you were dead, so I just..." She shrugged helplessly.

"I can't believe they didn't tell you the truth." Neesha scowled and kept walking. "They've made a few choices I'll have to reckon with. O and Nandara have already gotten an earful out of me. Once Dionelle has had some time to recover, I expect she and I will have a shouting match in our future."

"Mamma, no!" Spark gasped.

But Neesha smiled. "Shouting at each other is our love language. Honestly, I'm not sure how else to communicate with her."

"But she doesn't talk."

"She was quiet, yeah. But that's to be expected after all she's been through."

"They didn't tell you."

Neesha rolled her eyes and waited.

"Nanny hasn't spoken since the day you beat Draxli. Maybe two or three sentences in total, all at once, right before Loch came after us."

"Well, I guess it'll be a lopsided argument." Neesha had probably meant it as a joke, but her demeanour had changed. At least Spark wasn't the only one angry about all the half-truths spinning around the two of them.

"I'm glad you're here, even if you don't know what you're doing."

Neesha grinned, her eyes shining with tears. They'd reached the edge of the town, and a shadow fell over them just before Abyss landed not far off.

"Mistress!" Neesha called. "I don't think I'll ever not be relieved to see you."

Abyss snorted and lowered her head closer. Neesha ran up and hugged the dragon's snout. Feeling like she had a ball of lead in her gut, Spark stayed back. But Abyss lifted her head to Spark and regarded her with a faint nod.

"Neesha, your return has been quite dramatic," Abyss said.

"I heard there was a huge flash of light, but I don't remember much until Nandara started talking to me."

"It's more than that," Abyss said. "Many of my kin are talking again. In human languages."

Spark stared. Neesha tilted her head.

"The dragons all stopped talking when Nanny did," Spark explained. She supposed she'd be doing a lot of that. "Not a word out of any of them until I got here. Even then, it was only Abyss, and only sometimes."

"What...?" Neesha shook her head.

"We have much to discuss," Abyss said. "It's not all the dragons, but many."

Spark watched Abyss for a moment. "Would you say it's two-thirds talking again? Any pattern to their ages?"

Abyss raised her head. "I will investigate further. Will you need assistance with your plans to return to Pasdale?"

"I think we will, but for today we're going to need some rest. Is that all right?"

"The eggs here remain quiet, and the Superiors are still assessing. A brief delay is acceptable."

Neesha glanced between the two of them, looking more perplexed.

"There's a lot to catch you up on. Maybe after you've had that cry?"

Neesha gave her a shrewd look, followed by a half-smile. They said their farewells to Abyss, who returned skyward, and Spark brought Neesha to the house that was supposed to be theirs, but was barely a house at all.

But Shadow was curled up on the front steps, and he barked at their approach.

"You have a dog!" Neesha grinned and knelt down to pet Shadow, who very enthusiastically gave her all of his doggy attention before giving Spark a very interrogatory, thorough sniffing. What on earth did she smell like to him? And maybe he recognized a bit of Nanny's scent there? He'd be so happy to see her again.

Spark gave Neesha a quick tour, pleased by how impressed Neesha was, while Shadow trailed behind them.

"You built this all yourself?"

"Nandara helped a lot. Stone and some others, too."

Neesha's mouth fell open. "Stone? He's here?"

Spark rolled her eyes. "More they didn't tell you. He says he promised you he'd look after me. Nanny wouldn't let him when we were in Pasdale, so he came here, and he was here for me when Loch…" She took a deep breath against the sob trying to escape.

Neesha nodded wearily. "I am going to do *so much* shouting when we get back to O's."

Spark made a garbled noise, a yelped laugh choking on a sob, and closed the gap between them to hug Neesha. "I don't even care if it's all a mess. I'm so glad you're here."

And it was a mess. Spark didn't know what to say or how much affection to show or when to hold back or when to press forward. She had no frame of reference for her mother's needs, only knew the gaping maw of loneliness didn't ache quite so badly now, even if the woman standing before her was a complete stranger.

Well, nearly a complete stranger. All the irritated but fond stories she'd heard about her mother while she was growing up had prepared her some. But it was obvious, even after so short a time, that the other adults hadn't really understood Neesha. There were years to make up for and a chasm of unfamiliarity to cross, but there was already a bridge there. So it was weird, and Spark still felt strangely lonely, but the despair didn't have the same teeth as it had had even that morning.

Spark ended the tour with her bedroom, leaving some linens and a basin of water for Neesha to wash up when she was done with crying, and then went up to the roof. She had a room to finish and unspilled tears of her own to shed.

CHAPTER FIFTEEN

Neesha slipped out of bed barely past dawn, having slept back to back with Spark all night, with the dog lying across their feet. It had been nice, but fraught. Neesha had just wanted to wrap her arms around the girl—nearly a woman—and hold her all night, to cup her body around Spark's and make up for seventeen lost years of mothering. It almost seemed like that was what Spark wanted too. Maybe she needed it. But they were still strangers to each other. Neither of them had the words for their emotions yet.

It shredded her heart.

Spark's dog lifted his head to watch Neesha go but didn't follow. Ondias's trash heap had contained a few of Neesha's possessions, ones that had been cleared out of the old farmhouse to make room for Spark, so she had some clothes, including an old nightgown. She was grateful for the few small comforts and tiny familiarities.

And she had done plenty of shouting at both Ondias and Nandara, though mostly Ondias. Dionelle had been sleeping—Lina had bathed her and helped her dress and gotten her into the spare bed in the house. Neesha would shout at her mother eventually, but Dionelle was so fragile. Neesha had never seen her like this, even after everything she'd put her mother through years before.

It broke her heart to know she'd never get the reconciliation with her father that she'd hoped for.

But this morning was about a different man—one she'd made a promise to, though it was one she couldn't fathom keeping. Everything felt like yesterday, and yet none of it really mattered anymore.

It gave her a headache if she thought about it too hard, so she pushed it out of her mind as she stepped out of Spark's stone house and quietly shut the door behind her.

She truly understood what Spark was going through, and it was why she had forced herself through the awkwardness to spend time with the girl, but godsdamnit did she want her own mother to comfort her and tell her there was a plan. She wasn't certain what was going on with Dionelle or if it was temporary. The silence in particular was difficult.

But Neesha needed to piece her life back together, which was complicated when her brain insisted it *was* together—she'd just figured it out a few days ago! Would she ever acclimatize to the seventeen-year gap? Should she even try?

Probably.

She stole through the streets—trying not to trip over things as she kept gazing up at the city glittering in the dawn light—with only the vaguest idea of where she was going. Hopefully it was early enough to catch Stone at home, otherwise she'd have to find him in the market. Once she found the market. She really only knew how to get between Spark and Ondias's houses.

But she didn't even have to go through the village proper, because Stone's farm was on the northern outskirts, fairly easy to get to from Spark's. Which, if what she'd overheard was true, might have had a lot to do with Stone's daughter.

A smile played across her lips.

She passed a few people, mostly from a distance. They smiled and waved, barely paying any attention. One of them even called, "Morning, Spark!" to her, and she supposed that at a glance the two of them looked similar enough, especially with Neesha's long hair pulled back. Up close, though, aside from the fireborn attributes, there was little resemblance. Spark had taken more after Reiser's side of the family, and after her father.

Neesha brushed those thoughts aside and arrived at what she hoped was the right farm. This would be even more embarrassing if she had to knock on multiple doors to find him.

She got to the doorstep and paused. And paused.

Finally, she decided it would be worse if she stood here until Stone or Ember opened the door to leave for the day. So she knocked. And her heart stopped when Stone called out, "Just a sec!"

It felt like an eternity before he opened the door, neutral pleasantry pasted on his face. She didn't move, didn't speak, didn't breathe, watching as his face went through a flurry of emotions: confusion, surprise, grief. That face—like so many others—was both familiar and alien in how it had aged. Stone had new wrinkles, and his hair streaked with grey.

"Neesha," he breathed. "Can it be?"

"It's me."

"We all saw the light, and I'd heard rumours. But when I went up to your post last night and found it empty, debris on the ground... I thought you'd finally died."

"Seems it was better than that. Or worse? Depends who you ask."

He gave her a sad look, and then they stood there staring at each other. She thought it would stretch on forever, that they'd grow old and die before either of them managed to move or break the silence.

But Stone finally shook himself and stood back, opening the door wider. "Will ya come in?"

"I'd like that. I think we need to talk."

Stone's smile turned brittle, but he nodded and led Neesha into the house. It was lovely, with a large open space of kitchen and dining area and parlour stretching from one end of the house to the other, and closed doors to other rooms along one side. The north side, Neesha suspected, as there were large windows on the other three walls with stunning views of the valley and the mountains beyond, all of them dappled with shining light reflected off the city.

The way the light reflected around the valley was something Neesha had forgotten—and it had been gloomy when she'd last been here. There'd been a lot of other things to pay attention to.

The house itself had stone floors and brightly polished wooden walls, with furniture that was oversized and comfortable-looking. They took up seats across from each other at Stone's kitchen table, confirming Neesha's suspicions about comfort levels. She still couldn't figure out what to say. It was like her mother's silence was wearing off on her. Where to even begin?

"Just so you know, I can't take all morning," Stone said eventually. "If I don't get to the market, Ember will come looking for me, and that's maybe not the interruption you need at the moment."

Neesha gave him a wry smile. "No, perhaps not. I'm sure Spark would like to be the one to introduce me to her. I hear she's grown up to be a lovely woman."

"Aye, she turned out all right, despite my efforts. Seems you've heard a lot already."

"Plenty of some things, not enough of others. Seems our families were meant to be united after all—we were just trying to force it a generation too soon."

Stone chuckled. "Ain't it the truth. You know you don't owe me nothin'."

"Thank you." Neesha hadn't realized how tense her shoulders were until she relaxed at his assurances. Stone always was infuriatingly comforting. "I think that's the main reason I came here. I made you a promise, but circumstances have rather changed."

"I should say so. You needed someone to help raise your girl, but she's just about a woman now. I can't see what you'd need me for."

"Friendship." The admission left her mouth unbidden, startling them both. "I could use a friend. I've got a daughter who's the same emotional age as me, and so much I missed out on, and a mother who won't speak, and a mentor who's conflicted, and bleeding *Ondias,* and, well..."

"She's a damn ornery woman and meddles in everything."

Neesha laughed, full and deep. Despite the awkwardness, she was relieved she'd come here.

"Thank you, Stone."

"I didn't do anything."

"You tried. Spark told me how you've been there for her since Loch took everything from her. From us." Neesha sagged. She'd cried out most of her grief yesterday, curled up in Spark's bed. "And I'm sorry my parents and the rest of them were so hard on you. I went up one side of Ondias and down the other when I found out they didn't believe you about our agreement. That they wouldn't let you help with Spark."

"Spark's doin' all right. She didn't need me. Though I can't help but wonder how much stronger the girl would be if she'd had you there, fierce as ever, helping her through it all the whole time."

Neesha knew he was trying to ease her guilt, but it only made the sting worse. She collapsed against his table, forehead on the surface and arms around herself, wracked by great ugly sobs again. Apparently she hadn't quite finished crying herself out yet.

"I'm sorry," she sobbed. "I failed all of you."

Stone came around the table and sat next to her, his big, warm hand rubbing her back. "You did the best you could."

"And what good did it do? All I wanted was to keep her safe."

"And she *is* safe. It could have gone better, yes, but that wasn't on you. Dionelle and her crony old friends, those fools at the Guild—they were too busy worrying about decorum and civility and tradition to do what you needed to succeed. You did the best you could with what you had, and if you didn't have what you needed to do better, well, that was the fault of those supposed to be teaching you."

Neesha sat up and gasped. She didn't know where this version of Stone had been hiding, but she was glad to have his wisdom.

"And I think Nandara, at the very least, understands that," Stone said. "Since they both got to this valley, she's been helping Spark with the things she never helped you with."

"I heard a little about that. A little about what they think happened to me."

"Spark has been bent on bringing Di home and waking you up, and now she's gone and done it. She's doing all right, Neesha. You don't need to feel guilty for that."

"But she's gone through so much and been so lonely. I wasn't there when she needed me."

"But yer here now, and she still needs you. You can't get the time back, but you can make the days from here going forward better for her."

Neesha leaned over and hugged him.

"I envy the wisdom all these years have given you, Stone. Apparently I'm thirty-five, but I still feel like a teenager. So much has changed, and I've just been sitting stagnant in that godsdamn column for a lifetime."

Stone took her hand and smiled. "I know it's hard for you to see right now, especially when Pasdale is still a wreck and the dragons are in danger, but you changed things plenty. There's new rules for gettin' into the Guild, and some of the old timers in the market stopped being so nosy about what consenting adults do with their time. And maybe it's a small thing, but I kept my promise to you. I raised Ember and River as equals. I gave her everything I gave him, didn't expect different from either of them, and then refused to saddle her with a betrothal."

"You should have had a word with *my* idiot family." Neesha clenched her fist. After all the misery trying to force her to marry someone had caused, here they were trying the same with Spark. "You really don't mind that Spark and Ember are a thing?"

"Nah. Age and everything that's happened—bein' in this place—it's all given me perspective. Our girls love each other, and it'd be wrong for anyone to try to come between 'em."

Neesha nodded slowly, feeling wrung out but a little more grounded. The topic made her think about a particular piece of mail that had ended up in the crate of things Ondias had stashed away.

Yenette, the only woman Neesha had ever loved, had written—recently, only a few years before. There were all sorts of rumours, some accurate, that Neesha hadn't died after all. So Yenette had tried her luck and had posted a letter for Neesha via Ondias, declaring her support—that she didn't believe Loch's lies, and that if the rumours of Neesha's well-being were true, she'd love to be in touch again.

Neesha mentioned it to Stone.

He watched her with an amused twinkle in his eyes. "Nee, you should be happy. If there's ever a day it's safe for you to return to Pasdale, maybe you should. See if Yenette is still around. I remember her—fine lass. She bought strawberries from me for preserves every year until I moved here." He stroked his beard and watched her. "She was married, last I saw her. A betrothal I don't know she was completely happy with."

Neesha snorted. "Who ever is? You were lucky with Talienna, even if it was brief, and so were my parents. But really, it seems so many of them end up like Ondias. Or even more bitter because they never get the release of divorce."

Stone gave her hand a squeeze. "I think maybe you've got a starting place on helping your girl out. Ember's been torn up about that betrothal. Thinks Spark'll take it and Ember will lose her."

"Not if I can help it." Neesha stood and gave Stone another hug. "Thank you, for everything. For all the years I missed, for the promises you kept and the ones neither of us could. And thank you for this. I think I know what I need to do, where I can start building my life again."

"You don't got to thank me. And I'm happy to keep being a part of it in whatever way works best for you."

"Friends?" she asked.

His smile was broad and warm and genuine. "Friends."

He walked her to a fork in the road and then turned toward the village and the market, where his daughter waited for him.

Neesha looked to the distant shape of Spark's house and hoped it would be a home soon.

CHAPTER SIXTEEN

Spark wiped tears out of her eyes so she could see to fuse the stones. It had been awful waking up to the empty bed, to her mother gone without a word, like Spark had done something wrong. She couldn't bear to search the village for her, either. She kept telling herself that Neesha had probably gone to see how Nanny was doing, or maybe to get some real food, since Spark kept forgetting to go to the market.

But it still felt like a rejection.

It didn't help that she also felt she was somehow betraying Nanny by focusing on Neesha. Nanny had raised her like a mother, but it was Neesha who was at least trying to do what Spark needed and saying what Spark needed to hear.

Not that what she needed to hear fixed much. Loch still had Abyss's egg, still posed a threat, and Spark was still the only one who could do anything about it. Maybe she wasn't so lonely now, but the weariness sank into her like her bones were a moon.

Her insides twisted, and she choked back a sob. But the tears were too much to see through, so she set down the stone and sat against the unfinished wall and let the grief wash over her.

She'd just taken a deep, steadying breath to pull herself together when she heard a scrape from near the stairs. A moment later, Neesha poked her head up through the gap.

"Are these the sorts of tears that need company or solitude?" she asked softly.

"I'm so tired of being alone." Spark barely got the words out through the tightness in her throat.

Neesha came and sat next to her, wrapping an arm around Spark's shoulders. Spark curled against her mother, sobbing even harder, not even sure why anymore. Except for the last year, she'd always had Nanny to comfort her like this. Nanny and Pappy had filled the roles of parents for her.

But Neesha was different—more open-minded, less judgemental. And in a lot of ways, she was the same age as Spark.

"So this is my room, is it?" Neesha asked.

"It's for whoever wants it first."

Neesha ran her fingers through Spark's short tangle of hair. "Well, looks like that's me. There's no way I'm living in O's trash heap, even if part of all that clutter was mine to begin with."

"She doesn't throw anything out. Ever. Lina's gotten her to get rid of some things that were definitely absolute rubbish, but I heard it was quite the battle."

Neesha wiped away some of Spark's tears and gave her a sad smile. "Ondias needs to exert control somewhere after she lost so much of it."

Spark sighed. "You lost more and you're not a jerk about it."

"Give me time!" Neesha laughed. "Can I help you build? Seems only fair if I'm going to live here."

Spark suddenly felt light and warm. "You're really staying?"

"We're sort of both in the same mess, aren't we? Nowhere else to be. You've been here nearly a year now, so tell me: what's it like?"

"Winter is awful. It's shorter than in Pasdale, but the cold gets right into your *bones*."

Neesha laughed. "Shouldn't you be trying to sell me on this place?"

"Oh. Well, the winter is the worst part. It's, uh, still a bit of a dump, but I've built this place to feel more like the farmhouse in Pasdale. But it's not boring, even if it's tiny. The dragons are always circling and making noise, and some of them bring us to the trading post south of here, which is a lot like the market in Pasdale. Always something new!"

"Oh, good! It's always been so isolated."

"Yes, but it's so beautiful."

Neesha nodded, gazing dreamily up at the dragon city. "I don't think I'll ever get tired of it."

"I'm not! And even if winter is terrible, the sky is so clear, you can see the stars and the dancing lights. And there's a star shower near the winter solstice, and the dragons have a big festival for it. It's just... I can't even describe it. I hate how I ended up here, but I love this place."

"Pasdale is all I've ever known." Neesha glanced at her. "But I can't think of anywhere else I'd rather be. Even if I can go back to Pasdale, I'm not sure I want to. There's a real community here, one that doesn't care what I did or didn't do, whether I'm married or not."

"I don't want to get married." It came out as a horrified whisper.

"Not at all, or not to who Dionelle picked for you?"

"I don't know. Maybe not at all?" She took a deep breath. She needed to know how much she could trust Neesha before she made herself any more vulnerable. "Mamma, I don't like men. Not in a marrying them kind of way."

Neesha smiled and touched Spark's cheek. She pressed her lips together and tilted her head thoughtfully. "Honestly, neither do I. Men are a bit of fun now and then, but I don't love them. Sounds like maybe it's a little different for you, though?"

Spark nodded carefully, braced for some kind of "but" to ruin it all.

"All right." Neesha patted Spark's arm and stood. "Show me how you're getting these rocks together, and let's get to work."

Spark stared. That was it? But Neesha had said didn't like men either. No one had mentioned that in all the stories Spark had heard about her mother, but maybe the other adults didn't know? Spark couldn't see any reason why Neesha would lie about it. So that was something else they had in common, something that allowed Neesha to understand Spark where the other adults didn't. Spark inhaled against the hot tightness growing in her throat. She wiped her face on the hem of her shirt, still sniffling a bit, and then got up to show her mother how she'd fused the pieces of stones together.

"Ah. I can't pull fire out of the air," Neesha said. "Have you got a candle or something I can use to draw from? Or are you going to give me some fire whenever I need it?"

Spark fetched a candle and left it in a corner sheltered from the breeze. Neesha watched her work a bit more before picking up a small block, setting it down on the row snug against the one Spark had just fused, and drawing some fire from the candle to her hands.

"Bit of terramancy to it too, right?" Neesha asked.

"Oh, I guess? I mean, I've never used terramancy for this part, just worked with Nandara to build the foundation."

Neesha sat back, her head tilted and blue-amber eyes alight. "Well, that's something. I think I'm going to have to use terramancy if I'm going to have a hope of keeping up with you."

Spark smiled and watched while Neesha melted and moulded the block to fit in with the rest—smooth on the inside and just whatever jumbled mess on the outside, like Spark had been doing. It did take her longer, nearly half Spark's speed, but they got a rhythm going.

"So..." Neesha paused her work. "Most families grow naturally, like a garden coming into bloom. But I think we're going to have to build ours instead—the two of us—and I have no idea where to start, or how, or if I'll even be any good at this when I've got seventeen years to catch up on. Maybe... it's best if you let me know what you need and we can go from there?"

Spark swallowed and grabbed another brick. They were almost done this side.

But what *did* she need? She'd needed someone to ask her that, for starters, but she wasn't sure she had an answer. She fused the brick and grabbed another.

"I think that Nanny did her best to raise me the way you would have, but there are bound to be gaps." She set the brick in place, heating it while she spoke. "Maybe... that's where we can start? Correcting where Nanny deviated from choices you would have made?"

Neesha smiled, a knowing gleam in her eyes. "Should we start with the betrothal, then?"

She stretched to get her brick up on top of the one Spark had just fused. It was almost time to bring the ladder up. They'd be done within the hour.

"You can do something about that?" Spark's heartbeat sped up.

"You're my daughter. They all seem to have decided you're my responsibility for the next year, until you're an adult. So yes. You don't want to marry Nandara's grandson?"

"Jatt. No. I like him, but we're *friends*. I don't want to be anything but that."

"There's more, though?"

Spark gathered up a new brick. "He thinks it's a good idea."

"Well, he's wrong. I'll talk to Nandara. Then I'll talk to him."

"I don't want to hurt him. He's acting like I'm rejecting him and not some stupid idea of how we should live."

Neesha took the block from her hands, nodding. "Listen, Spark. If he's really your friend, then he'll respect your choices. And if he won't, then you need to move on. It's not worth jeopardizing what you have with Ember."

Spark swallowed.

Neesha set the new block in place. "I had a chat with Stone this morning."

"You're... not still going to marry him, are you?"

Neesha laughed and finished the fusing. "No, and he was the one to admit the bad idea that was. That's what I mean about respect. Stone knew what he was getting into when I agreed to get married—he knew why I was doing it and what he was getting. And it seems like all the years I've missed have changed his mind in other ways. There's freedom here. I think we should both take it."

"Everyone's going to be angry about it."

Neesha picked up another block and smiled. "Then let them be angry with me. I'm used to it. We live in a world that makes it difficult to follow your heart, but try."

Spark felt a warm sense of peace, lighter than she'd felt in over a year. It didn't bother her that Neesha clearly felt as lost as Spark did. There was someone else to share decisions. Or to take them on entirely.

They got to the end of the row, so Spark fetched the ladder, and they quickly finished off the second exterior wall. They were also nearly out of stones. Neesha spoke more about the betrothal and how arranged marriages worked in other cultures. She'd taken time out of studying for her Guild exams to learn more about it the first time Dionelle had tried to arrange a marriage between her and Stone.

"The worst was how no one cared what I wanted," Neesha said. "At first, not even Stone."

Spark nodded, knowing exactly what Neesha meant.

But Neesha explained how other cultures did it—how it was about both families, about building community, and less about control.

"I've never been to any of these places, you have to understand, but the accounts I read sounded lovely. It was a decision both families were fully involved in, with the final say belonging to the two people ultimately getting married. And not something arranged for babies! Usually, the conversations start when both parties are teens. That's how it's supposed to be for us, but there's always that pressure. It seems absent elsewhere."

Part of Spark wanted to travel and see other places and find somewhere that would let her just be who she was. But she loved the valley and the dragons, and with most of what remained of her family here, she had even less reason to leave.

When they ran out of bricks, Neesha seemed disappointed. "Where do we get more?"

Spark pointed north to the quarry, and her mother stilled.

"We're using the old mountainside." Neesha stared, swallowed, and gave Spark a desperate look. "It's hard. Unbelievable. For me, that mountainside came down in the flood only days ago."

Neesha eyed the walls with new scrutiny. "So we have to go out there to get more? Do you have a cart? That's a lot of trips!"

"Oh…" Spark's cheeks grew hot. "Abyss fills that old travel wagon and brings me a load now and then. I… don't think I can ask her for anything right now."

Neesha nodded slowly. "Right. We need a plan. Well, you had a plan. We need details? I think I have some things to learn?"

"Is that safe?" Spark went cold. "Everything I've been learning is what took you from us in the first place."

Neesha put a reassuring hand on her shoulder. "Nandara gave me a good idea of what you've been working on, and it sounds like you're figuring out the things I was trying to do. You're making the dangerous spellcraft safer. I don't remember much before the fire took me, and nothing afterward until I woke up here, but we might be able to dig up some more answers."

"Shouldn't you rest more?"

"I assure you, I've had seventeen years of it. I don't know what exactly the dragon magic did, but don't think of it as some illness. It's like I woke up from a truly excellent night's sleep. Any damage is, well, spiritual I guess, and all from learning just how long it's been. Sitting idly while others finish battles I started doesn't seem right."

Spark flexed her hands. She didn't like the idea of pushing Neesha already, but didn't want to argue. And she really wanted someone to help her with everything.

"We should talk to Nandara about it some more, then."

"You can really just open fire portals any time you want?"

"Helps that I can pull fire out of nowhere to get it started." Spark smiled and snapped a small flame into the palm of her hand.

Neesha grinned at her and headed down the stairs. It was midday, and Spark's neglected stomach let her know what it thought of her forgetting food existed.

If her mother wanted to practice the dangerous pyromancy Spark had been working on, she had to assume Neesha understood the risks. Still, Spark would need to improve to protect them both.

CHAPTER SEVENTEEN

Spark stood with Abyss amidst the black dragon's clutch of eggs, looking up at the two looming in front of her. Abyss insisted they'd changed. They weren't any bigger or noisier, but they had a pull to them. Spark didn't like the way it made her feel frantic once she was away from them.

"What does it mean?" Spark asked as Abyss set her down outside her house again.

"We only have days now."

Spark cursed. "How many?"

"The Superiors are still assessing. But this is unexpected."

Neesha came out as Abyss left again, and Spark told her what she'd learned.

"We should probably go talk to Ondias about this," Spark said.

"As much as I'd rather never go back to that house again, she's the best source we've got. And we should probably check in and see how Dionelle is doing anyway."

Spark felt a pang of guilt over how little she'd thought about Nanny today. But Nanny just wasn't the same. It was like Spark had rescued a shell in Pasdale.

They quickly arrived at Ondias's, but Lina said Ondias was in the southern field, talking to one of the dragons. Spark grumbled. She hadn't even thought to check there first.

"Why don't you come in and have some tea while you wait for her?" Lina asked.

"How's Dionelle?" Neesha asked.

Lina's face crumpled. "Still no change."

Neesha went into the back room, while Spark followed Lina through the stacks and around the piles of stuff to the table in the kitchen. Lina made her some tea and then left for the back room as well. Spark heard the soft murmur of Lina and Neesha talking.

Ondias returned not long afterward, startled to see Spark waiting for her. Spark launched into a description of the new sensation she felt around the eggs.

Ondias closed her eyes and sank into the chair across from Spark.

"It's bad?" Spark guessed. She wasn't sure she wanted to know how bad.

"It's two-thirds good."

"They're hatching?"

"Yes. When the egg emits a pull like you've described, it means the egg is days away from hatching."

"How many days? How much time do we have?"

"Five days is the soonest. A fortnight is the longest I've heard of, and that was only once. Ten days seems to be the norm."

Spark cursed, closed her eyes, and rested her forehead on the table next to her cup. "Five days isn't enough. Ten probably isn't either."

"It's still two-thirds good."

"Right, well, we had a plan and it half worked already, so I'll go back... tomorrow? It's probably too late over there today. What's the time difference?"

Spark stopped talking when she saw the dark look on Ondias's face.

"You can't keep running off like this."

"I'm not running off! I'll take Abyss and whoever else she wants. A fire portal to sneak in is all we need, and I can already do that."

"This isn't your fight. You have plenty here to attend to, with the state your mother and grandmother are in. And you still haven't spoken to Jatt."

Spark growled in frustration. "I'm not marrying him! Or anyone else!"

Ondias scowled. "You can't keep repeating your mother's mistakes. That arrangement is for your own good."

"About that," Neesha said, coming out of the back room. "Where do I find Nandara?"

"Oh, don't you start with it now, too. You need to be a better influence on Mita."

Spark realized she'd taken the bait, falling into the usual pattern of argument. She did not have time for this. Five days. The eggs could hatch in just *five days*.

"Right. Well, I've got work to do," Spark said, pushing herself back from the table. "Thank you for the tea and the information."

The denial of the anticipated argument left Ondias off balance, and Spark was out the door before the woman could say anything else. Besides, Neesha was still in there and had sounded plenty ready for a world-ending argument. Spark rushed straight home and into the forge.

She paged through her designs, her thoughts chasing themselves in circles. She had so many things started or half-finished, and no idea what she should actually work on. Or if she should work on anything at all.

If it was a stealth mission for only the eggs, she had everything she needed already. But freeing Nanny would have Loch on high alert. Saving the eggs might not be as simple now as it had seemed the first time. What kind of fight would it be?

Spark floundered around her forge, still not having come up with a better design for the dragon-riding sling, and she wasn't sure yet how to make the gliding suit she'd envisioned after practicing with Raia and her blaze. She'd pulled out some of her scrap pieces to try to make some cutters to free the chained dragons. She'd have to practice with some of the chains she'd previously made to make sure she got the cutters right.

The day was getting old, and Neesha hadn't returned from Ondias's yet. No one else had come by. Spark tried not to let it get to her—she knew her mother had a lot to catch up on—but the loneliness crept in again.

She pushed the feeling aside and glanced at her notes. If they were going to do any sort of pyromancy work, they should probably get started on it soon, unless they were just going to completely abandon Abyss's egg.

Spark hadn't seen Abyss again, but doubted any of her eggs had hatched. There'd been quite a ruckus when another dragon's clutch of eggs had hatched over the summer. The dragons had erupted with noise and flame, dancing across the sky in celebration.

So, probably still time. Just not enough.

Spark tossed the length of iron onto the worktable, dusted herself off, and headed into the village. She stopped at Nandara's first because it was closer, but no one was home. That left going back to Ondias's. Spark steeled herself against it.

"—think she can fight?" Neesha was asking as Spark pushed into the house.

"You've got to get her out of bed first." Ondias sounded tired.

They paused and looked up as Spark came into the parlour. Neesha was hunched in one of the overstuffed chairs with a bundle of stunning amethyst dragon skin on her lap. Her eyes were red and puffy. Spark held her breath, but Neesha offered her a genuine smile when she saw her and beckoned her over. Spark slid into the chair next to her mother.

"Ondias found another crate of my things. Look at this!" Neesha unfurled the purple bundle and held it up so it was recognizable as wizarding robes. "It was an early Guild entrance gift. Of course, I never officially got in, but—"

"Oh, you can get in under the new tiers now, like I did," Spark said.

Neesha's smile twisted into something Spark couldn't quite parse, but her tone held a note of amusement when she said, "Of course you got into the Guild before me."

"We can worry about exams and tiers when we're safe," Ondias said. "If you really think you're ready for this, I'm not going to report you to the Guild. I don't think your temporary entrance was ever officially revoked, since it was set to expire once Draxli's forces were turned away, and, well... Loch might have misled a lot of fools in Pasdale, but the Guild always knew better. It's completely reasonable to extend it to now."

"Tell me more about these tiers."

Ondias rolled her eyes and disappeared deeper into the house, but Spark let Neesha know about what changes had come as a result of Neesha's battles and Loch's very existence.

"Excellent," Neesha said. "It's about time the Guild had some sense. I'll see if Nandara will give me the specialist exam for pyromancy. How long does it take? Do we have time today?"

Spark startled. "Today?"

"It can be my warm up before we start working on the problems with demon possession."

"You're a fool!" Ondias called from deeper in the house.

"A fool who's saved your hide more than you deserve!" Neesha called back, that note of wry amusement still in her tone. Then she rolled her eyes. "Ondias told Dionelle about what you all think happened to me—the demon pulling my essence into the fire realm when she un-possessed me. I think she meant it as a 'hey, look, we can keep that from happening again' sort of thing, but now Dionelle won't so much as get out of bed, so that's going great."

"Should I try talking to her?" Spark asked.

Neesha shrugged. "You probably know her better than I do, at this point. She and I never got along before. I think we were getting close to it. Kind of sounds like you ended up being the daughter she always wanted."

This time, Neesha's tone was bitter, and a sheen of tears covered her eyes before she blinked them back. Spark sank deeper into her chair and went still.

"Sorry," Neesha said. "It's all still a lot."

"I'm sorry, Mamma. Is there anything I can do?"

That same bitterness twitched across Neesha's expression before a sad smile settled on her features. "No, Spark. You've made more of a contribution than anyone can expect from you already."

"So did you. Seventeen years' worth."

"Fair point. But I'm supposed to be the adult here. So you let me worry about me and you and Dionelle, all right? If you want to talk to her, I won't stop you, but you don't have to."

"I haven't spoken to her since I brought her here. It couldn't hurt, could it?"

Ondias came into the room. "She's brittle, Mita. I barely recognize her anymore. Lina didn't train much in spiritual ailments, so we're all making it up as we go along."

Spark's breath caught in her chest, trapped by a weight as heavy as Abyss.

"Has she seen Abyss yet?" Spark asked. "She hasn't even left the house, has she? When I first got here, you got me to snap out of the shock by forcing me out of bed and out into the village. Maybe the same thing would help her?"

"I don't know that it can make her much worse." Ondias shrugged. "Good luck getting her out of bed, though. You at least ate and used the toilet. It's like she's not even there. Not as bad as with Neesha before yesterday, but damned close."

"Well, I'm bigger than her. What if I just carry her outside?"

"And what? Drop her in the dirt?"

Spark shrugged. Hopefully it wouldn't come to that, but between her and Neesha, maybe they could get Nanny moving.

Spark squeezed through the hallway lined with crates, trunks, and piles into the same room where Spark had spent her first days in the village. They'd been a blur, full of grief, thinking she'd lost Nanny. They were all together now, and it had already healed so much of her own pain, even if there was no getting Pappy, Bren, and Breen back. She had to hold hope that it would help Nanny eventually too.

The room smelled stale and musty. The curtain across the window made it dim, and the walls seemed much closer together, like the stacks around the edges of the room might collapse and bury her. Spark itched to leave again.

Nanny lay with a thin blanket over her. She was dressed in borrowed clothes. Her hair was clean but, even though someone had clearly put effort into detangling some of it, it was still partially matted. Nanny had never been a large woman, but she seemed so small and frail and old now. She had dark bruises of exhaustion under her closed eyes, and her cheeks were sunken and far too pale.

The sight stole Spark's breath. Her heart ached. Nanny needed fresh air and sunshine.

Spark fled the room, back out to the parlour.

"Bring one of the chairs outside," Spark said. "Somewhere with a view of the city—somewhere Abyss can join us. And what have you been using to comb Nanny's hair?"

"We've all been taking turns at it," Ondias said. "Lina brought some lavender-scented oil to help things along."

"Bring that and the comb outside too." She turned to Neesha. "Come help me carry her."

Neesha's smile was sad again, but she hastily draped the bright robes over her shoulders and followed Spark into the back room.

"Is this how you've been taking charge all this time?" Neesha asked.

Spark didn't say anything. She didn't *want* to keep taking charge, especially when Neesha kept promising she would.

Nanny opened her eyes when the two of them entered, and Neesha showed off the robes. "Guess I'll get to use them after all, Mamma. I'm going to get Nandara to give me a specialist exam as soon as she gets back. I'll be a Guild wizard yet!"

Nanny turned her haunted gaze on them. Spark stilled.

"Come on, Mamma," Neesha urged, holding out a hand. "You need some fresh air. It's too cramped in this room for all of us to properly visit."

Colour rose on Nanny's cheeks. Her eyes went bright and wild, with the hint of flame around the edges. She settled her pained gaze on Spark.

"They saw you," she rasped. "They'll come."

Spark's body buzzed with electric cold, and the darkness in the room encroached on her vision. Neesha swore, then grabbed Nanny's shoulders and pulled her to sitting.

"Curse them anyway," Neesha said. "We've got five days, dozens of dragons, and the three best pyromancers in the world. Let them come. We'll end them."

Spark half expected a shower of sparks around her mother, like the way Spark herself used to get when she was younger and more emotional.

"Nobody's ending anything until we get some more practice," Spark said. "I can do more than portals now. Let me show you."

They got Nanny out of bed, and she shuffled along with them, her face streaked with silent tears. Outside, Ondias had set up one of her soft chairs and a spare side table with the comb and bottle of oil on it, as well as some soap, a basin of water, and a towel. Nanny dropped into the chair.

While Neesha worked the oil into one of Nanny's knots, she leaned closer to Spark and lowered her voice. "I thought you said she didn't talk."

Spark shrugged. "Everything is weird right now."

Neesha didn't disagree and worked away at making Nanny more presentable while Nanny stared sightlessly into the space between Ondias's home and the next house over. It was a gap big enough to accommodate Abyss. Spark looked up to the city and the few dragons circling the valley, but there was no sign of the black dragoness. Spark pulled a fire out of the air and used it for a summoning.

It took longer than she would have expected for Abyss to appear out of the city and glide down to where they waited.

As she landed, Nanny's expression cleared, and she sat up straighter, a ghost of a smile on her face. She didn't move from her chair, but Abyss gently came in closer, hunching to fit in the space and resting her chin on the ground just in front of Nanny. She nudged Nanny gently before settling in.

"I grieve your losses," Abyss said. "And regret that I did not arrive in Pasdale in time to aid anyone but Spark."

Nanny closed her eyes, shedding a few tears, and nodded slowly. She opened her eyes again, offering Abyss a real smile.

"I am relieved that you are here with us now," the dragoness added.

Nanny gave her head a little shake. Spark interpreted it to mean a touch of disbelief.

"We've all got some things to get used to," Spark said.

"I have news from the Superiors," Abyss said. "While not everyone in the valley has been surveyed, of those who have, approximately two-thirds of them have found their voices again, including my mate. Of these, most of them are younger dragons, though not all. The Dragoness Superior speaks human languages once again, but a couple of the juveniles, including a hatchling, remain silent."

Spark looked from Abyss to her mother to Ondias.

"There's more," Abyss continued. "All of the eggs are much closer to hatching than they were even yesterday. Some of them are much bigger. The Superiors suspect that whatever power was released from the fire realm on Neesha's awakening has affected all of us, including the eggs."

Ondias leaned forward, head tilted. "That furthers my theory that the fireborn are affecting the dragons."

"The Superiors agree, and would like to speak with the three of you when there is time."

"Your egg doesn't have much time. And neither do we," Spark said. "Loch's people saw me, and he'll be sore that I got Nanny out. They'll attack soon—if they're not on their way already."

"The Superiors worry that another battle—and any injury to one or all of the three of you—could further weaken our kind."

Neesha looked around at them. "I know I'm missing a mountain's worth of information, but it seems we have two options: fortify the city and wait for the attack, or fly out to meet them."

"We're not really ready for either," Spark said. "I've been trying to build weapons and things that either the dragons or people flying with them can use, but it's not much. There's the armour I've made, but it's not enough for the numbers we need. It's just... None of it's enough, and now we're out of time."

"We really need to decide what we're going to do before we make a plan," Neesha said. "Is it possible to split our forces and do both?"

"That depends on how many dragons Loch has captive," Ondias said. "I don't have a recent count, but Nandara might."

"Where is she?" Spark asked. "I thought she'd be here."

Abyss snorted, promising to return when they were ready to act, and left in a torrent of wind and dust. Still working to clean up Nanny's hair, Neesha pressed her lips together, suddenly more focused on her work.

"Don't be shy about speaking your mind now," Ondias bit out.

Spark's mind tried to jump between a dozen different scenarios as to what Neesha might have said to Nandara—and why—before her mother spoke.

"I called off the betrothal like you wanted," Neesha explained. "I spoke to Nandara first, then Jatt. She was still talking with him in his studio when I left."

Spark buzzed, her pulse thundering in her ears. She was instantly relieved and guilty and maybe a bit horrified.

"Was he okay?"

Neesha shrugged. "Can't say—I don't know him well enough. He was quiet, but based on his body language, he seemed equal parts angry and sad."

Spark held her breath, tapping her hands against her thighs.

Neesha paused her detangling to put a hand on Spark's shoulder. "Remember what I said about being worthy of friendship. It's hard losing someone you thought was special—it hurts, and it's not any fun—but it's better in the long run."

After watching Abyss fly off, Nanny had been staring up at the city glittering in the late afternoon sun—a bit of wonder and joy briefly returning to her expression—but she sagged, the lock of her hair slipping out of Neesha's hands as she worked at the knot.

"It'll be okay, Nanny." Spark knelt in front of her, a hand on her knee. "You did your best, and now Mamma's here to help you with it. We can worry about my future when we're not in immediate danger."

Spark didn't actually want to talk about any betrothals at all, but she wanted to offer something to make Nanny feel better. Nanny only nodded wearily, staring down at her hands while Neesha went back to working on her hair. Ondias left, claiming she had work to do.

A familiar voice called from down the lane. "I wondered if I'd find you here!"

Spark's stomach fluttered. Neesha chuckled, no doubt because Spark had some stupid look on her face. She stood quickly and turned to see Ember practically bouncing down the lane toward them.

"Pa told me the news." She came right up to Spark and took her hands. "It's true? About the betrothal?"

"She didn't want to do it," Neesha said, not looking up. "I called it off."

Ember glanced her way, then back to Spark with raised eyebrows.

Spark took a breath. "Right. Ember, this is Neesha. And Nanny—er, Dionelle. I've finally got an adult making decisions for me that aren't terrible."

Neesha snickered. "She thinks I'm an adult."

"Well, the rest of them do, and that's what counts, I guess," Ember said. "How's Jatt?"

"I haven't seen him," Spark said. "He'd better get over it, or I'll slap him."

"I'll hold him down." Ember grinned.

"Mamma's helping me with the house, so we're getting through it faster. Of course, since I completely bungled the rescue yesterday, they're going to know where Nanny ended up. They'll come here."

Ember's grin disappeared. "On high alert again, then?"

"Yes. Lots to prepare for. And I didn't get Abyss's egg back, so we still need to figure that out, too. We need to try to get Mamma caught up on all the magic I've been working on with Nandara."

"Oh, I don't think I can help with that?"

"No, I don't think so," Spark agreed. "But maybe we can do something later?"

Ember's expression fell. "I'll try to stop by after dinner."

"I'd like that. Maybe if you come across some spare chairs…?"

Ember grinned. "I think Pa probably has a couple in the shed. Maybe I'll bring some wine, and your ma can tell me what it was like almost being my stepmom."

Neesha snorted another laugh while Spark sputtered and choked. Nanny sighed audibly, but it sounded more like the false exasperation Spark remembered when she and Bren had been on a tear, full of energy and driving the adults crazy. Nanny's colour did look a little better.

Ember glanced over Spark's shoulder, and her face fell again. "Well, I leave you with that awkwardness. I don't envy you what's to come."

Spark turned to see Nandara on her way to join them and swallowed. But Nandara smiled, reaching them as Ember disappeared down the lane.

"How's Jatt?" Spark asked.

"His pride's been stung, but he'll get over it. And we had a good talk that gave me more understanding of his situation. There's plenty of time for you three to talk about your futures later."

"Definitely bigger things to worry about right now," Neesha agreed.

Nandara nodded. "Spark, may I have a word in private? We'll be back in a moment."

Spark followed Nandara farther down the lane, glancing back once to see Neesha watching them carefully, still combing Nanny's hair.

"What is it?" Spark asked.

"I haven't had the chance to talk to you since Neesha woke up and you brought Dionelle back. I wanted to make sure you're actually okay. I know this is what you wanted, but it's also not how you envisioned things."

Spark glanced at Neesha again.

"It's just all… weird. And we're still in so much danger."

"I know you'd hoped this would give you a break, and it looks like you've got a bit more work ahead of you. But you seem comfortable with Neesha despite being essentially strangers."

"Yeah, that's the weirdest part! It's awkward, and I can't explain it, but we manage to feel simultaneously like strangers and like she's always been part of my life."

Nandara smiled. "Family takes on so many different shapes. Sometimes, the family we choose is the one that was there all along."

When they returned, Neesha put the comb down and placed a kiss on Nanny's head before coming around the chair to speak more directly with Nandara. "I meant what I said earlier. I want to see what Spark's come up with and see if the two of us—or three," she said, glancing at Nanny, "can sort it out properly."

Nandara clasped her hands in front of her.

"I really have recovered from whatever that was," Neesha insisted.

"Physically, yes," Nandara said.

"And we won't know the rest until I practice. And I'm serious about the specialist tiers."

"I know you are. I've got everything ready. We can evaluate your ability after dinner."

"Sure." Neesha winked at Spark. "That'll give you a bit of privacy."

Spark's cheeks warmed. "Mamma, what are we going to do with the spells I've been learning? They're only good against the ice dragons, and there are only three of those left. There are far more captive dragons."

"We'll do the same as you and Dionelle did when they attacked the house—target their riders. Their riders aren't fireproof."

"Neither are ours..."

"No, but you've got some armour," Nandara said, drumming her fingers against her chin. "That proved to be an advantage last time, so there's no reason to think it won't help this time. While I can't guarantee Loch hasn't figured out something similar, I haven't heard anything from my sources."

"Do you have more than Unari?" Spark asked.

Nandara smiled. "I've got half a dozen I trust who provide me with information regularly."

"Ondias wanted to know how many dragons Loch has."

Nandara nodded. "I'll speak with her and meet you back here. Abyss can take us up the mountain again."

Neesha applied more oil to Nanny's hair and picked up the comb again while Nandara went to find Ondias. Spark fetched a stool to sit in front of Nanny. Cautiously, she withdrew the pendant from beneath her shirt and held it out to Nanny.

"You should have this, shouldn't you?" Spark asked.

Nanny first stiffened, then sobbed, shaking her head so that Neesha lost the knot again. Spark disappeared the pendant back under her clothes and squeezed Nanny's hand. She changed the subject, but Nanny's silent gaze returned to the dragon city. Was she thinking about how it had fallen once already? That it was in danger again?

Or was she just marvelling at the beauty of it?

Spark hoped they could save it. She'd been so certain that the three of them together would be unstoppable, but Neesha was overwhelmed and Nanny wasn't herself at all. They both had so much to learn, but there was no time.

CHAPTER EIGHTEEN

Spark did her best to hide how tired she was as she and Nandara went through all the magic theory again, up in front of the armoury, this time for Nanny's benefit.

Nanny hadn't come with them yesterday evening, which was probably for the best. When they'd practiced, Neesha had been trying to un-possess Spark, but she'd lost focus once Spark had let the demon take over, and she hadn't been able to cope at all when Nandara had once again pulled the demon—and Spark—right out of Spark's body.

It was becoming increasingly easier for Spark to take herself back and expel the demon on her own, even without Neesha there to help coax her, but it continued to be deeply exhausting.

After Neesha had panicked, they'd had to quit early. Which was fine, because it had meant an early dinner and a visit from Ember, who'd brought more chairs, and it had meant time for Nandara to administer Neesha's specialist exam to the Guild, which she'd easily passed, despite being a bit shaky from the demons.

But then she'd had nightmares all night long. Spark had pretended they hadn't woken her, but neither of them had slept particularly well.

Now, trying the same exercises, Nanny looked about ready to panic. Spark felt like her insides were too heavy while her body was too light, and like she was going to let Abyss down. Like they would never be safe.

Abyss stood patiently nearby, in her usual protective role. Nandara wore a spare firecloak for these lessons, but it would only protect her from so much. While Neesha had been doing her exam, Spark had tempered more leathers to be dragonproof, adjusted the tempering on her axe, and worked on her gliding suit.

"Are you ready for a demonstration?" Nandara asked.

Nanny's eyes widened as she looked around at the three of them, then glanced at Abyss.

They hadn't decided yet whether they would meet Loch's forces head-on or fortify the valley. It would depend on how things went today. Based on Nandara's sources, they could probably risk spreading out their forces and doing both. But only if the three fireborn women could master some dangerous magic.

"It's not safe to try any of this if you're not ready." Nandara directed that comment at both Neesha and Nanny.

"I'm good today," Neesha said. "I think practicing and using some magic for the exam helped shake a few things loose."

"I wish I had time to teach you how to harness each other's power. It might save you from needing demons."

Spark had only heard a very little bit about wizards drawing magic from each other. But as she understood it, they could amplify magic so that, when harnessed, they would be far more powerful than each working individually.

"You're going to have to confront demons and the fire realm." Nandara's tone was doubtful, and the expression she laid on Neesha matched.

"Don't know if I can do it till I try. Let's stop wasting daylight. Spark can damn near get the demon out on her own, and I'm the one you lost this way. I need to learn how to do it right."

Spark held her breath in order to keep from bursting out that she should start again, but Neesha was right. Spark had been practicing this all for longer, and she nearly had self-exorcism down to an art.

"I'll guide you through it," Spark said.

"We start with you still in control of the demon," Nandara said. "If you can't handle that, you can't handle a full possession."

Neesha scowled but nodded. Spark opened a portal to the fire realm and Neesha interrupted. "Shouldn't I learn that too?"

Spark looked to Nandara.

"That might be a safer place to start," Nandara agreed. "If my memory serves me, you had some skill with portals when you summoned trueflame."

Spark closed the portal again but kept the fire going while Neesha immersed herself in flame, tearing at it like she was furiously pulling weeds, until it flared with the light of a portal. Spark grinned.

"Has Spark learned to work trueflame?" Neesha asked.

"I haven't done anything with portals except use them to free Nanny."

Nandara sighed. "Nee, are you stalling out of fear, or do you have a good reason for switching the order we agreed on?"

"Spark's said how exhausting the possession is. I don't know if we'll have anything left after working with the demons, and learning to work trueflame would be helpful."

Nandara let Neesha continue, and she taught Spark how to pull trueflame through a portal. A column of fire thicker than the old firs deep in the mountains spiralled skyward, flame licking the clouds. It was a dazzling, roaring vortex, hotter and brighter than anything Spark had seen this side of the fire realm. It turned out all Neesha was really doing with it was pulling through parts of the fire realm itself and unleashing it.

Spark gave it a try. It was easy enough when she was already an expert at opening fire portals.

"Spark, stop," Neesha gasped. "Close it. Now."

Spark didn't like the panic in her mother's voice. She closed the portal, cutting off the source of the vortex. It dissipated with a hiss.

"What happened?" Nandara asked.

"Spark, did you hear it?"

"The roaring?" Spark asked.

Neesha shook her head frantically. "The column of fire... It... It wasn't quite talking, but it felt like words. They wanted me. I felt like a moth around a lantern."

"Oh!" Nandara said, rushing to Nanny's side. "Di, are you all right?"

Nanny, who'd been standing back near Abyss, had her eyes squeezed shut and her hands over her ears.

"I heard the call as well," Abyss said.

"Why didn't you hear it?" Neesha asked Spark.

"She's been resistant to the demons' trickery and the pull of the realm," Nandara said. "Maybe we've adequately inoculated her against the dangers?"

"Or maybe I'm so much demon it doesn't even recognize me as different," Spark said.

Neesha let out a low whistle. "I wonder... I'm going to stand back. You try again and pay more attention this time."

Spark waited until all three women were back next to Abyss and then opened a portal and pulled another column of fire out. It raged in a spiral skyward, roaring like a wildfire. The danger it presented was clear, though it was beautiful, like the dragons themselves in a lot of ways. If Spark felt drawn to it, it wasn't any different than when she was drawn to any beautiful thing.

"It could be how much alike you are with the fire realm, but I also wonder if it's because you've already worked to resist the pull in a real way," Neesha said. "You made a safe place in your thoughts where the demon can't reach you, right?"

Spark stood straighter. "Yes. Could that be the difference?"

Spark and Neesha had spoken about it before they'd fallen asleep last night, when Spark had shyly admitted where she mentally retreated to.

"Do you have a safe place?" Spark asked. "Somewhere peaceful and protected? Even if only temporarily?"

Neesha's gaze wandered until it focused on Abyss. "I think I've got something. Abyss, I'm going to need your support."

Abyss lay her chin on the ground, and Neesha sat with her back against the dragon's neck. Nandara moved off to the side so that Abyss was between her and Neesha. Nanny was nearby and watching. Spark knelt in front of her mother and started a fire.

Neesha closed her eyes, and took a breath. "I'm ready. Pull up some trueflame."

Spark did, and Neesha's eyebrows shot up, but she didn't seem alarmed. She sat with her eyes closed a little longer, then opened them and looked at the thin column of fire rising into the sky. She smiled.

"That's much better," Neesha said. "It's still enticing, but more like a fancy dessert after a meal that maybe I don't need, and less like a cool drink of water after being lost in a desert."

"So that means you were double doomed all those years ago," Nandara said. "It's no wonder we lost you to the call of both trueflame and demon trickery."

"We've got our answers, now. And a way I can protect myself."

Spark cut off the trueflame. "Do you want to keep going?"

Neesha smiled at her, resting a hand briefly on Spark's cheek, then she closed her eyes again. "Now a demon."

Spark pressed her lips together, suddenly more fiercely protective of her mother than she'd ever been. But they needed this. Abyss needed their help. Spark lit another fire, and her mother summoned a demon.

"Do you recognize this one?" Spark asked. They'd talked about that part, but she wanted to be sure her mother remembered.

Neesha shook her head, and the demon vanished into her. "I've got it. This is the best and worst feeling."

Spark chuckled. She beckoned Nanny over. "I can go first, if you want, to show you."

Nanny shook her head and then gestured back toward Nandara. The two of them had worked through the theory that Nandara and Spark had come up with to make the process of removing the demon easier.

"Okay, Mamma. Nanny's going to try. Are you still feeling okay?"

Neesha nodded shallowly. Nanny started the banishing spell. Spark thought it was going okay, but it was hard to tell when she wasn't involved in the magic. But Neesha gasped and winced and jerked away.

"Should we stop?" Spark asked.

Nanny paused.

Neesha shook her head. "Keep trying. It's weird. I don't like it."

"Remember, it's not as bad if you can keep yourself separate from it. Just let us know if you need to stop," Spark said.

Nanny continued the banishment, and a weird glow emanated around Neesha, like an aura of sunshine. But Neesha was gritting her teeth. Nanny looked worried.

Suddenly, Neesha screamed, and Nanny leapt away. The glow disappeared.

Spark got in closer and summoned the demon, giving it a more interesting target than Neesha before it got control of her. The demon launched itself from Neesha toward her. The gap between them was small, but Spark was ready—she caught the demon with a spell and banished it.

Neesha sat with her head bowed, panting. She swore, startling Spark.

"I'm sorry, Spark. I don't know if I can do this. Nandara was right—that's exactly what happened back in Pasdale. That demon wasn't leaving without me." She shook her head angrily.

Nandara came back around, a comforting hand on Nanny's shoulder. "If we can't get a demon out of you safely, then you can't use demon possession anymore. You know that."

"Yes, I realize. I hate this." Neesha stood up and stalked away to the mouth of the armoury, shaking her head and swearing into the darkness beyond.

"Am I really that much stronger?" Spark asked. "Am I really the only one who can do this?"

"It's hard to say," Nandara said. "We'd have to get the both of you into the Guild with Grand Chancellor Dira and the full council to really figure it out."

"That doesn't help us today."

"I don't think it's the power difference," Neesha said, coming back. Her words were clipped and her tone hard and bitter. "I'm just a godsdamned coward. I can do it, theoretically. I just don't know how to tame the fear of losing another seventeen years."

"We know how to remedy that, in the unlikely event you get pulled in again," Abyss said. "And in the even more unlikely event that both of you are lost to the realm, dragons can open a portal. *Someone* can come for you."

"Fine," Neesha said with a resolved nod. "We try again."

Nanny grabbed Neesha's shoulder, shaking her head frantically.

"Mamma, I have to. We can't keep letting Spark do all the dangerous work herself. I can do this."

Neesha sat against Abyss, taking time to mentally prepare herself before repeating the process. This time, Nandara successfully separated the demon from Neesha.

Breathing harder than normal, Neesha insisted they try again and that Nanny do the banishing this time.

"You have to learn," Neesha said. "The likelihood one of us will need you is high."

Spark gripped her hands in front of her and watched on as Neesha took another demon, and Nandara walked Nanny through it. It didn't go quite as smoothly as when Nandara had done it, but it worked. Nanny didn't seem relieved, though. Neesha was ashen, a sheen of sweat on her brow, and she sat with her head hanging between her knees.

"This is awful." She looked up at Nandara. "We should—"

Neesha's words were lost to dragoncries, the whole valley erupting with them. Spark clamped her hands over her ears, but it still felt like it would split her skull.

The worst of the racket was to the south. The cry was answered by the entirety of the dragon city, all of them flocking out to circle the valley while a host of them went south. A short time later, they returned, escorting six new dragons.

"Again!" Spark watched them descend into the valley while the others piled into the supply wagon Abyss had used to ferry them up in the first place.

The dragons were gone and a new group of riders were present when Spark and the others arrived in the field with Ondias. The new group contained only five riders—two men and three women—and Spark wondered if they'd lost someone or if they just had a different dynamic between the dragons. This group all had varying degrees of tawny or beige skin and straight black hair, epicanthic light brown eyes, and short wispy builds—except for the one quiet man in the back who was a head taller than the rest and nearly as wide as tall. The others wore their hair longer, all of it neatly braided or tied back, but his was short and spiky, almost comical in how it stood on end. Spark didn't recognize the accent they spoke with.

Ondias was delegating, getting one of them to head down to the southern trading post. "If that's where you're all coming from, I want one of you down there to hold any more there until the Superiors have a handle on the situation."

"There's going to be more?" Spark asked.

"Could be." Ondias was deeply annoyed. She only introduced their leader, Jin, one of the women. "Rumours have spread pretty far, and this lot is painting a rather dire picture of lands beyond our borders."

"It's not just Golden Hill," Jin said. "This Loch has been working with the king, expanding down the continent all the way to the southern and eastern seas."

"They're building a dragon army," the large one added. "Training hatchlings they raise from eggs and breaking adults they've managed to capture. They've taken riders and dragons together, turning the bond against them and forcing them to do Loch's bidding."

A cold buzz raced up and down Spark's spine. "An army? How many?"

Ondias held out a placating hand. "We don't have a good idea of numbers, but there are only so many in captivity, and they're far outnumbered by those who are free."

"And Loch can't send all of them here, or he'll lose what ground he's got," Jin said.

"Still, if he sends any of them, we're looking at far more than the seventeen in Pasdale right now," Spark said. "We can't defend against that!"

Ondias gave her an annoyed look. "I'll bring this news to the Superiors. They can always recall the remaining free dragons to come defend the city. If we can confirm Loch's numbers and movements, we can appeal to the Guild to send more wizards for aid as well."

"They've been so resistant to get involved," Nandara said. "I tried when I was there, but Loch has amassed so many powerful aquamancers to his cause that I think the Guild is intimidated."

"So we go back to Pasdale," Neesha said, her voice hard. "I killed Draxli. I'll get rid of this new one."

"You know it won't be that simple."

"Guess I should get back to practicing." Neesha looked to Spark and then back at Abyss. "This has been enough rest, I think I can try one more demon."

The buzzing cold returned until Spark felt numb, but at least Nandara took up the argument that Neesha should rest. But Spark was getting a good look at where her own stubbornness came from, and so she found herself back up the mountain with her family and Nandara.

Spark wanted to walk all the way to the ocean and just lie down on the shore. She tapped her hands against her thighs, looking everywhere and nowhere. "Everything's a mess," she muttered.

"Certified disaster," Neesha agreed. "We should still go to Pasdale. Or, I guess, maybe you should. With some dragons. You need to get Abyss's egg. Whatever plan you had for that, you should do it."

Nanny went rigid with alarm and Nandara started to interrupt, but Neesha plowed straight over them both.

"If Spark takes dragons through the fire realm, they can get that part of things over in a few hours. If it's going to be days before there's an attack here, you can be ready for both."

Spark blinked a lot. "They were right. You really are reckless."

Neesha burst out laughing. "Tell me I'm wrong, though."

"No, you're not wrong," Nandara sighed, giving Nanny an apologetic look. "Getting the eggs back and freeing any dragons there will work to our advantage. It will be easier when the bulk of Loch's forces are likely already on their way here."

"Glad we've got that settled," Neesha said. "I want to practice this more, but what if Spark goes tomorrow?"

Nanny was still shaking her head.

Nandara looked like the dragon city had already fallen again. "I'll talk to Ondias about some specifics, and we'll see."

Neesha looked to Abyss. "What do you think?"

"My eggs stir, but the Superiors believe there is a day or two yet."

"All right. Let's get on with this." Neesha gestured to Spark.

Spark lit the fire, and Neesha summoned the demon and invited possession.

But Neesha had gone too still. Something was wrong.

Flame burst all around her. Nandara screamed, but Spark was already holding the blaze in a tight circle around her and her mother. Abyss coiled herself around the two of them, folding her wings in around them, and grabbed Neesha when she lunged for Spark with her hands extended like claws.

Only Neesha's head poked out from between Abyss's fingers. She snarled and struggled, fire bursting out where it could.

Spark had fallen back when her mother had attacked. She sat on the cold hard rock, breathing heavily.

"Nandara, are you and Nanny okay?"

"We're all right. What's going on?"

"I'm on it. Mamma is safe for now. We'll get the demon out of her."

Spark tried summoning the demon, making herself a target again, but this time it didn't work.

"Oh no," she gasped.

"If you cannot draw the demon out, you must draw your mother out."

Spark remembered how Abyss had given her something to focus on. "I need your help," she told the dragoness. "Come in closer and talk to her."

"Neesha, hear me," Abyss commanded in a tone that made it hard for Spark to focus on anything else. "You must fight."

Spark was left wanting to pick up weapons and go to battle, but this was a different kind of fight. She got right up close where Neesha could see her.

"You're stronger than the demon. Mamma, you can do this. You're safe. Abyss and I are here, and we've got you. You need to make a safe place inside." Spark tapped her own forehead.

Neesha stopped struggling. Spark hoped it was a good sign, but she backed up just in case the demon changed its mind about her as a target.

"If you're in your safe place, you need to make a separate space, somewhere for you to put the demon or shut yourself away. Even if you can imagine a fireproof trunk or something."

Neesha's gaze focused on Spark for a moment. Then she hissed, baring her teeth. Her eyes filled with fire again.

Had this been what it had looked like to Nandara when Spark had lost control? She shuddered.

"Then you've got to push the demon out of your space entirely," she continued, hoping Neesha could still hear her voice. "Push it out of the house, or throw away its box."

Nothing changed. Spark came closer, wondering if she should try using herself as bait again.

"Oh! I used aeromancy! Mamma, you can't use fire on the demon—it doesn't work. Pick a different kind of magic."

Neesha's expression cleared a moment later. She roared furiously, and the demon stood between them. Spark jumped back, but Neesha was already banishing it.

"Shitting moons," Neesha gasped.

Abyss let go of her, and she staggered and fell into Spark before bouncing away. Spark caught her by her upper arm and kept her from going down too hard.

Neesha's expression was distant and unfocused again, but in a different way. "Maybe I wasn't as rested as I thought," she wheezed.

"But you did it! You got the demon out on your own."

"By a generous definition of 'on my own,' but sure. Good tip about the aeromancy, though. That did the trick."

Spark grinned and then immediately burst into tears.

"Yeah, that's exactly how I feel too, kiddo." Neesha shoved herself to sitting and got an arm around Spark's shoulders. Spark leaned against her and squeezed.

Abyss had stepped back, and Nanny rushed in to join them. She sobbed against Neesha's shoulder, her arms wrapped around Spark and Neesha both.

"That's enough for one day," Nandara said. "You're both pushing too hard. And Spark already has everything she needs to go back to Pasdale. I think an evening of rest won't set us back."

Neesha shook her head angrily but didn't argue. She couldn't even stand on her own yet. "We don't have time for this," she grumbled.

They didn't, but they couldn't manufacture more energy for Neesha to push through. She needed rest—the natural kind. That she'd done so well so quickly was promising, but Spark didn't think they could face down Loch's forces without both Neesha and Nanny learning more.

CHAPTER NINETEEN

Spark watched Neesha break off bits of bread and toss them to Shadow, certain the dog was getting as much dinner as her mother was. Well, at least she was eating the meal Nandara had brought for them—simple chicken and fresh vegetables, not something cured or dried or otherwise preserved like the hard bread Spark still had around. It was far better than anything Spark had eaten in a week.

She shovelled the food in her mouth, wishing she'd taken some time to appreciate it. Who knew when she'd get real food like this again? She'd be back to Pasdale tomorrow, and then who knew what would happen.

And it was still just Spark and Neesha here. Not that there was anywhere for Nanny to stay even if she'd wanted to, but it really *didn't* seem like she wanted to. Was it just that she'd missed Ondias so much? Was Nanny angry with Neesha, and so was avoiding them both?

As much as Spark loved having someone else argue with the adults, it did seem to be keeping them away when Spark desperately wanted more guidance than Neesha could give.

She sighed, picked up her gourd of water, and headed out of the kitchen.

"I'm going to work on some armour. There's not much here, but you're welcome to it."

Neesha flashed her a warm smile, scritched the dog, and broke off some more bread—one bit for her and one for Shadow.

Spark had finished up her gliding suit late last night and now inspected it with fresher eyes. Everything seemed in order, but she needed to test it before she'd know if it required adjusting. She pulled out all the leather armour bits she had, some of them still unfinished. The others could work with it after she'd tempered it, and while any elemental could do that part, she was the only one who could do it for days on end. The concentration and staying awake were the only parts sapping her energy. Even working with other elements didn't tire her the way it ought to, and she could only assume that working with fire demons gave her a boost.

With everything laid out, she called up the demons and set to work. It was easy but tedious, the process repeated for each piece. While Nandara didn't know how to enchant more than one object at a time, she suspected there was a way, but Spark didn't really have time to figure it out and couldn't afford to screw things up while she experimented.

She was just sending the demons away when the door opened. Shadow came trotting in, and she had to scramble to keep from losing control of everything.

"Oh no! I didn't mean to distract you," Neesha said, taking control of the earth demon while Spark dealt with the fire demon.

"You're supposed to be resting."

"I'm bad with being alone. Can I rest in here?"

"You're going to actually rest and not try to do half the work for me?"

Neesha tilted her head and glanced around the room. "I wouldn't even know the first place to start."

"Most of this is just for show." Spark shrugged. "I don't like people knowing just how easy some of this is for me."

"How do you mean?"

Spark sighed and picked up the forgotten blob of a spearhead she'd been working on an eternity ago. "How do you think I turn this into a weapon?"

Neesha opened her mouth, but closed it immediately, looking at the piece and then scrutinizing Spark. "What I know of a blacksmith's work involves putting the bits in the fire until they're hot and then hitting them with a hammer until it's whatever the thing is you want. But I'm guessing that's not what you do."

"When I don't have to, no." Spark used her hands to heat up the piece of metal until it was glowing and malleable.

Neesha came over and poked at it. "Huh. I wouldn't have thought to use my hands. But then again, I can't do the heat part of it the way you do."

"It's faster this way, and I'll use the hammer for the finishing touches. Once I have the time to figure it out, I can probably get a good edge to the blades with only my hands. But I don't have a lot of time to experiment right now."

Neesha sat in the chair near the worktable and watched Spark finish the spear.

"What's with the armour?" Neesha asked.

"It'll withstand a dragon strike."

Neesha's eyebrows went up. "Well done!"

"This is all we've got. I'll see tomorrow if Ember has more. This is for people. The leather works all right on a dragon, but it's just so small."

"Right, you've got dragon-skin armour."

"It's more lightweight and doesn't slow the dragons down."

"And I assume you've tempered all the rigging as well?"

"Yes. It won't do a whole lot of good for Pasdale, since it'll just be me, but it'll be helpful to face whatever is going to happen with Loch's forces."

Neesha helped Spark store the pieces for Ember and her team to finish later. Then she settled back in the chair while Spark dug through her pile of iron scraps until she found what she needed to fashion bolt cutters.

Spark would have to do a lot of tempering them to cut the chains on the captive dragons and also survive the trip through the fire realm, but she suspected that being able to steal into the pen and quietly free dragons would be to her advantage. The more she freed before anyone noticed, the better.

She'd have to talk to Abyss and Nandara about specifics to make sure she wasn't going in blind this time. She wasn't going to fail again.

She didn't realize how long she'd been at it until Neesha startled, having fallen asleep in the chair and then almost toppled out of it.

"You going to work on this all night?" Neesha asked.

"I don't know when else I'll have the time."

Neesha shrugged. "I'm going to bed. You should soon too."

Spark got back to work, ideas for succeeding in Pasdale running through her mind. If she was right about the time conversion and when they'd send her again, there'd be a good chunk of the day for more preparation. She'd have to talk to Nandara, but she suspected Neesha would want to get more practice in as soon as she'd eaten, and Spark would need to be ready.

Nanny wasn't going to be dealing with any demon crises. Spark worried Nandara and Abyss might not be able to help Neesha either if something went wrong.

"Ugh, so I should have some energy tomorrow, shouldn't I?" She glanced over at Shadow, who was curled up under the worktable. He didn't even twitch an ear. "Traitor. Maybe I'll make *you* go pull demons out of Mamma."

She needed energy for Pasdale, as well as for helping her mother. But she didn't think she should risk going without some tools, either. She had to at least finish these bolt cutters, then she could sleep.

CHAPTER TWENTY

Neesha came back from breakfast with Nandara to find Spark was still in bed. She had no idea what time the girl had finally gone to sleep, but she doubted it was much before dawn. But it was getting late in the day, and there was a lot to practice before the Pasdale mission in the afternoon.

Nandara had gone to Ondias's to get Dionelle prepared for more of the demonwork they'd be doing, and Neesha was happy to leave her to it. Both Ondias and Dionelle were barely recognizable, and not just because they'd both aged. Dionelle was still, understandably, in shock, gone deep inside herself. She was possibly only now having the space to process losing half the family. She didn't seem to have fully accepted that Neesha was awake and walking around and every bit as... *herself* as she'd been the day she'd defeated Draxli.

Had they expected her to wake up changed? In a lot of ways, she had—maybe not the way they'd wanted, but maybe in the way Spark needed. And that was fine with Neesha.

The change in Ondias was the starkest. Ondias had always been opinionated, but she'd never been miserable like this. Or cruel. None of the others saw it, except maybe Spark. Neesha could only guess that Ondias had grown bitter gradually enough for everyone else to get used to it.

But Spark and Dionelle had also been through terrible loss, and from what Neesha had heard, it had made Dionelle gentler and Spark more selfless. Maybe it was because their losses had been final—they were Neesha's losses too, she supposed, but they didn't feel real yet—while Ondias had to see (or at least hear about) Zev still alive and walking around, enjoying first a string of new lovers and now comfortable bachelorhood in Pasdale, where his role as a double agent allowed him to remain at court with all the influence and power he'd had before.

Neesha really got why Ondias would want to see him eaten by dragons, but she couldn't understand why Ondias had to make it everyone else's problem.

So Neesha was steering clear of the place. She wasn't ready to support Dionelle in whatever she was going through, and especially not if she had to listen to Ondias telling her how all of her life choices had been—and continued to be—the wrong ones. Neesha had no idea what she'd have done without her old mentor around. Let Nandara deal with the other two; Neesha could focus on Spark.

And on herself.

She had a lot to learn and a lot to catch up on, and it looked like they had a couple of hours this morning before Nandara would be ready to work on pyromancy with them. Neesha knew exactly how she wanted to fill the time.

She pushed the door to Spark's room open a crack and peeked in. Her daughter lay sprawled across the bed on her stomach with her face in the pillow, one pale leg jutting from beneath the blankets. Neesha smiled, but her chest tightened, and it took her a moment to breathe through it.

"Spark?" she whispered.

"Nnnngh."

"Do you think you can function yet?"

"Zah."

"I have a terrible idea. You're going to love it."

Though she moved in slow motion, Spark rolled over and squinted in the general vicinity of the door.

"I want to try dragon-walking," Neesha said.

Spark blinked, then froze, then sat up suddenly, throwing back her blankets.

"I can test my gliding suit. Do you want to summon Abyss and see if she'll do it? I need food."

Neesha grinned while Spark stumbled around her room, trying to get ready as quickly as her gangly limbs would let her. Neesha went to the forge, where a few embers still burned. She spun them up into a proper fire and used it to summon Abyss, then waited in the side yard for her.

It took a while—Neesha assumed because of the new pull from the eggs—but Abyss dropped down in the field next to Spark's house. Was it Neesha's house yet? She supposed it was, though it would feel more like it if they ever got her bedroom finished.

Neesha greeted the dragon formally, then asked, "Have there been any changes with your eggs?"

"None yet."

"Good, that gives Spark time to be properly ready to go back to Pasdale. It will be some time before we're ready to try any more demon possessions, and I had hoped that while we waited you might agree to letting me try aerial combat."

Abyss watched her for a moment. "I believe I can spare some time."

"Wonderful!"

Spark came out not long afterward, dressed in leathers Neesha hadn't seen before, buckled over her dragon-skin flight suit.

"What the hell are you wearing?"

Spark grinned. "I got the idea from Raia after she mentioned how they don't have an aeromancer to keep them in the air anymore."

To demonstrate, Spark stretched her arms wide, pulling the new leathers—attached at her wrists and ankles—taut in a mimicry of dragon wings.

Neesha just barely managed to hold her expression neutral. "Do you think you can fly?" She didn't keep all the incredulity out of her voice. Nandara said the girl was clever, but also that she was desperate.

"Not exactly. More like gliding? Graceful falling? I have no idea until I fall off of Abyss and test it out."

Neesha blinked. Right. She hadn't paid as much attention to that part of Spark's tale of dragon-walking. Once they'd gotten up in the air, it had involved an awful lot of falling. Neesha desperately wanted to try anyway.

"We may certainly practice on the ground," Abyss said, "but I will need accompaniment in the air if we truly wish to be certain neither of you falls to your doom."

Neesha nearly reconsidered, but it had been a terrible idea all along, and she wanted to at least try, even if only on land. If she was any good at it, they could keep practicing after the Pasdale mission. She needed to learn more.

And she needed to help Spark.

"Do you wish to use the sling?" Abyss asked.

Spark considered Neesha. "I didn't end up using it a whole lot with Raia. I think we need to see if Mamma can keep her balance before we worry about getting her to climb out of the sling."

"You're the expert." Neesha shrugged, keeping her tone light as she struggled not to be bitter. From her perspective, no matter how much time had really passed, *she*'d been the expert, the one calling all the shots, only a week ago. Rather than get used to the change, she'd rather go back to being in charge.

It had quickly become obvious to Neesha that Spark had been deeply sheltered growing up. She lacked the sort of experience Neesha hoarded like one of the dragons. Spark was very, *very* good at pyromancy, metalwork, and convincing the dragons to go along with her mad schemes. She was also a skilled engineer, it seemed. But beyond those skills, Spark was driven more by desperation than any real desire to lead. And she was soft.

The hard decisions Spark had been forced to make had clearly taken a toll on her in a way they didn't with Neesha. Neesha needed to get ahead of this and take that burden from her daughter.

Abyss stood very still and, unhelpfully, did not crouch down to make the climb shorter, as Spark showed Neesha the sorts of handholds to look for on the dragoness as they scaled her leg. Only about halfway up, Neesha's arms began to ache, and the true, terrible shape of this idea came together.

Neesha leaned her body tight against Abyss, letting her legs take most of her weight for a moment before she resumed following Spark. She had to stop one more time before reaching Abyss's broad back.

"Oh, this isn't so bad," Neesha said. "More like crossing a steep hillside full of scree than trying to climb a wall."

"Yeah, it's pretty easy. But once the dragons start flying, well..."

"That's when people start falling?"

"Something like that."

Spark, bafflingly, shifted from standing on one leg or the other, while Neesha paced down one side of Abyss's back and up the other. It was the most physically taxing thing she'd done since Spark was born.

Her body was still convinced she'd given birth only a few days ago. Neesha's muscle memory was still calibrated to account for being heavily pregnant, and she was perpetually surprised by how small her body was now. Her size and shape had returned to pre-pregnancy normal while she'd slept, but the fact of it hadn't sunk in yet.

Once Neesha was used to the feel of having a dragon underfoot, Abyss spread her wings like she meant to take flight. The ripple of muscle took Neesha off her feet. Spark had her arms out for balance and swayed, shifting to stay upright.

"I suppose that's a bit what it's like to be in the air," Neesha said, unable to keep the surprise from her voice.

"A bit, but there's wind, and her body tilts as well. It's unpredictable. Well, it feels unpredictable, but the way Raia and her crew are so nimble at it, I assume that with practice they learn to anticipate how the dragons will move and react."

Abyss gave another little shake. Neesha caught hold of one of the taller spikes at the middle of her back to keep from falling. Spark held her balance on her own.

Abyss trotted off across the field.

Neesha had to wedge herself between two spikes to keep from falling, one against her back and her arms wrapped around the other. Spark, meanwhile, very slowly made her way along Abyss's back without holding onto anything at all. Neither of them was particularly graceful, but at least Spark could move around. Neesha was certain that if she left her spot, she would fall and not get back up again until the dragoness quit moving.

Abyss hadn't gone very far when a dragon cried out from overhead and a shadow fell over them.

Neesha didn't recognize the dragon, but as it swooped across the sky, she noted some rigging on one of its arms.

"Oh, that's Jin!" Spark pointed.

Jin's dragon climbed higher into the sky. Abyss cried out in return and spread her wings.

"Oh no!" Neesha gasped.

"Hold on," Abyss told them.

Spark darted between two of Abyss's spikes just ahead of Neesha. A heartbeat later, the dragoness launched herself into the air, angling into the sky. Neesha nearly lost her grip, her legs slipping out from under her and dangling out over nothing.

The ache in Neesha's arms burned, then spasmed. She kicked her feet, trying to brace herself against the spike behind her and take pressure off her arms, but it was abundantly clear that she had all the physical prowess of toast.

"Shit!" she gasped, an instant before she tumbled away into the bright blue emptiness.

Wind shrieked all around her as she cartwheeled through the air. She caught fleeting glimpses of Abyss getting smaller, the city glittering, and the green of the valley floor rising to meet her.

Suddenly, there was warmth all around her. She'd been cradled in the secure grip of a turquoise and canary-yellow dragon. A moment later, she dropped again, slamming onto Abyss's broad back. The black dragoness was gliding in a circle, and Neesha's legs immediately failed her. She fell down, but thankfully didn't slide off into the sky again.

Spark helped pull her close to Abyss's spines. The entire new blaze of dragons and their riders swooped around them, a safety net of wing and scale, but Neesha's pulse raced and she felt wobbly and a little like she might vomit.

Abyss tightened her spiral, angling down, and Neesha nearly lost her grip again. Spark grabbed her arms, fingers digging in with startling strength. When Abyss swooped, Neesha lost her hold on the spike and jerked out of Spark's grip.

Neesha clawed frantically, and Spark caught her wrist before she could fall off entirely. Spark braced a foot against the spike and pulled. But when Abyss shifted direction, Neesha was again dragged away from her daughter.

Neesha tumbled off the dragon, while Spark fell off the other side.

Two of the new dragons were there to catch them both immediately.

"Let me fall a bit next time!" Spark called as they were both set back down on Abyss.

Without Spark already braced to help her, Neesha slid along Abyss's back until the dragon shifted direction, and Neesha was once again sent flying out into nothing.

She used her favourite curse and kept her eyes squeezed shut until a dragon caught her, bringing her back to Abyss. Spark was ready this time, dragging Neesha higher up Abyss's back.

"Here, Mamma. The gaps are smaller, and you can wedge your body in between. As long as she doesn't do a flip, you won't fall off."

Spark all but shoved Neesha into the space and climbed away, making it look easy. Neesha glared at the spike in front of her and tried very hard not to move. Her ego might not survive another fall.

She was aimlessly furious. She hated herself for being so utterly terrible at this, and she struggled not to begrudge Spark the ease with which she clambered over Abyss's back.

But with the flight suit fitting more closely than Spark's usual loose shirts, the strength in the girl's wiry frame was more obvious, particularly the muscle definition in her arms and shoulders. And she had a man's grip from a lifetime of hard labour at the forge. Neesha would need to train months to have anything nearing that kind of strength.

So this had been a waste of time. A terrifying one.

Abyss shifted direction again, pumping her wings to gain altitude, and Neesha pressed herself deeper into the space between spikes. But Spark cursed. Neesha craned her neck to see not only that the girl had fallen off, but that one of the leg attachments on her gliding suit had come loose. She couldn't reach it to fix it and fell uncontrolled. Neesha's chest tightened.

She reached out a hand. A gust of aeromancy burst under Spark, catching the membrane of her flight suit, keeping her aloft until one of the other dragons dove in to grab her.

"Hey, that's what Raia said her brother used to do!" Spark said, settling next to Neesha.

"Is that thing actually going to work?"

"I almost had it." Spark adjusted her buckles and tugged the ankle strap. "Are you going to just stay here?"

"Seems best, unless Abyss wants to carry me for the rest of the flight. I'm awful at this."

"You were good with the aeromancy, though."

Neesha's smile was wry. "At least I'm good for something."

Spark patted her arm and climbed away, over to Abyss's shoulder. "Gonna test it for real now!" she called, and then leapt, arms and legs spread wide.

Neesha's entire body thrummed with cold electricity as she watched Spark fall away. But it wasn't really a fall, and as Abyss looped back around, it was clear that the suit was doing something—slowing the fall, if nothing else. Spark would be pleased, even if it wasn't perfect.

Neesha was frustrated with her own lack of success. But Spark was right about the magic, and that's what she needed to stick with.

CHAPTER TWENTY-ONE

Spark hoped, for so many reasons, that this was it, that they'd figured out the magic that needed figuring out, because she didn't think she could stand looking at this patch of mountainside—glittering and red and lovely though it was—ever again.

Nandara wasn't with them this time, which had Spark both nervous and excited. Abyss was here to keep things from going too wrong. Spark had given Nandara some suggestions for battle plans when she and Neesha had come down from their flight test, and now Nandara was with Ondias, trying to figure out their best options. Ondias had apparently spent most of the previous day speaking with the Dragoness Superior to smooth things over even more with the dragon riders and make some plans.

All the dragons were on edge with the newcomers and the promise of more on the way. The Superiors didn't like the idea of somehow being indebted to humans for help, and that indigo dragoness was really raising a fuss. It probably didn't help that Spark and Neesha kept training with Jin's blaze. Ondias was trying to make the city dragons understand that these were special circumstances, and that they benefited as much from the arrangement as anyone.

Given the circumstances, it would be foolish not to pool resources. That seemed to be the tentative agreement they'd reached.

Today, Neesha wanted Nanny to do more spellcraft. Nanny was hesitant, but Nandara had apparently worked with her in the morning to prepare her.

"We're going to need you to learn this eventually, so it might as well be now," Neesha said.

Nanny had her arms wrapped around herself, shaking her head and looking out toward the dragon city.

Spark came forward and put a hand on Nanny's shoulder. "You're afraid because of last time? And because of what happened when I was a baby?"

Nanny glanced at her and nodded. She gestured helplessly toward the city—the western column. Abyss gently nudged her nose against Nanny's side.

"Right, but I got her out of it. You weren't here, so you didn't see it, but it was actually kind of easy? I did it entirely by accident, and we can do it again. But there's no reason to even lose someone like that again in the first place. We know what pulling someone out of themselves looks like now." Spark looked to Neesha. "If Nanny pulls you out with the demon, are you going to be a wreck again when we put you back together?"

"Definitely," Neesha said.

"Mamma, that doesn't help."

"Of course it would be a disaster. But as long as it doesn't take you another seventeen years to fix it, I'll be fine."

"Okay, but what we're doing is a little different. You were unconscious in the diamond. I was aware of everything when Nandara pulled me out of myself. You need to be calm when we stuff you and the demon back in, if that's what it comes to."

"Unless one of us figures out how to do this right."

Nanny rolled her eyes.

"What's that supposed to mean?" Neesha snapped.

"Mamma, we have to get to that part. If we get it wrong a few times along the way, you need to be ready for how awful it might be."

Neesha turned away and looked at the dragon city. She was silent for so long, Spark thought she might stall until it was time for Spark to go to Pasdale.

"Fine," Neesha said eventually. "I'll deal with it. I'm coming with you to Pasdale, so let's get this over with."

Spark stood straighter. Nanny took a step back, her face twisted in dismay.

"That's far too dangerous!" Spark said.

"So dangerous I should let you go alone?"

"I've done it once already. I'm resistant to the fire realm's trickery."

"I guess I need to learn to be too. You've got that safe place. I just need to trust in mine more."

Nanny shook her head, backing farther away.

"What if something goes wrong?" Spark said. "Neither of us would be here to help the city when Loch attacks."

"Then we'd better get this right." She glared at Nanny. "This thing where you try to protect me from the danger instead of teaching me how to deal with it is exactly the problem. I need to learn this. We all need to learn to deal with whatever fears we have as we go. Spark can't do this alone, and I have business left in Pasdale. I won't have them think I'm a coward or a failure. We're going to free those dragons and save those eggs, and we're going to do it in enough time to protect the city. So let's get to it—we're burning daylight."

Nanny looked horrified, hugging herself tighter and shaking her head.

"Neesha is right," Abyss said. "Mastering your gifts and your fears will ensure success. I will be with Spark, but I cannot do all of the magic she needs."

Nanny sagged and came closer, almost folded in on herself.

"We're practicing as safely as possible, Nanny. I think the worst that can go wrong already has, and all it means is taking a break before trying again."

Spark started a fire. Neesha called a demon before Nanny could object further.

"I've got the demon." Neesha looked at Nanny. "Just like Nandara taught you."

Nanny went through the spell. Spark stayed close, with a hand on her grandmother's shoulder, and Abyss watched intently. Neesha winced, and Nanny's mouth pressed into a grim line, but she was breathing slowly and remained focused.

When the demon reappeared, Spark nearly started cheering. But Nanny hadn't finished the banishment. First, she had to be sure.

"Mamma?" Spark asked.

"I'm okay. Let the demon go."

Nanny had barely pushed the demon back into its realm when Neesha summoned another.

"No breaks. We go again until it's easy."

And so it went—twice more, Nanny pulled demons out of Neesha. The third time looked easy.

"Nanny, are you ready to try with a full possession?"

Nanny immediately shook her head, but Neesha pressed on.

"We need to. You're doing well. Remember, Spark and Abyss can fix it if you lose me. We need to do this."

But now, when Neesha called demons, they all felt familiar—three in a row, not a stranger among them. It was getting difficult for Spark to control them all. When a fourth was also familiar, Neesha and Spark exchanged a worried glance.

"How many do we try?" Spark asked.

"How many can you control at once?"

Spark flexed her hands. "Maybe one more?"

"Then we'd best hope this last one is new."

Another demon materialized. Neesha glared at it, nodding. "It's new. Let those ones go."

Spark worried that her mother was lying. Would she do that? Was she that reckless? Spark tapped her hands against her thighs. Yes, Neesha was absolutely that reckless. Did it matter? Could the demon figure out something they couldn't counter?

Spark cast a glance at Abyss, but she was already lunging to restrain Neesha, who'd let the demon take control.

Nanny had her hands pressed over her face, shaking her head and taking a step back.

"Just try, Nanny. If you can't, I can. And she can probably recover on her own, but that takes more out of her."

Nanny went through the summoning, and the demon came out with less fight than Spark had anticipated. But Nanny gasped and backed away. When Spark saw the empty expression on her mother's face, she knew why.

The demon tried to run, but Spark snatched it and held it in a summoning.

She stood in front of Neesha, cautiously meeting her gaze. "Mamma, I know you're still at least a little bit in there. I'm going to put the demon back in. Collect yourself and get to your safe space as fast as you can. I'm going to do this quickly. Maybe we can catch it off-guard, okay?"

She had no way of knowing how much Neesha heard or understood, but she stuffed the demon back into Neesha's body. She caught a glimpse of her mother's furious intelligence a moment before it was all washed over in flame. Spark was already going through the spell, teasing the demon out.

It was difficult work, different than when Neesha had been in control. Spark concentrated on those differences, on where and how the demon remained anchored, slowly working to pull it away.

She wasn't sure if Neesha had been able to isolate herself in her safe corner, but she kept going anyway. She'd stuff the demon in and try again if this didn't work.

"It has to work," she grumbled through gritted teeth.

Spark wanted to use herself as bait to draw the demon out, but that wasn't something Nanny or Nandara could replicate. It was important that one or both of them learn how to do this.

She went deeper into the magic, feeling out where the spell and demon met, where the demon mingled with Neesha. It was all different—the demon was hot and angry, like when it had taken over Spark, but Neesha felt warm and safe, like when Spark was in her own mental safe corner. Spark focused her spellwork on that safety.

Finally, the demon stood apart. Neesha pitched over, hands braced against her knees, gasping and swearing.

"Mamma, what's your oldest brother's name?"

"Bly, that asshole." She chuckled. "It worked, Spark. I have no idea what you did, but you did it. It felt weird, but not painful like before."

Spark sent the demon back into the fire realm, and Neesha stood and swept Spark into a hug.

"You are remarkable, and I'm so furious I missed so much of you."

Nanny stared at them, her hands pressed over her mouth and her eyes wide.

"It's okay, Nanny. I figured it out. I can show you what I did."

Nanny closed her eyes. Tears fell silently, and she turned away.

"It's all right, Mamma," Neesha said, her voice gentle. "You can do it when you're ready. When we get back from Pasdale."

"You've all done well today," Abyss said.

"We can do a little more, and then we'll go see how Nandara and Ondias are doing with the preparations. What do you think, Spark?"

Spark took a steadying breath and agreed.

Worryingly, it took four demons this time before they found one that didn't feel familiar. The third hadn't felt familiar to Spark, but it had to Neesha, which Spark hadn't even thought to look for. She retreated to the safe farmhouse in her mind, closing out the demon, and waited. It seemed so easy now to push the demon out. But here on the plateau, there were no distractions, and she wasn't sure how well this would work in the chaos of a battle.

Neesha needed to be able to do this.

Spark wasn't sure how long she waited. Did time pass differently when locked away in her own mind? It seemed like an eternity before the demon's heat receded.

"Spark?" Neesha's voice was high and tight.

"I'm okay."

Neesha sighed with relief, audible over the crackle of fire and the hiss of the demon she held. When Spark opened her eyes and focused on her mother, the demon was gone. But the daylight had changed, and the sun was lower in the sky.

"Sorry, that took forever," Neesha said.

Spark glanced at how the shadows had changed. It had been around an hour.

"But you did it. Should we try again?"

"We'll do one more, just to be sure. But I think I've got it now. Then we should take a break so we're rested when it's time to go."

Nanny looked awful. Spark wanted to comfort her, to reassure her, but everything was chaos. She wanted to believe Neesha, but there were a lot of ways things could go wrong and only hours left to prepare.

CHAPTER TWENTY-TWO

Spark stood on the roof of her house, which would soon be the second floor, staring in bewilderment at the pile of red blocks Abyss had just deposited. She was still in battle mode, still ready to attack Pasdale. It took a lot of her willpower not to open a portal and leave.

But Abyss, after leaving them at Ondias's, had come back to say that the eggs were still quiet. They had time—it looked like they'd get the normal five day minimum at least—and Ondias had spoken more with the Dragoness Superior and had decided that the eggs were the current priority. It would be a small mission, stealthy and quiet. Neesha and Spark had one more day of rest and preparation.

Meanwhile, four blazes of dragons were heading for the shores of the Great Sea to intercept Loch's forces there. Jin's blaze had just left. Others were preparing, their best warriors outfitted with the armour Spark had made.

Once Neesha, Spark, and Abyss retrieved the eggs from Pasdale, they would come back to the valley and practice dragon-walking and any battle magic they felt they'd need. Once Loch's forces appeared, Abyss would be summoned, and the three of them—plus backup blazes—could use a portal to reach the battle in plenty of time.

Timing would be important, but this new plan took advantage of portal travel's speed. If Neesha and Spark could become competent at aerial combat in time, it would help free dragons from Loch's forces during battle.

Spark was no longer sure what was going on today, but it wasn't anything like she'd expected. After so many days of going so hard, slowing down didn't feel right.

Heaving a sigh, she picked up a block and brought it to the new wall. She'd hoped her mother would be around to help with it. She'd really enjoyed the companionship yesterday, and wasn't sure why she was here by herself. Nandara had told her to rest. Neesha said that maybe they'd practice the demon extraction some more, but she wanted to talk to Ondias and Nanny first.

Spark made it through two rows of blocks, constantly thinking about going down to the workshop to make something, or going to find Nandara and convince her they really shouldn't change their plans yet again.

"This is ridiculous," Spark muttered.

"Hey, now, that's my bedroom you're talking about." Neesha appeared on the stairs, carrying a bread bowl of stew in each hand. She offered one to Spark. "It would appear Nandara doesn't believe we've had enough to eat ever in our entire lives."

"This is better than the old cheese I've got."

Neesha chuckled and sat next to her in the shade of the south-facing wall. Spark scooped out bits of the thick stew with chunks of bread and watched the light off the city glitter across the valley.

"So have you got enough tarp left to give me a bit of a roof, or have you cannibalized it all for armour?"

Spark had a moment of panic to wonder if she had left any tarp. She stopped with a scoop of bread halfway to her mouth and glanced around at how much space there was to cover. What had she done with all her supplies?

"I think there's some in the studio." Spark stuffed the scoop into her mouth. "I've got some extra wood I can use to cover over the windows and use that tarp up here. You're going to camp?"

"For tonight, at least."

"You don't have to. I don't mind sharing."

Neesha gave her a sly grin but didn't argue. "Best to be prepared."

"I don't know. I'm prepared to *leave*. I can't get out of time-to-go mode."

"You've been through so much. I think it will take some time for that urgent voice to quiet. But maybe, in a few days, we'll have taken away the excuses it's giving you, and you can have some peace."

They finished their meal in silence. Shadow reappeared to help with the last scraps of their bread bowls and then curled up to sleep in a patch of sunlight.

Neesha picked up a block, grinning at him. "How's he the only dog here?"

"Are you kidding? It took nearly three days of walking through the mountains before he'd let Abyss pick him up. It's the same with most animals. The chickens came as eggs. The goats and the couple of mules are the only ones who really don't seem to mind the dragons."

Neesha frowned as she set her block down on the row. "We'll have to look harder for more animals that can tolerate the trip. Shadow needs some dog friends."

"The apprentices and their food scraps are more than enough for him." Spark snorted a laugh and picked up another block. "There's no herds for him to manage or dangerous wildlife to protect against. Wouldn't more dogs just end up bored?"

Neesha stopped halfway through fusing her block. "Some dogs need jobs, yes, but others can be just pets. You didn't have friends in the city with dogs just meant to lounge around and be adorable?"

"I didn't have friends." Spark set her block down and turned away.

"Oh, love. I'm sorry. I didn't realize it was that bad. You've got friends here, though."

"Jatt hasn't spoken to me since you called off the betrothal."

"He'll come around."

"And Ember is cross with me for... I'm not even sure what. Not having this place done yet? Not spending enough time with her?"

"You weren't exactly supportive about her brother."

"Mamma, he's a toad. And how did you hear about that? Are you tapped into the gossip already?"

Neesha smiled and went back to fusing her block. "I *am* friends with Stone. That's got to count for something. I think Ember could use a little sympathy about losing her only brother, even if he is a toad."

"She was cross with me before that anyway."

Neesha nodded sadly and went for another block while Spark set hers on the row and fused it.

"I get the sense that maybe Ember has been trying to expand her definition of family," Neesha said. "And I think you retreating into this place to focus on your more traditional definition of family has made her feel unwanted."

"But that's ridiculous!"

"I never said your lady love was rational." Neesha laughed. "She's something of an impulsive creature, isn't she? Ruled by her emotions, that one. And you did withdraw your attention, no matter the reason."

Spark sighed, sitting on the low wall they'd built. "Mamma, she knows how important you and Nanny are to me. Especially when she got so upset about River."

"If you can remember that, while Ember understands things on a rational level, her emotions always outstrip sense, I think that will go a long way to helping you repair things with her."

"So she understands this is important but still feels upset?"

"Yes. You've got to appeal to how she feels. Woo her a bit."

Spark scowled ahead at nothing. She shook her head and went back to work.

"I've asked her repeatedly to come join me here."

"Spark, you barely have space for *you* here. It doesn't matter how much you *say* she's welcome here—you've got to *show* her. Give me some space up here so I'm not crowding in your business. Get some comfortable furniture for her to sit on and work at. And for heaven's sake, stock your pantry with more than hard bread and cheese and dried meat."

Rather than argue, Spark glared at the pile of blocks in front of her.

"Listen, you're faster with the fusing, so you keep at this," Neesha said. "I'll go do some bartering in the market, all right?"

"What have you possibly got to barter with?" Spark stood and faced her.

"Well, I'll barter your services, for starters," Neesha laughed. "But I have useful magic of my own. And there were a few lovely pieces of jewellery in those crates of things Ondias kept."

"You shouldn't barter your keepsakes so I can feed my girlfriend."

Neesha chuckled, but it was mirthless this time. "These are hardly keepsakes. They're things suitors bought to try to woo me, things my family bought to try to make me more presentable as suitors became harder to come by. All lovely things I will never take out of those crates. Might as well get myself a bed with them and help you along too."

Spark pressed her lips together. Neesha's mood had taken a turn, and she didn't know what to say, so she nodded. Neesha started for the stairs.

Spark caught her hand. "Mamma, I'm sorry they did that to you. It wasn't right. Thank you for stopping them from doing it to me."

Neesha's eyes shone with tears. She pulled Spark into a hug. "We'll get through this yet."

As Neesha left, Spark went back to building the wall, occasionally wiping errant tears, and tried not to think what her life might have been like with her mother there fighting for her all along.

Spark had to wonder what, exactly, that jewellery had been made of—or how many promises her mother had made—as she watched over the side of the house while Neesha and Ember unloaded supplies from Stone's wagon. In addition to two baskets of fresh food, a sack of rice, another of potatoes, and a block of cheese, there was more cutlery and crockery, a bed with linens, a wardrobe, a brazier, a large tarp, three more basic wooden chairs, and two mismatched oversized armchairs—one of which Spark had last seen at the bottom of a stack in Ondias's house.

How much of the smaller pieces had been rescued from Ondias's trash heap?

Spark went down to help put some of the things away—the food and dishes, mostly. She had no idea what her mother intended for the furniture, though she watched on in confusion as Stone walked down the hall with a load of lumber that he left in the unfinished studio.

"It's for a worktable," Ember said, watching her. "Some assembly required."

"Right. Maybe we can work on it later tonight?"

"I think maybe getting your ma somewhere to sleep should be top priority?"

"Sure. She'd definitely like her own space."

While Ember went to help her father unload more supplies, Spark pulled Neesha aside.

"Mamma, did you promise them I'd rebuild the whole village or something? How did you barter for all this?"

Neesha's eyes twinkled and her lips twisted into a smile. She pulled what looked like a second sack of rice from the pantry and beckoned Spark closer.

"Not a word of this to anyone," Neesha whispered, glancing at the door. She opened the bag full of glittering gems and Spark gasped. "It's the diamond I was encased in. Stone went up and collected all the fragments and brought it to Ondias to give to the dragons, but they've got no use for it. So he gave a handful to Ondias to keep her quiet and gave the rest to me."

Spark's mouth fell open. "Mamma... How—what...?"

"Exactly!" Neesha laughed, high and wild. "I could buy all of Pasdale with this! I already gave a small satchel of it back to Stone because what am I going to do with all of it?"

"Fill the house, for a start."

"Well, yes. But four of these gems bought me all of this, Spark." Neesha blinked and shook her head. "It's pure diamond, the best quality in the world, and touched by magic. Its worth is immeasurable!"

Spark laughed, "And you used it to buy some groceries!"

Neesha cackled and tied the bag closed again, heaving it back into the pantry. "The four of us and the Dragoness Superior are the only ones that know about it. It stays that way until I have some notion of what I'm going to do with it all."

Spark and Neesha joined Ember and Stone in hauling the rest of the supplies inside. It took all four of them to wrestle the bed up the stairs, but at least without a wall in the way, it was easy to get in the room. Neesha shoved it off into the corner for now and stashed the brazier under it.

She went back out to see Stone off, but Ember stuck around.

"Can I help?" she asked, gesturing to the wall.

"Not sure? We're using magic to fuse the pieces together." Spark picked up a block and demonstrated.

"Oh, well, I can bring the blocks to you. Make it go a little faster?"

Spark was glad to have Ember around but nervous about upsetting her again. Even with Neesha's advice, she wasn't sure how to give Ember what she needed without feeling self-conscious and overthinking every word and action. But Ember brought over blocks and stacked them next to where Spark worked, piling them up faster than Spark could fuse them. There was a nice tidy pile by the time Neesha returned to continue working on the wall.

"How do you get the ceiling to work?" Neesha asked. "The old farmhouse had wooden rafters, even if the rest was stone. I didn't notice any downstairs."

"I just fuse it, same as with the wall. Takes a bit more work to hold it in the right place and fuse it at the same time."

"Good thing you've got extra hands."

Spark kept working, amazed by how much faster it went when she didn't have to keep getting up and fetching more blocks. It was easy enough to work around Neesha, who went at half Spark's pace. They finished the wall with plenty of daylight to spare.

Spark refilled their water and brought up some of the fresh fruit to snack on.

"So do we stand on the ladder to fuse the roof?" Neesha asked.

Spark blinked. "You want to keep working?"

"Can't hurt." Neesha shrugged. "It would be nice to get at least a bit of a roof over the bed in case it rains before we get back."

Spark draped a tarp over the bed to keep it clean, and she and Neesha stood on it. Neesha held each block in place while Spark fused it to the rest, and then Ember would fetch the next one and hand it up to them. It was a little past a decent dinnertime when they ran out of rock pieces, but they'd finished the third wall and about half the room's roof.

Spark left Neesha to secure the tarp around the sides while she and Ember went to make rabbit and potatoes for dinner. Ember prepared a bowl of greens while Spark cooked the potatoes and grilled the hare.

"Your ma's all right," Ember said, setting out the plates.

"Sure beats arguing with Ondias."

"Oh, your ma is a delight at that! You should have seen her bartering for the furniture she snagged from the trash heap. Mostly she picked items out of the crowded room your nan is staying in, to give her a bit more space."

"You know, for how reckless and selfish everyone has said she is, she's been awfully thoughtful."

"I wonder how much of it was just plain old clashing? Your ma was ahead of her time. What Ondias thinks of as selfish just seems to me like not letting herself get pushed around."

"She knew exactly what I was going through with that whole mess with Jatt. It made her so angry to see them all repeating the same mistakes that got her where she ended up." Spark glanced at the door, half expecting Neesha to be standing there listening. "I'm so glad she's here."

Ember came around the table and put her hand on Spark's shoulder. "I'm really sorry that I gave you such a hard time about wanting her and your nan. I see why you needed her so much now, and I'm glad you've got her."

"I still could have done more for you while trying to help them."

"I realize now that maybe you were already doing too much."

"That doesn't make it easier on you. And I could have been kinder about River. Did he ever turn up?"

Ember's face pinched up like she was in pain, and then she put on a brave smile. "Yes, and alive, even. He's heading off with the next caravan out, or that's what I've heard fourth-hand or so through dragons and Ondias and whatever."

Spark squeezed her hand. "Well, he's still alive, and that's good. You can see him again when he ends up where he's going. Or maybe being away will help him grow up a little and he'll come back?"

"Maybe."

"Or, when this is all over, Abyss and I can take you out and follow that caravan."

Ember smiled and took Spark's hand. Spark swept Ember's hair away from her face and drew her closer, kissing her gently.

And that was how Neesha found them, clearing her throat from the doorway. "Dinner first, ladies. And maybe a bit of planning."

"For tomorrow?" Spark asked, bringing the food to the table.

"I think maybe tonight we should practice a bit of terramancy, or otherwise figure out how we're going to tip those eggs into portals."

"Isn't that why Abyss is coming?"

"Spark, she won't fit in that room. It'd be better if they didn't know we were there at all until someone eventually goes in to stoke fires and finds an empty room. Nandara thought it might be better if Abyss stayed in the fire realm. We can push the eggs through to her, and she can push them back out the other portal, right into the dragon city."

"Well, yes, that does seem efficient," Spark said, though anything beat the inefficiency of her last attempt.

"And Ondias said Dionelle wants to come with us. But she didn't seem very eager when I was there."

"You just haven't learned how to read her yet," Spark said.

"Could I come?" Ember asked. "Not through the fire realm, obviously, but after?"

Spark looked startled and threw her mother a look.

"You're ready to fight?" Neesha asked.

"I am."

"Well, I suspect that's something for you and Spark to work out, as long as you're prepared to handle yourself through the danger and there's a dragon willing to take you."

Ember looked thoughtfully at her plate, poking a cut of potato with her fork.

"Is Abyss really coming with us?" Spark asked. "Surely her eggs will hatch before we reach the ocean."

"It's still hard to say. Between her and her mate, she's the better fighter, so I assume he'll stay behind with the eggs and another dragon can use his armour."

Spark set her fork down hard and sat up straighter as a realization hit her. "Mamma, you don't have any armour."

"Don't worry, love. I've got my robe. I can use belts and ties to make it fit a little more closely, but it'll do."

"Only against fire. Leave it here and I'll make it dragonproof before bed."

Once they finished dinner, Neesha got out her lovely purple robe and brought the rest of her things up to her room.

"Why don't I help you with your ma's robe?" Ember asked.

She'd seen Spark do it a few times, and Spark welcomed the continued company.

"You get it set up," Spark replied. "I'm just going to talk to Mamma for a minute."

Neesha's tarped-off room was small, with barely any space beyond the bed, but it was enough for a side table and the stack of her crates to one side. She had a pile of books and a lantern on the little table, and was sitting on the corner of the bed nearest the light with a book open in front of her and Shadow curled up next to her.

"Everything okay?" Neesha asked.

"Mamma, it's too dangerous for Ember to come with us."

"It's too dangerous for any of us to go, if we're being honest."

"She's not a wizard."

"No, but she's familiar with all of your weapons, and she's determined to stay with you. I think you should let her."

"I couldn't stand it if she got hurt. Jatt got hurt when he came with me to save Abyss in the spring, and it was awful."

Neesha gave Spark a pitying look and shifted forward on the bed to touch her arm. Spark sat next to her, Shadow leaning against their backs, and she touched Spark's cheek.

"Caring about people makes us vulnerable, but it's far better than to be cold and alone. You've been alone long enough, Mita."

"What if something happens to her?"

"It will be terrible, and you'll get through it."

Spark felt cold and prickly. "I don't know if I can do that again, Mamma. Losing Pappy... I still hear it."

Neesha gathered Spark into her arms, and she leaned her head on her mother's shoulder.

"That was terrible," Neesha said. "Just hearing about it shattered my heart. Being there... I'm sorry you had to go through it. I'm sorry you were alone. You're not alone anymore, but you've got to look beyond me and Dionelle. You've got us back for now, but we won't always be here. You need to build your own life."

"But what about you?"

"I'll get this nonsense with Loch squared away and then figure out my own rebuilding. But you must know family comes in all shapes and sizes, that it's more than who you share blood with. And you can be part of many families at once. You didn't really get that growing up because you were so isolated in Pasdale, but this is a fine place to learn how it works, and Ember's a fine person to start with."

Spark sighed. "It hurts to even think about something going wrong, of losing someone again."

"Then don't think about it," Neesha said, amusement in her tone. "Go spend an evening with your lady love, and forget the bad things in the world. Be a teen, make some bad choices, and enjoy them."

"Did you enjoy your bad choices?"

Neesha cackled, and Shadow lifted his head to glare at his nap's interruption. "Every last one. And you're the best bad choice I made. I've been through a lot. I don't regret my choices—I just wish some of my options had been better, that things had worked out better. It's hard not to think that with the training I've got now—just a few days more than I had before—I might not have lost myself to the fire, might have stopped Loch from turning the whole city against our family, might have been there to watch you grow up and to teach you and protect you. But that's not how it worked out, so we do the best we can with what we have now. And right now, you've got a lovely girl downstairs waiting for you."

"Thanks, Mamma." Spark kissed her cheek, patted Shadow on the head, and went back downstairs.

Ember grinned when Spark came in, everything set up to enchant Neesha's robes. Spark took Ember's hands, kissing her knuckles before settling in to work. Once Spark was done and in the process of sending away the demons, Ember picked up the robes and shook them out, examining them.

"Too bad we don't have another day. I could make this into a suit like you've got." Ember looked a bit shy and went to the wardrobe they were stashing in the forge until Neesha had room for it upstairs. She pulled out a folded pile of leather and spread it out.

"More armour?" Spark asked.

"It's mine. So I can come with you."

Spark felt that cold buzz again but managed a smile. "Thought of everything, have you?"

"The armour will keep me safe, and I'll stay with Abyss. I can use your weapons to help her and otherwise stay out of the way."

Spark nodded slowly. "Let's not worry about that right now. We've got a few days and so much to get through tomorrow."

Ember smiled and put the armour aside, pulling a pack of supplies out next. "I'm ready to go whenever it's time. I'd just need to run and say goodbye to Pa. I could stay here, if you wanted."

Ember couldn't meet her eye. Spark buzzed all over, but the cold was a distant memory. She came closer, took one of Ember's hands in hers, and stroked Ember's long tresses with the other. Ember leaned closer, her body soft and warm as it pressed against Spark's. Spark moved her hands to the side of Ember's face, pulling her closer yet, and kissing her urgently. Ember made a satisfied little noise in her throat and all that buzzing heat condensed in Spark's belly.

Still in each other's arms, Spark led Ember down the hall to her room, closing the door firmly behind them.

CHAPTER TWENTY-THREE

Spark awoke feeling like she'd only been asleep minutes. The room was dark, though she was so warm, wrapped in a tangle of limbs with Ember. Spark never wanted to wake up alone again.

But a knock at the door had woken her.

"Spark, you need to get up," Neesha called, urgency filling her tone.

Ember stirred next to her, and Spark lit the lantern on the side table. She regretted getting out of bed, the cold air prickling at her skin as she collected her clothing from the discarded items draped around her room. She washed up and dressed quickly, then slipped out the door to join her mother in the hallway.

"What's going on?" she asked quietly, so as not to disturb Ember.

Neesha gestured down the hall to where the front door stood open and the usual racket from the dragons had changed tenor. Spark recognized it and gasped.

"Battle cry," she said. "But how? Loch couldn't possibly have gotten here already!"

Neesha pressed her lips together and shook her head. "I don't know the details, but Nandara was just here with the message that an attack is coming up from the south."

"What? The south?" Spark shook her head.

"I don't know more than that. Hurry now."

Abyss was outside waiting for them, blending in with the darkness. Spark wasn't sure what time it was, but there wasn't even a faint blush of dawn on the eastern horizon.

"Raia's blaze was scouting," Abyss said. "They flew through the night to get the message to us. It's Loch."

"How is that possible?"

Abyss shook her head and urged them out to the field where Ondias held a lantern and conversed with the Dragoness Superior herself. They paused their conversation as Neesha and Spark drew near.

"How is it Loch?" Spark demanded.

"Raia confirmed only that it was him before racing back here with Dragon and Flame to warn us. The Mistress Superior and the council suspect he left some time ago. Nandara's contacts have noticed Loch's inner circle behaving oddly for around a month now."

Spark felt cold. She stared into the night.

"So we go south and meet his attack," Neesha said.

Spark startled and stared at her mother. Would she ever get used to having someone else ready to jump straight into a problem?

Ondias sighed. "We have little choice in the matter. We cannot let him reach the valley. The Superiors have already recalled the dragons that left yesterday. The ones scheduled to leave today are accelerating their preparations. You need to be ready to leave when they are."

"But what about the mission to Pasdale?" Spark gave Abyss a desperate look. "What about your egg?"

"Merciless Winter Sky will remain with the eggs here, as planned," Abyss said. "I will go with you to battle Loch, but my mate will use a summoning to signal when the eggs begin to hatch. If it is safe, we will go to Pasdale then."

"We could go now!" Spark shook her head, feeling like she'd already failed again. "We can go while the others prepare. It won't take but a few minutes!"

"It's mid-afternoon in Pasdale by now," Ondias said. "You'd be seen. It's too risky."

"We must stop Loch," Abyss insisted.

Spark opened her mouth to argue, but Neesha squeezed her shoulder.

"Come on, let's go get ready." Neesha gestured back toward Spark's house.

"We can't just give up on Abyss's egg!" Spark protested as they walked through the darkness. Distracted, she held some fire in her hand for them to see by.

"We're not giving up," Neesha said. "We're changing tactics. This is Abyss's decision in the end, and she's made her choice."

Spark scowled into the dark and stomped along the path to her house.

"I don't like it either." Despite her claim, Neesha sounded like she was smiling. However, her amusement was fleeting, and her voice strained when she said, "But we can't let the city fall again."

Spark slowed down and glanced at her mother. Spark had heard from the other adults how despair had driven Neesha against Draxli in the end. She'd been fuelled by guilt that she hadn't saved the dragon city when she had the power to do so. And while that battle had happened when Spark was hours old, in Neesha's mind, it was last week.

Spark stopped, took Neesha's hand, and squeezed it. "We'll stop him, Mamma. There's three of us now."

Neesha squeezed back and glanced toward the village proper. "Well, two of us, at any rate."

Spark hadn't considered that Nanny wouldn't come with them. She had to, didn't she?

Spark woke Ember and told her what was going on. Something sad flitted across Ember's face before she pushed it behind a determined wall.

"All right, I'll say goodbye to Pa and be ready to leave when Abyss returns for us."

Spark kissed her and let her get ready, no matter how much she wanted her to stay behind.

A lot of danger lay ahead, and Spark resented it. She resented having to leave the safe cocoon of this home she was building, this new expanded family she had. But leaving it was the only way to keep it all safe, to be free. She had to help bring Loch to justice.

Not knowing how long they'd be gone, they ate what wouldn't keep and put everything that would travel into a pack. Ember had hers ready to go. Neesha didn't have much, but she'd used spare straps and buckles to make her robes less of a hazard. Shadow stamped nervously around all of them with his ears flattened, knowing the gear they packed, picking up on their nerves.

Ember had barely been gone when she bustled in with Stone, both of them carrying weapons and supplies.

"The whole village knows, and they're preparing," Ember said.

"Everyone who knows how to work the weapons you've made is bringing slings out to the field to ride with dragons," Stone said.

"Pa's coming with us."

Neesha stopped dead and stared. "You can't be serious."

"Mamma, he came with Jatt and Nandara to help me free Abyss in the spring."

Stone put a hand on Ember's shoulder. "Afraid I've inspired my girl."

"Huh." Neesha shook herself. "Well. I'm sure at some point the changes the years have brought will catch up with me."

Stone gave her a knowing smile. "They're not wee babes anymore. I suppose I can take risks now I maybe should have then."

Neesha shook her head and finished packing her bag. As they hauled their gear out to the side field, Nandara and Jatt both showed up. Nandara went straight to speak with Neesha while Jatt cautiously approached Spark and Ember with his hands stuffed in his pockets.

"You came to see us off?" Spark asked.

Jatt shrugged his bony shoulders. "Don't sound so shocked."

"Figured you'd still be off sulking," Ember joked, giving his arm a light jab.

"I'm sorry," he said. "About everything."

"We can talk about it when we're back," Spark said.

He shrugged again. Then he came closer and gave each of them a hug, sending Spark's emotions into chaos. But they really didn't have time for her to make sense of anything she was feeling.

"Be careful," he said. "I'll keep an eye on your place and keep your dog fed."

"You could come with us," Ember ventured.

He stuffed his hands back into his pockets and stared at the ground. "After last time—I nearly drowned in a swamp, and never mind my arm—I'm not sure I won't freeze up. You need steady hands right now."

Spark gave him another hug.

"It'll be worse than swamps this time," Nandara said, as she and Neesha joined them.

Abyss had landed at some point and loomed out of the darkness into the circle of lanterns that surrounded their preparations.

"He's coming up the river," Neesha said. "Nandara just brought more details. He's got a host, and there'll be more of those water monsters he brought to Pasdale. The dragons have sent a scouting party north to make sure it's not a diversion, but I don't think he expected to be spotted so soon. He was nearly three days to the south when those riders spotted him."

Spark cursed. "That'll put him nearly to the trading camp by the time we get to him."

"They've had warning," Nandara said. "And they've always known to stay well back from the river."

Spark looked to Stone. "Is that why you're coming? River's in direct danger."

"We all are," Stone said. "But it won't hurt to find the boy and see to it he's made the right choice in leaving."

"We'll have a bit of time to prepare on our way there, but we must be quick," Nandara said.

"Aren't we prepared?" Spark gave her a sharp look.

"Those river monsters he's got have magic of their own."

Abyss leaned her head in closer. "They are our only natural predator. Rarely a concern unless we are carelessly hunting in deep waters. But since Loch came to power, they have been unusually aggressive. We have lost many because of them."

Abyss turned to look directly at Spark and Neesha.

"They are why I failed to save your family." She snorted, angry smoke venting out her nostrils. "There are always one or two of them on our main routes across the ocean. I had to go a day's flight north to avoid them."

Spark closed her eyes, flushing hot and cold and struggling to breathe. She turned to Neesha. "You incinerated Draxli, didn't you?"

"Abyss had the honours. We'll take care of this one. He'll pay for what he did." Neesha turned to Abyss. "They're smart enough to know your migration routes?"

"They've been directed," Abyss said.

"By Loch?"

"That is our theory."

"So we'll have to fight them. What works?" Spark asked.

"Fire demons help. That was how I killed one in Pasdale," Neesha said.

A thunderous cry rang out from overhead, the sound of it nearly driving Spark to the ground—panic at the memories of dragon attacks and the murders of her family in Pasdale inundating her senses until Ember came to one side of her and Neesha to the other, both drawing her back to the present.

"That was our dragons," Ember said.

"We're still safe," Neesha added.

"It's time to go," Abyss said.

"Let's get the slings on and get everyone to a dragon, then," Nandara said.

"You're coming with us?" Spark asked.

Nandara gave her a wry smile. "I'm entirely too old for this, but you're going to need someone with experience."

"Where's Nanny?"

Nandara's smile turned sad. "She can't do it, Spark. I'm sorry. It's too soon. Her mind hasn't healed enough to face Loch and his dragons again. Ondias and I have taken turns staying with her since Raia raised the alarm. She'll be here to protect the city if that's what it comes to."

Nandara went off into the dark with Stone to find whichever of the dragons was bearing them into battle. Ember and Neesha helped get Abyss into her armour and the sling, and then squeezed inside with Spark. Once the battle was underway, Spark would climb out to do what she could. Neesha would have her magic, and Ember had weapons.

Abyss took to the skies. Spark saw the shapes of many other dragons against the starlight. Nuzzled between Ember and Neesha, Spark fell asleep as the dark mountains zipped by below them. The dragons were flying low and fast and silent. They'd reach battle before midday.

CHAPTER TWENTY-FOUR

Spark watched the plain ahead of them, where the traders were in the process of retreating as best they could. The dot of the camp itself was visible to the south as the traders made their way northwest, farther away from the river that glittered near the horizon.

Eltir and Ice had joined them not long ago, and Raia had dropped onto Abyss and climbed down to the sling to update Spark, Neesha, and Ember.

Loch was well south of the camp, but maybe only another hour or two away.

"He moves too fast and against the current," Raia said.

"He uses demons, same as we do," Neesha said. "He can make water do anything he wants."

And he had three water beasts, a dozen ships packed with dangerous aquamancers, and a blaze of dragons a dozen strong. Eltir recognized some of the ships in the armada as ones they'd fought before, including when they'd lost Raia's brother and his dragon.

Raia leapt off her handhold when Dragon flew beneath Abyss, and the two disappeared into the sky.

Neesha seemed grimly determined, but not worried.

"You think we can beat him?" Spark shouted over the wind.

"Absolutely. I already did once, and on my own."

Neesha told Spark about how she'd used trueflame—not knowing then that that's what she'd done—to vaporize the floodwaters Draxli and Loch had inundated Pasdale with. The demons she'd unleashed then had helped with some of the water beasts too.

"Nandara told me about what happened with those," Neesha said, her expression dark. "There's less risk of the fire demons running amok out here, but we'll have to make sure we collect them all again afterward so they don't make trouble for the traders."

"Will I be any use in a water fight?" Ember asked.

"Maybe less against the water, but aim for the boats if we get close enough."

"And knock off any enemy dragon riders," Spark added.

While their dragons outnumbered the dragons on Loch's side, they didn't outnumber all his dragons and wizards combined, even if the dragons from the city who'd gone east returned in time. And there was the possibility that this was a diversion and the real attack would come from another direction.

The Dragoness Superior would summon them all back if they were needed. Though the threat in the south was dire enough as it was. Spark didn't think they could successfully fight a battle on two fronts. And as they flew ever closer to the swollen bulge of river water where Loch's forces approached, Spark wondered if they could fight even *this* battle.

As they drew nearer, Raia and her blaze pitched higher into the sky, far beyond the reach of any of their strategies. Spark wondered what their plan was.

Long before they reached the water, enemy dragons reached their advance. Spark scrambled up the handholds to wait on Abyss's shoulder, where she had a better view. This left more room for Ember and Neesha to manoeuvre in the sling. She wrapped a handhold around one fist.

When the first dirty-brown dragon approached, Spark waited until it nearly collided with Abyss, then called up a furious gust of aeromancy to knock away one of its riders. A lance of fire pulsed from under Abyss—Neesha's pyromancy. It consumed another one of the riders, while a venom ball launched by Ember caught the third in the face.

But there were five of them in total. Spark's skin buzzed. It would be impossible to free all the dragons.

Abyss clawed another human off the dragon they faced as she scrabbled to grip its wings. For a sickening moment, the two dragons tumbled through the air. Finally, Abyss threw her opponent from the sky and swooped away, her focus turning toward the river.

Flame, Ice, and Dragon circled above Loch's forces, casting fire downward, but they were too high for any of it to reach its target.

"What are they doing?" Spark muttered.

Loch's forces grew closer, with only one dragon left circling, and it seemed too concerned with Raia's blaze to confront Abyss. The ships below looked far more imposing than Spark had anticipated, and the water beasts seemed impossibly huge—three times Abyss's length. Two of the beasts were at the front of the armada with one in the back.

"That's got to be him back there, the coward," Spark growled.

"He will sacrifice everyone here to save himself," Abyss said.

"Well, those are wooden ships. Let's drop them a fiery gift. Then maybe you can make a nice snack out of Loch."

Abyss growled and dove. Spark gripped her handhold in both fists and got as low against Abyss as she could, trying to wedge against some spikes. The crush of wind stole her breath, and her eyes watered as she watched their target get closer.

Behind them, dragons shrieked. Abyss suddenly pitched into the sky, spiralling back the way they'd come. It took a moment for Spark's brain to catch up with the input from her eyes.

The dragons scattered and roared, some of them climbing higher and others aiming dragonfire down at the water. A couple of them were caught up in what looked like ropes made of water.

Spark scrambled back down to the sling, her eyes on the view below. "What...?"

"There are water demons." Neesha pointed.

Spark had never seen a water demon and had no idea what her mother was pointing at. After what had happened to Neesha, Spark hadn't been allowed to work with them or go near any. She barely knew any aquamancy at all.

"Is this like Pasdale? Weren't there aquamancers controlling them then?"

Neesha's face had darkened with fury, and her eyes shone with fire.

"Abyss, get in closer!" As Abyss dove for the struggling dragons, Neesha elbowed Spark. "Give me fire. We need a portal."

Spark hissed, but there was no time to argue. Ember sank down into the sling, trying to keep out of the way.

Thankfully, Neesha didn't try using a fire demon to counter the water demons. Instead, she let trueflame fly, manipulating the flames and the portal within to point the fire vortex at the shafts of water tangled around three of the dragons.

She managed to vaporize enough for the dragons to escape, but more water filaments shot out like whips. Some of the dragons had climbed high enough to be out of reach.

And then one of those water whips lashed against Abyss. It wrapped around the dragoness, narrowly missing the sling. Spark cried out and ducked. Abyss's upward momentum jerked to a halt. She roared and struggled against the water's pull, but it was clear she wouldn't escape on her own.

Spark pulled fire from the air and concentrated it into a beam of light, so searingly bright that she couldn't even look at it. The beam sliced through the water at the dark blot beneath them, where the water whip originated. The whip collapsed.

Abyss flew higher, but a spout of water erupted below. A water beast—huge, lumpy, and greenish black—shot out toward them, giant jaws open. Abyss spiralled away from it, flying beyond its reach.

Neesha's trueflame vaporized more whips. Spark used her light beam one more time, the strength of the magic leaving frost on their faces and covering the sling as it sucked all the heat from the air.

Spark turned her whole body, leaning out to get a better view around Abyss's bulk. She felt cold, and her limbs were going numb as she searched the water. There were still water whips and those dark blots, but they were behind them. Spark exhaled long and slow.

"Okay, so that's why Raia and the rest are staying so far up there," Spark said.

"We can't do anything from that height," Ember said.

"No, there's one thing. Abyss, get higher and above them!" Spark met Neesha's gaze. "We drop fire demons on them."

Neesha's face lit up. "Yes! Aim for the boats more than anything."

"What if, when we get close to Loch, we drop trueflame on him?"

"It's not going to hurt anything—except maybe him!" Neesha cackled.

Ember did her best to give them enough space. As Abyss looped back around and made a run over Loch's forces, Neesha and Spark both dropped fire demons. They managed to get a few onto the first ship—one of the largest—while many others uselessly hit the water. Neesha kept dropping demons, while Spark opened a portal and poured out trueflame.

Abyss looped away so Spark and Neesha snuffed their fires lest they hit an ally, and it was another moment before Spark got a view of their handiwork. The large boat was entirely engulfed in flames. There were smaller fires on a couple of the others, but Loch's water beast was just resurfacing after having retreated deep into the river to avoid the trueflame.

"Godsdamnit!" Neesha cursed. "It's too far, and he's got too much warning to counter what we do. We need to get closer."

Abyss went in for a dive, but was immediately lashed with water whips again. Neesha and Spark spent all their time keeping Abyss from being pulled into the water. Ember, at least, had been able to hit one of the boats with some venom balls. The first boat, extensively charred and still steaming in many places, had mostly sunk. Its former passengers were little blots in the water, making their way to other boats.

Abyss made another pass with similar results.

Spark growled in frustration. "Once more!" she called. "I'm going to jump."

"Spark, no!" Ember gasped.

"You sure?" Neesha asked.

"Keep the water whips off Abyss and try to help me with aeromancy if you can."

Spark got her axe out of one of the storage pockets and strapped it to her back. As Abyss came around again, she double-checked the buckles on her gliding suit and climbed out of the sling, Ember gripping her to help steady her.

"Okay, now!"

Spark leapt, arms and legs spread. Her heart raced. There was only one other dragon nearby, and no one close enough to help if the suit failed. She didn't expect to survive if she hit the water instead of her target. Gasping against the tightness in her chest, she tried to tilt her body to stay on course.

A helpful gust of wind pushed her back on track. The water monster grew closer, and she saw Loch himself, that awful pale stork of a man, standing in the middle of a platform strapped to the beast, right there in front of her. His eyes were on Abyss.

He hadn't noticed Spark at all.

She slammed right into him. The two of them tumbled across the wooden platform and hit the railing on the other side. Stumbling on her glider, Spark got to her feet, but Loch was up first. He wore that monstrous smirk on his face, just the same as that day in his throne room a year ago when he'd taken everything from her.

Magistrate Turd.

Spark threw fire at him. He countered with a dome of water, so that her fire only sizzled on impact.

"Hello, beastie," he said. "I'd hoped to see you here. Though maybe not quite so soon."

He gushed water at her, slamming her across the platform. She'd already been opening a fire portal, and she called trueflame to counter. Fire roared across the platform. He diverted water underfoot to keep the wood from incinerating.

"Ah, I see you've learned some control." His voice dripped with malice. "It won't save you from a place in my dungeons with your waste of a grandmother. I'm going to cut you to pieces while she watches."

Didn't he know Nanny wasn't there anymore?

Spark didn't bother trying to engage with him or answer his taunts. Nothing he said mattered. She just needed to stop him.

She called a fire demon, but he blasted her with more water, then leapt from the deluge, snarling. He drew a dagger and lunged for her while she tried to direct the demon at him. She had no time to go for her axe.

Loch batted the demon away with some water and collided with Spark, ramming the blade into her side. Blackness erupted across her vision as all her thoughts were consumed by pain. She shook her head to clear it, and she could hear Loch cursing. She blinked until her vision returned.

Loch held a warped blade. Spark looked down at where he'd stabbed her and saw the dent in the chestplate over her dragonskin armour. His dagger hadn't made it through.

The pain made her want to vomit, but it was nothing like the broken ribs from the previous battle.

Spark wheezed, trying to command the demon to attack Loch, but he blasted her with more water. She sailed out over the side of the platform, dropping to the river below.

She called desperate fire to her hands and opened a portal before she sank beneath the surface.

CHAPTER
TWENTY-FIVE

Neesha went cold as Spark disappeared under the water. Beside her, Ember screamed. They were far too high up to do anything useful, but Neesha half wanted to jump from where they were and land on Loch. She would crush him and break every bone in both their bodies. Who cared if it killed them both, as long as she took that pale, soggy monster with her.

But Loch's sea beast shrieked and writhed. The water next to it boiled where Spark had disappeared. A column of fire erupted in a spray of steam.

"Trueflame!" Neesha gasped. "She's got a portal in the water. How in the hell...?"

And then it all winked out.

Of course. If Spark had a fire portal with her, she'd have gone through it and closed it behind her.

"Shit, she's stuck there without a fire."

"There's fires everywhere," Ember said.

"Yes, but she needs one here or we're doomed." Neesha called to Abyss for more flame and used it to open a fire portal just to the side of the sling. A few seconds later, it flared, and one white arm shot out, feeling around.

Ember startled and screamed, but there was delight to it this time. Neesha reached over and caught Spark's wrist, guiding her hand to the nearest hold. Spark was not graceful as she tumbled from the fire realm, her body swinging out into the open sky. But that vise grip of hers held, and she dangled from the sling for a moment before climbing back into it as Neesha gripped her forearm to guide her.

"That was madness!" Neesha shouted over the rush of wind as she gathered Spark into her arms and squeezed maybe a little harder than was necessary. Ember, sobbing next to her, reached over Neesha to grip Spark's shoulder.

"Never do that again!" Ember cried.

"No promises," Spark said.

Neesha released her and Ember leaned around to embrace Spark, kissing her sloppily on the cheek. Spark blushed and unsuccessfully tried to extract herself.

Neesha touched Ember's shoulder to get her attention. "You said you were ready for battle. This is going to get worse before it gets better. Are you sure you've got this?"

Ember nodded unconvincingly while she wiped away her tears. Spark held her hand and Neesha looked out over the battle below to give them a moment. Boats burned, dragons swooped, and Loch looked less smug. Had they rattled him? Good.

"We need more demons," Neesha said. "And better control of them. We'll need Nandara to do it safely."

"Mamma, are you talking about possession?"

"Yes." She took a breath to steel herself against the thought of being stuck in her own mind for another seventeen years. "I have an idea."

Abyss banked away from the river and out over the aerial battle, calling out until one of the dragons peeled away from the fight. Raia's blaze had joined the fray, Raia with her dragon who Neesha understood she had uncreatively named Dragon. Neesha watched her knock one of Loch's people from a captive dragon before leaping to Dragon's back for a quick escape. An orange dragon Neesha didn't know rose to meet them, bearing Nandara and Stone.

Their dragons moved farther north—where Loch's advance had slowed, if not completely stalled—and took a moment on the plains near the riverbank to swap Nandara and Ember, while Neesha went over her plan. Nandara didn't like it anymore than Spark did.

"We practiced!" Neesha snapped, wishing they'd just trust her half as much as she trusted them. "We'll get it right this time. It will give me the control I need. Now let's get demons into these dragons, and then me, and stop wasting time."

Spark made the fire, and Nandara summoned and sent a demon to the orange dragon, who launched himself back into battle, roaring to spread the word. One by one, the rest of their massive blaze came down to each receive a demon.

Demon-possessed dragons were unpredictable—even more so than normal—but the boost in power could counter the water beasts. And if Neesha was right, she could connect with every demon in the battle once she also called a demon into herself and opened a portal.

"Gods, no wonder it went so wrong last time," Spark said.

"It was a terrible idea," Neesha said. "Good thing you're here to save me this time."

Neesha hated that Spark was taking so many risks, and that she herself was right back to taking the same ones all over again. It would have been more reassuring to have Dionelle with them. Neesha tried to remind herself that she was prepared this time. She knew enough not to get lost to the flame. But she'd have to let the flame take her, at least a little, if this was going to work.

And they really needed it to work.

"Oh no," Nandara gasped.

Neesha followed her mentor's gaze to the storm bubbling from the river to the south of battle, maybe a league behind Loch's water beast. He was going to drown them all if he could.

"Shit," Neesha hissed. "We have to stop him. Spark, go with Raia. Get close to him. Use those light beams from earlier. Once I'm ready, I'll watch through Raia's dragon and guide him if I need to. But your goal is to get as close to Loch as you can."

Spark gripped her mother in a hug. The girl was trembling, and Neesha had to stifle a sob. "You won't lose me again."

Spark nodded and Dragon plucked her up, set her down next to Raia on his green-and-teal shoulder, and took flight. Nandara went with Stone and Ember in the orange dragon's sling, and Abyss deposited Neesha by herself into her own sling. Neesha quickly set to work buckling herself in, using components of all the sling's harnesses and making an absolute tangle of it.

If it was hard for her to escape with her mind in the right place, it would be impossible to escape with her mind in the wrong place. She'd be safe here with Abyss if something went wrong.

And it *would* probably go wrong.

Abyss took her half a league north while the orange dragon stayed nearby as backup. Abyss circled tightly over the river, closer than was probably safe, and Neesha opened a fire portal as wide as she could, pushing until it spanned the width of the flooded river.

She poured trueflame out of it, creating a dangerous wall of fire that hit the water's surface with a roar of steam.

Neesha plucked a single demon through the portal. Her body went cold and her thoughts tried to flee. Good. If she was afraid, she'd be more vigilant. But she'd done this before. It would work.

With a fortifying breath, she took the demon in. The heat lit her up from the inside. The scorching power gusted through her bones, and she shivered as it filled her. No wonder she'd lost herself to this. She felt like a goddess. She smiled as she brought her safe retreat into the corner of her mind, but didn't use it yet. She held the demon in check while sinking into its power, closing her eyes and expanding her awareness to remotely observe through the eyes of one of the demons they'd unleashed.

With every blink, she bounced from one demon's mind to another's, taking in the scene from their perspective and assessing it. There were some demons on boats that were sinking and others on boats where aquamancers were desperately trying to put out flames. She lingered among the latter, showing them the weak points in both the people and the boats. She directed them to target the strongest aquamancers with blistering infernos and to punch holes in hulls where demons had found their way into the ships' holds. Neesha looked through the demon in Dragon and saw that they were still trying to get close to Loch. There weren't any demons in range of him yet.

But the storm he'd called billowed around them. Rain began falling in a dangerous curtain behind him.

"Godsdamnit, it's not enough. They need to get closer! Can we drag this firewall toward him, do you think?"

Before Abyss could answer, a great cry rose up among the dragons. As Abyss circled around to face the northeast, Neesha caught a glimpse of a whole blaze coming their way—the dragons who'd left early in anticipation of this battle taking place on the shores of the ocean, not on the river in the middle of the plains.

Neesha pushed the demon possessing her to the very back of her mind and called out new instructions to Abyss. Jin and her dragon were the first to swoop close enough that Neesha could begin putting fire demons into the new dragons and sending them off. She sent Jin to follow Raia and Spark and immediately sent her awareness along too to keep an eye on them. Watching through the new dragon's eyes, Neesha's heart jolted in her chest as she saw an enemy dragon slam into Dragon. Spark and Raia both jumped from his back onto the back of their opponent.

Two men came toward Raia, but she was sure-footed as she threw blades at them. There were four men in total—then three, as one of Raia's blades sank deep into one man's chest, sending him tumbling out into the sky. She pulled some kind of short spear, more like a club with a knife on the end, off her back and swung and jabbed at the remaining attackers, leaping between dragon spines to dodge hits and come in from new angles.

Spark had her axe out, but she wasn't using it on people—she was cutting the chains off the dragon beneath them. Neesha didn't even realize the axe had been enchanted to cut through dragon chain. But one of the men broke away from Raia to attack Spark.

Cold fear and hot fury chased each other up and down Neesha's limbs as she helplessly watched her child in danger while she was strapped a safe distance from battle. Jin and Raia's dragons were too far back now to help, other than to catch the pair if they fell. They'd all known the risks. But Neesha's gut clenched as the attacker swung his blade, and Spark ducked out of the way.

It should be me out there.

But Neesha would have already uselessly fallen off. She was repeating her mistakes all over again, just like where this all started—fighting the water and risking her daughter. All she'd wanted was to avoid putting her family in harm's way in the first place.

She wasn't strong enough. But maybe Spark was.

Spark backed up, opening space between her and her attacker. She ducked under another swing of his sword, then drove the blunt end of her axe right into his gut. It doubled him over and he lost his balance, sliding out into the air.

Three more strikes to the chain, and the entire rigging fell away. Raia leapt off and was caught by Dragon. Spark had jumped too and glided using her suit until Jin's dragon, with Neesha still riding his demon's consciousness, swooped in to catch her before depositing her next to Raia. The remaining men on the captive dragon fell with the rigging, all tangled up in it. Could they not dragon-walk at all? It looked like they could hardly handle being on a dragon any better than Neesha could. The chains that had kept them on now pulled them all to their doom.

The newly freed dragon banked away from battle, roaring and heading south. Neesha lost track of it quickly because Dragon swooped low over the water, shrieking a battle cry while Spark used precision beams of fire, cutting one of the boats clean in half. A water whip came up at him, but when he exhaled fire, Neesha used it to knock the water away—she and Spark splitting the dragonflame.

Spark took a new beam of fire and sliced open the water beast attacking them.

The river came up like a reverse waterfall trying to drown them, and Neesha's fury erupted. She tried to open a fire portal into the dragon's flame, but the distance diluted her efforts. Without physical hands in the fire, she could do little more than make it bigger. Another of Spark's light beams cut them a path through the water, and the dragon banked up and away.

Neesha expected to see the sky as he pitched upward, but it was just all fire and heat. She had no sense of the dragon at all, or his demon. Only power to end it all. Glorious and consuming.

Oh shit.

Her demon's focus was scattered enough for Neesha to regain a tiny measure of control. It was enough to break her connection with the other demons in the battle. She opened her eyes—her real eyes, in her human body, with the straps of the sling digging into her shoulders and constricting her chest. But there was a giant blaze where her awareness had been.

Cold panic squeezed her chest, and Neesha remembered the safe place in her mind that she'd been saving. It was a struggle to recall the dragon chamber of the Wizard's Guild, but she forced herself to, one piece at a time—the high ceiling, the entrance in the ceiling where the dragons would descend, and the stunning, shimmering mural of a night sky crowded by silver stars. She remembered the peace and quiet of that place as she'd rested against Abyss and cradled tiny baby Mita, allowing herself a moment of true serenity before it all went wrong.

She brought herself back there, alone in the room, looking up at the glittering dragon constellation that decorated the ceiling. It was smaller in her mind than in reality, though plenty big enough for her to hide from the demon possessing her, and it was warm in the way Abyss's solid presence was—a contrast to the stifling heat of the fire demon.

Neesha settled into that comfort, knowing Abyss would keep her safe. Spark and Nandara would come for her.

CHAPTER
TWENTY-SIX

V oid Behind the Stars wheeled around over the river. The motion was languid, lazy-feeling, when really she was ready to burst out of her skin, wanting nothing more than to dive into battle and destroy Loch and his aquamancers and whatever other monsters thought they could keep her kin in chains.

And while her egg was not in chains, it was still beyond her reach and still in grave danger. Time was growing thin to retrieve it before it hatched into cruelty and corruption.

The sea serpent in the middle of the armada had recently been killed, and Imposing Shores bore down on Loch with Spark and the other human. As the new blaze, led by Jewelled Waters and his human, Jin, got involved in the fight and more of their kin were liberated, Boundless Glacial Lake and Lava Flow ferried their humans in behind Imposing Shores with Spark.

Consuming Fire, bearing Nandara and other humans, angled in as well. Demons dropped to the boats and beasts below. Demon power in the dragons boosted the reach of their flame, which helped considerably in burning humans off their imprisoned kin. They'd freed four dragons. Two had fled south and another had turned to fight them even without her masters driving her.

But the reduced numbers might be enough for Imposing Shores to reach Loch on his own. Spark drew on some of his fire to make a devastating concentrated beam of light—a blade made of the sun itself, cutting through boat, beast, and water alike.

And then one of her beams cut through the hide of Loch's beast. As Imposing Shores bore Spark past, Lava Flow and Boundless Glacial Lake swooped in behind him to tear at the wound and pour fire across the creature's flesh. Humans always wanted there to be a singular blow comprising victory, one belonging to a singular human—against impossible odds—rather than an efficient and concerted effort.

And they had the nerve to call *dragons* arrogant!

Void Behind the Stars could not be certain from this distance, but it looked as though Loch had been thrown from his beast into the water. Only three boats remained. Other dragons were the concern for the moment, though they were outnumbered.

The battle was not quite over, then, but this was certainly a reprieve.

And that was when the summoning from her mate, Merciless Winter Sky, tugged Void Behind the Stars's thoughts toward the city. Their eggs were hatching. Terror flashed across her scales—and another sensation.

Something was different about the demon currently possessing her. It seemed less in tune to the battle.

Still gliding, Void Behind the Stars craned her neck to look at her underside and the sling. Neesha strained against the harness, her hands ineffectively clawing at the restraints, her gaze lost to flame.

Void Behind the Stars did not sigh out loud, though she felt it through her bones. She lifted her head and roared to Imposing Shores, drawing him back to her. As he swooped close, she plucked Spark from his back and deposited her on the rigging near her mother, just beyond Neesha's reach.

A moment later, the fire portal closed, taking the wall of flame with it. Void Behind the Stars could finally move beyond this one cursed spot. Much as she wanted to join the battle or rush back to the city to be with her young, she landed near the shore, crouching so Spark could stand on the ground and tease the demon out of Neesha.

Consuming Fire swooped past, releasing Nandara to come help. A moment later, Imposing Shores returned to whisk Spark back into battle.

Void Behind the Stars paid little attention to what Nandara was doing, instead watching the battle progress and pining for its end. They were close.

Spark used trueflame to incinerate the final sea serpent. The battle focused on fighting and freeing the remaining dragons.

And Void Behind the Stars did not care. She needed to be away from here. But Nandara was still coaxing the demon and none of the other dragons were paying attention.

Merciless Winter Sky's summons grew in her mind. The eggs in a clutch never hatched all at the same time. The females always broke through their shells first, and the egg in Pasdale contained a male. But it wouldn't be more than half a day before all of the eggs hatched.

Would it be more than half a day to end the last of this fight?

This was exactly where Void Behind the Stars feared she would end up, with the fate of her egg pitted against the fate of her kin. Ocean Deep, whose endlessly argumentative nature had filled every meeting of the Superiors for months, expected Void Behind the Stars to abandon all dragonkind for one hatchling, which was so deeply insulting Void Behind the Stars wouldn't let her thoughts linger on it. But the pain of it hurt no less.

When they had lost so many dragons to Loch and his allies, the thought of losing one more—one of *hers*—was unbearable. She hadn't heard from her brother, Summer's Eve Lightning, or his mate, Bruised Horizon, in far too long. Only rumours. Their eggs were gone, destroyed or worse.

It looked like Loch would suffer a defeat here today. But even killing him now would not end the misery. These attacks went all the way back to the king in Golden Hill, whose influence had consumed half the continent and continued to grow. Loch was the king's most powerful minion, but certainly not the only one. Not by far.

There was time yet for her stolen egg, and maybe for others, but they needed to go very soon. Void Behind the Stars let Ocean Deep's criticism slide away and remained at her post. Ocean Deep was shortsighted in her biases and didn't believe the humans could make a difference. Maybe few of them could, but Void Behind the Stars trusted *these* particular humans.

She trusted that, with their help, she could uphold her duty to her kin in this battle while *also* saving her egg *and* freeing more of her kin in Pasdale.

So she was not surprised when a short time later, Neesha began swearing, sounding every bit like herself as she unclipped from the sling to tumble out and stand in the grass next to Nandara, and when another of the boats sank, hissing and steaming as the fires aboard met the river water. The remaining captive dragons turned away from battle and fled south, and the two remaining boats that had not yet been sunk flowed into a hasty retreat, carried more swiftly than the current could bear on its own—nearly faster than dragons could fly.

Strangely, only three of the six freed dragons remained, all restrained at the moment. The others had fled south, as Loch and his remaining people now did.

Void Behind the Stars didn't know when Spark had made the leap from Imposing Shores to Consuming Fire, but the latter landed first. Spark climbed down from his shoulder, jubilant, looking for her mate Ember, making sure Neesha was okay. Neesha waved the girl off as she spoke in low tones with Nandara, but Ember's voice was pitched high with panic as she collapsed into Spark's arms.

"It's River! Did you see him?" Ember sobbed.

"What? Where?"

"He was on that last boat with Loch's people!"

Spark blinked a lot, like she did when she found something deeply confusing. "But how did they know? And why—I don't even like—Okay, we can go after them. We've got lots of dragons to spare. Maybe Jin—"

"No, Spark. He's not—they didn't *take* him. He *went*. On purpose." She collapsed into tears again.

Stone was with them, and as Spark gathered Ember into her embrace again, he draped his arm around Ember's shoulders.

Neesha swore again, this time a particularly foul oath. Spark was focused on her mate's emotional well-being and likely not thinking, but Neesha clearly was. Void Behind the Stars had to wonder how much the boy knew of Spark's power. How much had he overheard? How much had Ember told him? If Neesha and Spark had made it through this battle without revealing any secrets to Loch, they certainly wouldn't have any left now.

Boundless Glacial Lake and her blaze landed. Raia immediately leapt from Imposing Shores and ran to Spark.

"Did you see?" Raia said. "It was my brother's dragon!"

"Wait, the one you lost?" Spark turned her head as if to find him. "Where? He's here?"

Raia vibrated with emotion, constantly looking from Spark, to the gathered dragons, to the retreat in the south. "Eltir freed him of the chains, but Shell shook everyone off and shot off to the south. No sign of Creves anywhere. I don't understand!"

Still trying to console Ember under one arm, Spark extended the other to hug Raia.

Void Behind the Stars had to wonder. Why flee south? She understood the ones who'd surrendered and the one who'd turned to fight. But the one fleeing south again that she'd seen had been distraught and distracted. Turning back the way they'd come had been a deliberate choice.

"We need scouts to follow Loch," Void Behind the Stars said, bringing her head down near the humans. She addressed Raia. "Go. Follow them and look for your brother. May you find him. We will need a report of those fleeing, and of whether Loch is truly among them."

"There's got to be some powerful aquamancers with them for those boats to move that quickly," Nandara said.

Void Behind the Stars just wanted Raia and her people to go. Work still needed to be done. Heart's Blood, the Superior who had aided Spark in Void Behind the Stars's rescue in the spring, was delegating some of it, seeing to the freed dragons who would need to go to the northern plateau until their minds could be healed from their ordeal.

And Void Behind the Stars could not bear a protracted wait while the humans grew distraught over events that could not be undone.

"The summons from my mate came some time ago. We do not have long," Void Behind the Stars said.

Heart's Blood stopped delegating to listen. "You cannot go to Pasdale alone. Even with the three fireborn women, you will be outnumbered. Six of the Pasdale captives were in this battle, two of them freed, but the other dozen are either part of the suspected diversion or lying in wait in Pasdale."

"And there's the ice dragons," Nandara said.

Spark groaned.

"Those ice dragons must be stopped," Heart's Blood said. "Their mistress can control the remaining captives, and you would have no hope of freeing them. And beyond that, she could lead them to attack the city even without orders from Loch."

"If that's not already what she's doing." Neesha rubbed her hands over her face. "Okay, so we've got to save eggs, kill ice dragons, and free captive dragons—about a dozen of them. And approximately in that order?"

"That is correct."

Void Behind the Stars was deeply tired of the talking, but she understood that Neesha was trying to turn the conversation toward a plan.

"If you take a fire portal, you can get there before Loch can alert Pasdale of any threat," Heart's Blood said. "It means you can take plenty of dragons with you, but only the three fireborn women."

"How many dragons from here can be spared?" Nandara asked. "You need scouts and guards."

"If there are a dozen captives, you will need that many to go with you."

"First, we've got to go back to the dragon city and get Dionelle," Neesha said. "That could take a minute. Keep a fire going here. We'll get her while you get your forces together."

"Raia's group is going to keep scouting Loch's movements," Spark said. "And Jin's group can stay here to guard and patrol, right?"

"We will make the arrangements," Void Behind the Stars said urgently. "Retrieve Dionelle. We must be swift if we hope to reach my egg in time."

CHAPTER TWENTY-SEVEN

Spark stumbled out of the fire alone into the dark of Unari's parlour. She wished someone had come with her, but especially Ember. Leaving her and Stone with strangers while they were so distraught over River's betrayal had not been easy. Spark had also had to leave Neesha and Abyss next to a fire portal, still trying to talk Nanny into their plan when Spark had come to get things started.

"Unari!" Spark called quietly, trying not to alert any neighbours.

"Spark," a soft voice answered from farther inside the house, "is that you?"

"I'm back, and I've got help this time. What was the original plan?"

Unari appeared with a lantern. "Well, you were successful with your grandmother, and well done!"

"Yes, but the dragons. We've got to hurry—one of the eggs is hatching."

"Oh no!" she gasped.

"I know how to get to the egg, but what about the other dragons? Where can I make a fire to free them?"

Unari made a quick diagram of the compound where Spark had already been, showing her how to get from the eggs to a spot in the dragon pen—one not easily seen, where Spark could open a fire big enough to bring Abyss and her blaze through.

Spark hugged her quickly. "Thank you. I hope we'll have this over with soon. Stay inside for now."

She dashed back into the fire, pulling a portal open as she went and making another from the fire realm to the room in the storage building at the back of the textile mill, where the eggs were being kept. This time, she opened the portal into the fire around the red and purple egg she remembered being next to Abyss's.

Despite walking into a room that was mostly on fire, she went cold.

The egg was spiderwebbed with cracks, little bits of the shell falling away.

"No, no, no, no...." Spark rushed over and put one hand against the shell, pressing like she could keep a dragon contained through the sheer force of her will. "No, please stay in there. Just a few more minutes."

The dragon inside stopped shuffling. Maybe the sound of her voice had distracted it? She had no idea. Her limbs buzzed, and her mind was too full and too empty all at once.

"I'll be back. Please just hold still."

Spark hated the idea of leaving it alone. She turned to the window and blasted it open with a fireball. Then, holding that fireball outside, she went through the open portal, bouncing herself from one place to another like a mouse being batted between a cat's paws.

Spark staggered out of the fire portal into the darkness—the afterimage of the fire realm blinding her—breathing hard and just needing to *go*. As the world slowly emerged back into sight, her heart rate ticked up a notch, gaze darting around. Her surroundings all looked the same, just brick walls and stacks of crates.

She spun back and forth, looking for something that matched Unari's description.

Around the corner, the informant had said. But there were corners to go around everywhere. The building's odd shape gave Spark nothing to work with.

But there was a glow in the darkness to her right. It was as good as anything else, so she bolted in that direction.

The space between buildings opened up into a large courtyard full of chained-up dragons, all of whom turned their gazes on her and heaved against their restraints. With their mouths clamped shut, they couldn't do much to alert anyone to her presence, though there was plenty of growling and wheezing.

She hoped they wouldn't alert the guards before she had the chance to get Abyss here, but she didn't have time to worry about it. Besides, even if she thought it was a good idea to free them first, the axe took forever and the bolt cutters were coming with Neesha.

Spark churned up a massive blaze, glancing at the nearest dragon for reference to make sure she had something big enough, then opened a fire portal and summoned Abyss.

And then she was back through the portal herself and back in the fire realm, hopefully for the last time until the dragons were free and their task was complete.

She returned to the room with the eggs just as pieces of the blue-black one fell to the ground around her, revealing the hatchling inside splayed on the ground.

"No, no, no! Your mother is almost here!"

She lunged for the hatchling, her hands shaking. It was bigger than a carriage, but all spindly and floundering, glittering black in the firelight, and shot through with cerulean like lightning bolts across a storm cloud. But it had hatched too soon.

Spark held her breath and stared. She had come all this way for nothing—come so close, only to fail at the last minute. Every choice she'd made had been the wrong one. Even with all the guidance she'd had, she still couldn't get it right. With the weight of a moon on her shoulders, she sank to her knees, her throat hot and eyes prickling with tears. Spark gripped her hands into fists. It was all too much. She had done everything she could and it wasn't enough.

"I'm so sorry," she whispered, tears sizzling on her cheeks from the nearness of the flame.

"Sorry!" the hatchling chirped.

Spark startled and looked up just as it pressed its soft snout into the side of her face. The hatchling knocked Spark down, falling over and pinning her for good measure.

"Sorry!" it chirped again, legs scrabbling at the stone around her.

Spark burst out laughing, before biting down on her fist to stifle the noise. Attracting guards was the last thing she needed.

"Sorry!"

"No, hush," she whispered, trying to give its chin a shove. It was like trying to lift an ox off of her. "We need to be quiet until your mamma gets here."

"Quiet!" The hatchling was not quiet at all.

"No, no!" Spark hissed. "Quiet means the exact opposite of what you're doing."

"No!"

Spark blinked. Did it not understand her words at all? Was it merely mimicking her? Either way, talking further wasn't helping. She kept wriggling to get free while the baby struggled to stand.

Angry voices shouted from beyond the doorway, far enough away that Spark couldn't make anything out—other than that they were definitely drawing closer.

Where was Abyss? Spark had expected to, at the very least, hear some roaring dragons by now.

The door rattled and the voices continued, hushed on the other side.

"Ugh, I need to get up! I can keep you safe, but not like this."

"Safe!"

"No, quiet, please! And just—just lift your head!"

The door burst open and three guards rushed in, wielding chains. Spark screamed.

"Sorry!" the hatchling chirped at them, finally lifting its head to get a better look.

Spark rolled to her feet and fanned a massive conflagration from the fires all around her. She pushed a wall of flame between her, the baby, and the approaching guards.

Someone shouted in alarm from the other side. One of them burst through the flames, wearing armour over fireproof clothing. He held a nasty-looking spear that, if Spark had to guess, was enchanted to pierce dragon skin. His armour was probably dragonproof too.

He charged straight for them.

Spark heaved a block from the floor, the terramancy making the ground beneath her feet shift as she drove the block forward, slamming it into him. She kept pushing it until he'd gone straight back through that wall of flame. She hoped it had landed on him and pinned him to the ground.

But she had no idea how many of these people were wizards, and she couldn't count on that doing much of anything.

"Sorry!" the hatchling chirped again.

"Yes, yes. We'll have time for that later. We have to go. They'll—"

At last, a dragon did roar from outside—a whole *blaze* of them roared as one. There were more human shouts from the other side of the fire, way more than the initial three guards. Spark wouldn't stand a chance against so many.

"Let's go!" She prodded at the hatchling, who promptly fell over again.

Spark went cold. She'd expected this to be easier. Just open another fire portal, and the hatchling could just walk through. No one had told her it wouldn't be able to walk yet.

"Right. Fine."

Abyss had to be out there somewhere. Spark summoned her again before pushing the wall of fire toward the door. She put a gust of wind into it to blow back anyone not driven away by the fire alone.

The shouts turned to screams—some terrified, some agonized. So not all of them had fireproof clothes. But her wall of fire parted anyway, so there had to be at least one good elemental among them. Spark poured more fire in their way, keeping the wall from snuffing out.

It would take an awful lot of elementals to get through her fire, but it required more of her attention than she had. They needed a way out.

Amidst the shrieking dragons outside, one stood out, growing louder. With a mind-splitting crack and a flurry of dust and debris, the wall behind Spark just... disappeared. Other parts of it fell outward. Parts of the roof caved in, while other sections were ripped away.

Stones rained down around her. Everything was fire and dust, dragons shrieking and men screaming. Those screams ending abruptly.

And in her mind, Spark was transported back to the farm. Throwing spells next to Nanny while men rained down from dragons, a firestorm in all directions. Cold and frozen to the spot, she saw the farmhouse come down again. Heard Nanny screaming her grief, knowing her son and grandson were gone.

And then Pappy was running in the open, and the dragon that would kill him was coming his way.

Screams cut short all around her, but the echoes of Pappy's death were all she heard.

Until she was pressed in on all sides by soft, hot darkness and the flashback fell away. Once Spark felt the ground beneath her feet again, she staggered across it, stumbled, and came to her knees, sobbing.

"Spark!"

She felt warm hands on her face, tender like Ember. But Ember wasn't here—she was somewhere safer.

"Spark, are you hurt?" Neesha asked.

Spark blinked away the past and looked into her mother's concerned face, those blue-amber eyes flickering like firelight, just like Spark's pure amber ones. Spark collapsed against her mother, dropping into a warm pool of safety as Neesha gathered her daughter in her arms and held her tight. Spark cried while Neesha spoke, but she didn't really register what Neesha said.

But then she heard Abyss's voice.

"No, there are enough of the others right now. I will stay and protect you."

"Sorry!" the baby chirped again.

"Dear gods, what has Spark taught him?" Neesha said.

"Quiet!" the baby insisted.

Spark eased out of Neesha's embrace and leaned back on her heels. Abyss stood over them, her baby next to one large foreleg.

"I'm sorry," Spark whispered. "I wasn't in time."

"Weren't you?" Abyss leaned in first to nuzzle Spark and then the baby. "But it hatched before you got here."

"He did not hatch into cruelty. And he was not in captivity long enough to understand it. He hatched into your love and protection until I came, and that is enough."

Spark collapsed into sobs again.

Neesha rubbed her back and crooned encouragement. "You remarkable girl," Neesha said. "You've done more than any of us ever could have."

Spark wiped her eyes and took a steadying breath.

Neesha watched her, that firelight sparkling in her eyes and mischief pulling at the corners of her mouth. "Let's find out what all three of us can do when we work together, shall we?"

Neesha helped Spark to her feet while Abyss gathered up her baby and took flight, disappearing into the dark sky. Nanny was nearby, bolt cutters in each hand hanging at her side. Her blue eyes shone wide and bright with barely contained panic.

Spark took one of the bolt cutters.

"It's just like the farm. I keep hearing it—" She swallowed.

Nanny nodded, a tear escaping down her cheek.

"But we're not alone," Spark said. "We'll do it right this time, Nanny."

Nanny's smile was lopsided and small, the bright panic still in her eyes.

"Abyss's blaze is taking care of the people for now," Neesha said. "And there's no sign of those ice dragons, but it looks like the full dozen captive dragons are here."

"Time for the bolt cutters."

"There's a problem." Neesha caught Spark's arm as she turned toward the pens of captive dragons. "Neither of us has the strength you do. It takes both of us working one set of cutters to break the locks."

Spark blinked at her mother, then glanced at Nanny as she struggled to lift her cutters. Right. Nanny had always been strong with all that work on a farm now gone to ashes, but had sat idle and deprived for a year. Spark knew her mother had helped minimally on the farm and been more of an academic, and none of them really understood yet what nearly two decades in stasis had done to her body. But she hadn't had the strength for dragon-walking. Her arms were like noodles.

Spark had meant to use the axe, all three of them working in tandem.

"Okay." Spark hefted a pair of cutters. "It'll take longer than we wanted, but it's the only way. Let's go."

Spark went to the nearest dragon but it lunged at her, straining against the chains. She noticed the state of it—wounds old and new, scarred and scraped. She had no idea how any of these dragons would react to freedom. They'd gotten some shocking reactions from the ones freed over the southern plains. Had enough dragons come with Abyss to handle them all? There were certainly more than she'd expected.

She backed away and looked around. A lot of the dragons heaved aggressively against their restraints. Would they view all humans in the same light after their treatment?

A glance back at Nanny and Neesha showed they were also taking stock of the dragons around them.

Spark found one that was sedate, barely paying any attention to any of them, and broke the lock at its jaw. It was one of the mill dragons, defanged and declawed, a sad echo of its glory. It didn't move.

"I'm going to get you out of here. Or set you loose to do as you please, at least." And she set to work cutting away all the restraints.

It still didn't get up, but she didn't have time to wonder. There were far too many dragons left. Given the number of chains, and using two tools instead of three, it could take an hour. She moved from one to another until Neesha came back holding her cutters. There was no sign of Nanny.

"She went to find the keys," Neesha explained. "This is taking entirely too long."

Neesha went back to work, bracing one handle against the restraints and using her body weight on the other in order to cut the bonds. She was going nearly as quickly as Spark had. Maybe they'd get through this yet.

Spark got back to work, frequently glancing around to look for Nanny, who had no idea about the layout of the mill and its outbuildings—no idea where a proper attack might come from. At least for now, Abyss's blaze was concentrating their efforts around the side of the building.

But as she and Neesha released more dragons, some of them fled, while a couple turned on Abyss's blaze. Abyss herself wasn't particularly easy to spot in the middle of the night, but there was enough firelight to illuminate her if she flew over. Spark hadn't seen Abyss since she left with her baby.

Spark opened the clamps over a dragon's muzzle, and it immediately snapped at her. She screamed, dropping her cutters, and shoved a gust of wind at it to put some space between them. She darted back, waiting.

This wasn't the first dragon unhappy about her presence, but it was the first to try to attack her before she'd even gotten it completely free.

And then a distant cry rose up from the southeast, toward the city. More dragons. A battle cry.

Spark went cold, even when the half-freed dragon washed her with flame. She parted the flame like swatting a gnat, trying to get a good look toward the city, to see which dragons were there.

The cry came again, louder. Closer.

The night sky dropped into her view, and Abyss landed, the baby nestled tightly among the spikes on her back just between her wings.

"The ice dragons are here," she said.

CHAPTER TWENTY-EIGHT

Spark stared at Abyss, mouth open, while her brain caught up with what she'd said.

"So there was no diversion after all?" Neesha said. "That was arrogant of Loch."

"And lucky for us," Spark said.

"Lucky!" the hatchling chirped.

"They do not appear prepared for us," Abyss said.

Spark thought of Raia and the others in pursuit of Loch, making him earn his escape—assuming he'd survived.

She shook her head to clear it. "We need to meet them head-on. Abyss, I'll open a fire portal so you can get your baby safely back to the city, and—"

"We cannot take him through the fire realm," Abyss said. "Its powers have affected some of my blaze strangely, akin to what you would call being drunk. We do not know what sort of long-term risk this may mean for any of us, particularly the young ones."

The cold whisper of failure prickled up Spark's arms.

Neesha cursed. "How do we get them out of here? There's five eggs left. And you can't fight with your baby on your back!"

"I will do what is necessary. We must take the fight to the ice dragons. Allowing them to reach these pens and take control of the captives here would be disastrous."

Spark trembled. Abyss's blaze would be outnumbered drastically. The whole plan relied on either getting in and out without being seen, or killing the ice dragons.

"I'll go," Spark said. "Keep releasing dragons here, and I'll use trueflame to get that dragoness. They're near the palace?"

Abyss nodded. Spark was already pulling up a portal when Nanny lay a hand on Spark's arm, shaking her head vehemently.

"Nanny, I can stop her. I can buy you some more time to be ready for the rest."

"There are three in total," Abyss said. "The two males will do anything they can to protect her."

"And trueflame can melt them all easily."

"Loch also has plenty of humans."

"We're wasting time arguing."

"We're stronger together," Neesha said.

Nanny nodded in agreement.

"Do we really have time for this?" Spark asked.

Neesha looked to Nanny, who stood resolute. "Look, Spark, I don't know how to read her the way you do, but I know that look."

Neesha was right—Nanny was determined. Spark hadn't seen that stubborn look in so long. She staggered forward and gripped Nanny in a hug, gasping to hold in a sob.

"Abyss, take Di. She can loosen the sling's straps while you fly and use them to secure your son. Spark and I will take a portal to the palace and meet you there." A flicker of something passed over Neesha's expression and was gone in a clench of her jaw. "The tower again."

Nanny gasped, but Neesha had already turned to Spark. Abyss plucked Nanny off the ground and took flight.

"But what about the dragons here?" Spark said. "And the eggs! We came to free them."

"And we can, once the immediate danger is dealt with. They're not going anywhere, unless the fools here free them for us. As long as we deal with that ice dragoness before we're outnumbered, we can still succeed here."

Spark still didn't like it. It felt like abandoning them all over again. Her gut seized against the potential failure, but she opened the fire portal anyway, grimacing against the blinding glare of the fire realm. She sought for a fire near enough the palace to open.

"Oh, there's one in the kitchens!" Neesha said, pulling open a portal first.

"What if it's a trap?"

Neesha scowled. "Then good luck to them." She glanced at Spark. "They're not expecting three of us, if they were ever expecting any of us to return at all. For all they know, I'm dead."

And then Neesha went through. Spark scrambled after her.

The palace kitchen was busier than Spark expected for the middle of the night. She was only half surprised to see Unari there.

"Yes, yes," Unari said, waving away Spark's concern before she even said anything. "You told me to stay safe, but I couldn't sit idly."

"You left the fire going for us," Spark said.

"Those ice dragons are in the courtyard right now, demanding reinforcements from Loch's cronies," Unari said. "Go quickly."

Neesha rushed off. Spark was torn between staying with her mother and getting more information from Unari—like how to find the courtyard. In the end, she chased after Neesha.

"Do you know the way?" Spark called.

Neesha shushed her, stopping at a junction and pressing herself against the wall. Spark could scarcely see her in the dark. All the lanterns were out, some of them hastily smashed in the process. Not a flicker of flame anywhere.

"Spark, I need fire—hurry."

Spark snapped a flame into the palm of her hand. Neesha whipped it into an inferno and pushed it around the corner. In the flare of light, Spark saw a guard in the junction, sword raised to strike. He cringed back, the fire racing past him.

Screams echoed in the hallway.

Before the guard could react, Neesha pulled a lance of flame from the blaze and drove it into his face. He didn't even have time to scream.

Spark gasped and stared, her whole body going cold and buzzing.

But there was no time, because Neesha sprinted down the hall again, hopping over the bodies she left in her wake. She held a bit of flame in her hand, not to be caught off-guard. At least they could see where they were going.

Not even hesitating at turns, Neesha went quickly enough that Spark felt she must know the way.

"Mamma, stop!" Spark whisper-hissed. "We were supposed to meet Nanny and Abyss!"

"If we take them by surprise in the courtyard, we won't need the extra help. Keep up."

They ran into one more patrol, which Neesha dispatched with equal efficiency as the first, but there were more than soldiers in the palace. Servants and members of court peeked cautiously from a distance, curiosity on their faces. Neesha regarded them warily, but gave the flame a bit more light—enough for the gawkers to recognize her face, and Spark's.

As they passed, they were greeted by gasps and left whispers in their wake. Shouts echoed in distant hallways, and voices filled with both horror and awe carried one word around the palace: *fireborn*.

Spark had no sense at all of where they were anymore as Neesha led her forward. She hadn't realized how large the place was. She'd been too terrified to pay much attention the only other time she'd been here. Neesha halted suddenly next to a window.

A dragon roared from entirely too close.

Spark pressed a hand over her mouth to keep from crying out, but Neesha pulled her hood over her head, crouched, and ran past the windows for a nearby set of doors that stood open onto the frigid night. Spark did the same.

An icy blast of wind hit her. She skidded to a halt just inside the threshold next to Neesha.

The ice dragons were leaving.

"Shit!" Neesha hissed. "Fire as soon as we're clear of the colonnade, and open a portal at an angle pointing right at them."

Spark didn't have time to reply—Neesha was on the move again.

As they cleared the colonnade, Spark pulled up fire for both of them to use. The ice dragons glittered, their chill freezing her breath. She'd hoped to catch a glimpse of Abyss, but of course their friend would be invisible as long as she stayed out of the light.

Spark got a fire portal open an instant behind her mother. Neesha poured trueflame out in a burst, catching more of the guards in the courtyard but too diffuse to do more than annoy the nearest ice dragon. The dragoness was nearly out of sight.

Spark adjusted her feet and the angle of the fire, summoning a pillar of flame high into the sky. But the ice dragoness banked around, having noticed Neesha's fire, and Spark's blaze only skimmed her.

Meanwhile, one of the males was diving straight for them.

Skin buzzing, gritting her teeth in concentration, Spark pulled the angle of the portal and aimed the trueflame right into the ice dragon's face.

Agonized shrieks filled the night, then the roaring hiss of so much water meeting endless blaze. The air grew warm and thick and humid—until a blast of cold air froze the stones next to her so solidly that they cracked. Neesha grabbed her arm and pulled her back.

Spark lost control of both the trueflame and the portal, the former winking out and the latter snapping closed. Before the fire went out, Neesha summoned a pair of fire demons, directing them both at the second male coming for them. She tugged Spark all the way back inside.

The stones outside—the ones not frozen solid—gleamed with water, mist filling the air. It was the only sign of the other ice dragon. Having killed one only made Spark that much more desperate to go out and melt the others.

"We're fish in a barrel out there without the element of surprise." Neesha stared out the door.

Spark followed her mother's gaze and spotted a tower across the courtyard—probably the tallest one in the palace.

"We need to get higher. Let's go." Neesha didn't wait to see if Spark was with her before moving.

Spark sprinted after her. "Mamma, why did suggesting the tower upset Nanny so much?"

Neesha tensed but kept going. Spark didn't think she would answer. But once they'd circled most of the way around the courtyard and had to be nearly there, Neesha explained.

"That's where it happened. With the trueflame and the demons. Last time. When I lost myself to the fire. Gods, it still feels like days ago."

Spark flexed her hands while her skin buzzed cold. She wanted to trust that Neesha knew what she was doing and where her limits were, but returning to that tower seemed foolish even if it was a good strategy. Spark wanted to argue, to suggest something else, but she wasn't familiar enough with the palace to come up with alternatives. Would Neesha even listen if she did?

Spark opened her mouth to try, but someone called out to them from down the hall. Neesha, fire in both hands, stopped so abruptly Spark nearly ran into her.

A man emerged from the darkness down the hallway, but Spark didn't recognize him.

Neesha groaned and rolled her eyes. "Unbelievable," she muttered. Then she called back, "I haven't got time for whatever it is, Zev!"

Spark blinked. Would she gain points with Ondias if she lit him on fire? (She wasn't really sure she *wanted* points with Ondias, but Ember probably would have told her to do it anyway.)

"I can't believe it's you," Zev said, out of breath. "When I saw that trueflame—so soon after Dionelle finally escaped—I wondered."

"Just like old times. I've got to get up the tower."

Zev reached them and shook his head. "After what happened last time?"

"I know what I'm doing now—got some training I could have used back then. We haven't got time for this. Let's go, Spark."

CHAPTER TWENTY-NINE

Nanny was in the tower when they got there, though there was no sign of Abyss. Nanny immediately pulled Neesha into a desperate hug, but caught sight of Zev and glared.

"I'm sorry, Di," Zev said, hands held out in surrender. "I hope they told you why I couldn't help you."

Spark blinked. "You've been the one giving Nandara information?"

"One of her informants, yes. I don't know the others, but she told me it was best I keep my distance, that I let the fallout with Ondias be cover for me to remain close enough to Loch to be useful to you." He looked from one of them to another. "It's remarkable to see you all together like this." He sighed.

"You've been here this entire time and let them torture her for a *year*?" Neesha snapped, the fire in her hands exploding with her fury.

Zev stepped back, but Neesha didn't advance any farther as Nanny placed a hand on her shoulder. In the brighter light, Spark saw just how old Zev looked, his face lined and dark hair frosting to white.

"Loch had her so well guarded, there was no getting in and getting her out again. Not until recently. We'd been planning, and then Dionelle disappeared one night. Was it you?"

"It was Spark," Neesha said.

Zev looked at her as if seeing her for the first time.

"She used fire portals to get out."

Zev shook his head. "Yes, I've heard she can create fire from nothing. Loch was very careful not to have any flame within two floors of Dionelle's cell—the guards used jars of glow worms for light. Since he left, a lot of his safety measures have fallen away."

"Wait, you knew he left?" Spark asked.

"Not until recently." Zev shrugged helplessly. "He's been gone over a moon cycle, as best I can tell. He'd left his top advisors performing a ruse to make it look like he was still here. I've heard he took a few of his most prized dragons and aquamancers and headed to the southern coast to help the king's expansion there."

Neesha stared into the middle distance.

"He came for the dragon city again," Spark said.

This startled Zev. "I had no indication he was going to actually do anything any time soon. What happened?"

"We stopped him," Neesha snapped.

"Good. I think his absence has led to lax security, even after you rescued Dionelle," Zev said. "I suspect it's helped you get this far."

"Whatever. It doesn't matter," Neesha said. "We need to stop these ice dragons now."

"All right, so you'll be wielding trueflame again," Zev said. "You're certain you're ready?"

"We've been practicing," Spark said.

"All three of us," Neesha added.

Zev was helpful, if nothing else, using his magic to help them unmoor the roof of the tower and send it plummeting to the keep below.

"Well, that'll get their attention." Neesha gazed out into the night.

"And that's my cue to get somewhere safer." Zev gave them all a nod, even if Nanny hadn't stopped glaring at him the whole time.

"Mamma, it was never going to work out with him and Ondias," Neesha said. "Maybe if your generation would get over marriage as the be-all and end-all of everything, you'd all be a lot happier for it."

Nanny turned her glare on Neesha, who grinned in return.

"Pappy always said how much Zev and Ondias loved each other," Spark protested.

"I think maybe he was projecting a bit too much of his own good fortune onto them." Still facing Nanny, Neesha glanced at Spark. "I mean, he's about old enough to be her father—that alone almost never works out. Zev was an ass for what he did, but Ondias was young and naïve, and he was her ticket out of poverty. She's entirely too proud to admit that, of course."

Nanny reached out and gave Neesha's thick braid a tug.

Neesha rolled her eyes. "I'm not wrong, and you know it. Tell me you didn't try to warn her? Anyway, she's your friend, not mine. I don't have to be nice to her."

Nanny clucked her tongue disapprovingly.

"Oh, come on, Mamma. You can't keep making excuses for her. She's way more pushy and overbearing than she was before Mita was born."

Nanny sighed, but it was the sigh of giving in, her eyes sparkling just a little. Spark grinned.

A dragon roared in the dark. Spark's skin buzzed and went cold. Neesha's expression turned serious.

"All right, time for trueflame and demons," Neesha said.

Standing in a loose circle with her mother and grandmother, Spark ignited the floor in the middle of them. The three of them each summoned a demon and held them steady. Spark opened a fire portal.

But Nanny shook her head.

"She's right," Neesha said. "Wait to use trueflame until the ice dragons are closer. We need to draw them in."

Nanny pressed her lips together. She snapped her fingers and pointed at the demons.

"Shit, that's risky," Neesha said.

Spark looked between the two of them, not quite following the conversation, but Nanny held out her hand and pushed the fire down smaller.

"No, you're right," Neesha said. "We can't let them know what we can do until it's too late for them."

"What does she mean?" Spark asked Neesha.

Another dragon cry came closer, sending Spark's shoulders up to her ears.

"Keep the fire small and don't use trueflame until they're too close to escape," Neesha explained. "We use demon possession for better control of the flame, but also to conceal them. Dionelle can call more demons and help us out if we lose control of them—or ourselves."

Spark lay a hand on Nanny's shoulder. It was still surreal that they were together. "Nanny, are you sure you're ready?"

Nanny shrugged helplessly in a manner that clearly said, "What choice do I have?" She shifted, putting herself between her family and the only way out.

"Good call," Neesha said to Nanny. "Not sure how much luck you'll have if it's Spark who loses control, though—she's like three times your size."

Spark touched Neesha's shoulder, smiling when she turned around.

"You're getting the hang of it—figuring out what she means."

Neesha grinned. "I grew up with her, too. It's only a matter of remembering which looks went with which words. I've got her disappointed face seared into my mind. But I guess I missed a lot, since we mostly shouted at each other."

Neesha's smile went lopsided for a moment before she shook it off, turning back to the task. The air was frigid, turning Spark's breath into opaque clouds. The ice dragons were silent, but they were close.

Spark wished like never before that she could see Abyss overhead, but she wouldn't until the flames lit up the dark.

Neesha drew in one demon and Spark did the same with a second, the heat of it filling every corner of her, bracing her against the cold. Nanny had another demon half-summoned, each of them poised to burst with fire at the first glint of ice in the low light.

And then Spark's demon tugged at her, trying to get loose—to turn her around. She turned on her own, sensing urgency to the demon's actions. She had to keep holding it—couldn't afford to lose control. Not now. None of them could.

There it was, a flash of ice in the dark.

Spark let the demon go. "They're here!"

She opened the portal wider and ripped trueflame into the air. After a steadying breath, she caught the demon Nanny had just summoned and invited another possession, bracing against the heat. Nanny kept summoning them, the ruined tower flickering brightly in the demonlight as they unfurled over the sides like deadly blooms, going after the ice dragons.

Spark tracked the ice dragoness, hoping her mother was watching for the remaining male. It was like she had new senses—everything was sharp and clear, the ice dragon a shimmering beacon. Rage bubbled inside Spark—a searing hatred coming from the demon. Spark staggered around, pulling on the fire portal to aim the trueflame at the ice dragoness as she looped past. In addition to a power boost, the demon's help granted Spark greater finesse, allowing her to target the column of trueflame with precision she didn't normally have.

She hit the ice dragoness's tail. Off to her side, Neesha got a hit on the male ice dragon's body.

Out on the edge of the palace compound, dragonfire erupted out of the darkness. Abyss must be out there, targeting something. Maybe reinforcements? But there was no time to worry about that. Wounded, both ice dragons faltered in the air, and Spark had a brief moment to hope that it was almost over.

But it wasn't enough. They were already recovering.

Spark roared and hauled on the portal, fanning trueflame up and out, trying to catch up to the ice dragoness. But the dragoness was flailing more than flying, her movement unpredictable. She dropped out of sight entirely.

Spark's fire evanesced. The demon inside her strained to go after the dragoness, but even with her fire down, the sky was still bursting with flame.

Neesha stood off to the side, her face strained and her teeth bared, and flung her arms wide as she cast trueflame out higher and wider, the hungry flame curling around a glittering shape lost to a roar of steam.

Neesha staggered, and a spike of fear buzzed down Spark's spine like cold lightning. But then Neesha lit up with fire an instant before the demon she possessed materialized in front of her. Neesha roared in triumph at taking herself back before she could lose control. The demon turned toward her, but a gesture from Nanny sent it where they needed it most—at the last ice dragon.

Or what was left of it.

"You've almost got it!" Spark cried. "Nanny, more demons!"

Spark focused her will on the ones they had loose, calling them back and sending them up with the trueflame. The demons latched onto the male dragon, pulling its wings and scrabbling at its scales as it struggled to fly away. More and more of the dragon was lost to vapour.

"Shit, shit!" Neesha hissed.

Spark glanced at her mother, whose eyes were closed tight and whose jaw was clenched, her hands bunched into fists. She reached out for the nearest demon Nanny had just summoned.

"Spark, hold them! I've got it!"

Neesha turned back to the flame—silhouetted by it, wreathed in it. Spark tried to exert her will on the demons, tried to make sense of everything around her to see how best to use them.

The demon in Spark tugged again and she let it go. She didn't need the boost, and not having to split her concentration would be valuable. Neesha had control of the trueflame, while Spark had the demons and the portal. Nanny helped with the demons, warily watching it all, her gaze darting to the periphery and back.

That ice dragoness was still out there.

Spark strained her senses, waiting for a whisper of cold. It would stand out even more now—the air was alive with fire and thick with steam. The roar of the fire faded to a hiss, and Spark sifted through flame like digging through sand. There was no sign of the ice dragon.

And then the fire all collapsed in on itself. Neesha lunged at Nanny, hands out like claws.

"Oh no!"

Spark took a step in that direction, and while the trueflame and fire were gone, the night was bright with the flame of demons, all of them scattering. Nanny's body was weak, but she used a vortex of air to hold Neesha back. Spark frantically banished demons, wishing Nanny hadn't called quite so many of them.

A gust of frigid wind struck Spark, nearly driving her to her knees. Two demons remained, and both leapt at the returning ice dragoness. They were the only thing that saved Spark from being frozen solid.

Abyss shrieked from overhead. Spark conjured a new fire, opened a new portal, and released the trueflame all around her. It washed over her in a crashing wave of heat, whispers urging her to step through the portal. But Spark renewed her focus and hurled more trueflame at the ice dragoness. She heaved flame out everywhere. Then she staggered back until she could see beyond the wall of fire.

The burst of trueflame had slowed the ice dragoness as she tried to swoop past, but she still climbed higher and would soon be out of Spark's reach.

Spark glanced over her shoulder, and her breath caught in her chest

Nanny lay on the stones, struggling to rise, and Neesha raced for the stairs. Spark felt the air all around her, sifting between her fingers as she gathered the wind and launched a gust at her mother's escaping body—catching Neesha at the knees and tripping her. Neesha crashed to the floor, but with the chaotic flail of a rabid beast, she scrambled to her feet.

The dragoness was getting away, and Spark desperately needed help, but she couldn't let her possessed mother down into the keep to release horrors onto the staff. Zev and Unari and other allies were down there.

Spark cursed, gave the trueflame one last flare, and ran for Neesha.

But Abyss beat her to it, swooping down between them. When she lifted out of the way, Neesha lay pinned beneath the hatchling, who chirped another apology.

Spark stifled a laugh.

Nanny was back on her feet, calling more demons. Abyss pitched upward, spiralling away after the ice dragoness. Spark grabbed one of the demons and flung herself at Abyss's tail an instant before it rose out of reach.

Spark had one horrified moment to realize that she'd worked with this demon before, and then pushed the thought aside. She needed to climb. Despite the heat of Abyss's body, the air all around was burning cold

Before Abyss carried her beyond the reach of the trueflame, Spark used the boost from the demon to bring it with them. As long as Neesha or Nanny didn't close the fire portal, she'd have all the fire she needed. She cast it out, looping it around Abyss like armour.

Through flame and steam, she saw Abyss raking her claws at the ice dragoness's wings.

Spark had nearly climbed as far as Abyss's wings and paused between spikes to wrap her friend's arms and hands in fire. She used the fire to summon two more demons and send them up to help Abyss.

And fire, always more fire.

Never enough fire.

Spark called more of it, until her every thought was flame, the dark slashes of Abyss a distant memory. She ranged farther, flying like she had wings of her own.

It was too much, too fast.

Spark snatched for a spike to brace herself and catch her breath, but her feet propelled her farther, carrying the inferno with her.

Oh no.

Spark retreated to the farmhouse inside her mind, but it was all flame. She shut herself in the mental kitchen, watching helplessly as the demon used her body to drive itself the length of Abyss all the way up to her head, pouring fire like molten earth over both dragons.

Slick with meltwater, the ice dragoness twisted away from Abyss, who struggled to follow.

Spark watched the demon fling her off of Abyss to land on the ice dragoness, bringing all the fury of the fire realm with her.

Okay, I probably would have done that anyway...

The demon used her to call more of its kin. That was going to be a problem. And she wondered if the demon had considered what would happen once the ice dragoness melted completely. Spark searched between flickers of flame, but there was only darkness and sky around them.

They were a long way up.

But the fire outside Spark's mental kitchen door wasn't quite as bright. She heaved it open with a gust of mental aeromancy, pushing the demon back and then out of her body.

And immediately wished she'd waited.

Her hands, bare and unprotected, burned against the cold of the ice dragoness, even as the fire raged and steam hissed and rose all around. The sound splintered her thoughts.

Just as meltwater had allowed the ice dragoness to escape Abyss, it eventually left Spark with nothing to hold onto. When the ice dragoness's wing melted away, she flipped, and Spark was flung into the night.

The fire waned, but there were still seven fire demons attacking the ice dragoness.

Spark threw her arms and legs out wide, trying to slow her fall. The air caught the material of her glider. Her tired limbs tried to fold under the pressure, but Spark held herself rigid, bracing against it. She tried not to think of her family and Ember and Jatt, of the unfinished house and Shadow. She'd see them again.

She trusted Abyss to catch her.

CHAPTER THIRTY

D ionelle's aching body went cold when Spark disappeared into the night, but went numb as her granddaughter reappeared in a barely controlled plummet, much too far from the tower for her to have any hope of helping. Her pulse rushed in her ears. She could not stand by and watch another member of her family die.

But she couldn't look away.

That night at the farm played in a loop in her mind—the finality of Reiser, the man she'd loved for decades, her soul mate, going quiet, and the way his shattered body had been left in the dirt as Loch's dragons carried her off to the worst sort of hell. Superimposed over all of it was the memory of the massive blaze the last time she'd been in this tower, and the way Neesha's eyes had been blank and empty. While Neesha's eyes were currently alive with fire, nothing about her expression was *Neesha*.

The night darkened, obscuring the stars and Spark's fall. Dionelle gasped as fire erupted from the darkness. There was no sign of Spark until Dionelle heard her call to the dragoness to get higher.

She'd been saved... while Dionelle had done nothing but stand on this tower and watch, just as she had when she'd lost Neesha the first time. Dionelle glanced back at Neesha, still lost to fire and struggling to get out from under the baby dragon, who appeared to be napping.

Dionelle took a shaky breath.

The ice dragoness managed to stay aloft even as more and more of her disappeared under the fire demons' onslaught. From such a distance, the struggle was little more than an orange glimmer in the dark. Dionelle could track *her* dragoness—Abyss, she supposed, not quite used to the nickname Spark had given her—by the way the stars disappeared as she moved.

Abyss climbed above the ice dragoness, then circled beyond her diminishing reach. Blinding fire erupted in front of Abyss and trueflame poured out like a waterfall, with the speed of a wildfire on a windy mountain. The icy shape plummeted, and Abyss chased it down.

Water rained around the tower, engulfing Dionelle in drizzly mist.

Then Abyss swooped out of the gloom, setting Spark down with such speed that the girl tumbled and rolled. Spark staggered to her feet, and Dionelle set to the task of banishing the fire demons.

Abyss circled once more and then landed, more gently this time, clinging to the side of the tower with her head peeking over, watching.

"I stay!" the baby proclaimed.

"You've done well," Abyss said.

A smile ghosted Dionelle's lips. She focused on her task, clinging to it. Giving it all her attention drowned out the rest. When she'd finished sending away the last of the demons, she turned to find Spark collapsed to her knees next to Neesha and the baby dragon, a gutting look of despair on the girl's face. Dionelle's stomach clenched.

"Mamma, remember what I told you?"

There was no flicker of recognition on Neesha's face. Bile rose in Dionelle's throat. She wrapped her arms around herself, closing her eyes and trying to breathe through the panic. When she opened her eyes again, Spark was watching her expectantly. The girl looked weak. Had she been careless with demons tonight as well?

Dionelle shook her head. The hollow look in Neesha's expression was too much.

"You can do it, Nanny," Spark whispered. "I can guide you."

Dionelle closed her eyes again, hot tears streaking her cheeks, and hugged herself tighter. What if she failed? After so much loss, after a year of torment, could she survive losing Neesha again? Spark and Nandara insisted it wouldn't be like last time, that Spark could open another fire portal and reverse it immediately. But Dionelle had failed them all so much, so thoroughly in the last year—and so many of the years before. She felt like all she'd done was fail Neesha her entire life.

Spark was the only thing she'd done right—getting her away from the farm, giving her the opportunity for escape. The girl had grown so much in the last year. She'd absolutely blossomed since Dionelle had come to the valley with her and Neesha.

Spark and Neesha both wanted to know what the three of them together could achieve.

Dionelle opened her eyes and looked around. Well, they'd handed Loch a defeat without her. They'd stopped those ice dragons. There were at least half a dozen of the angriest and most broken dragons left for them to free.

But first, they needed Neesha restored.

Spark was exhausted. Dionelle was the only one currently capable of extracting the demon. Dionelle took a deep breath and wiped her face. She knelt down with her daughter and granddaughter. Neesha struggled—or the demon in her body did.

Spark did the best she could to describe the differences between Neesha's essence and the demon's. While she spoke, the baby dragon leaned his head against her, and she absently stroked his chin. Dionelle's lips twisted, the sweet agony of it nearly too much. She took a deep breath and focused on Spark's words.

"They're both hot, but one feels like being angry all the time and the other feels safe. Like love."

Dionelle smiled, warmth easing the tension in her chest. She leaned forward to touch Spark's cheek. Then she pushed up the sleeves of her firecloak and focused on her daughter. She began the spell to drive the demon out, just as she had seventeen years ago, but her throat closed and her stomach roiled. Her hands shook as she struggled to focus, to hold onto the magic.

When she neared the point where she was supposed to command the demon out, she paused, holding the magic. Pouring her focus into it, she let herself feel it. She'd woven pyromancy into this spell, something she didn't normally do, but had been Spark's suggestion. It certainly made it easier to register differences in the magic around Neesha.

The summoning spell was light and flickering, and there was the angry heat of the demon. At first it was all she could sense as she moved her hands right into the spell, nearly touching Neesha's chest—but there, *right there,* was the difference. Flickers of overwhelming heat, angry and painful. But also a more soothing heat, like sinking into a hot bath on a frigid winter night.

It felt like Neesha.

Dionelle tilted her head. It was almost like she could hear the difference. Like hearing a song and trying to tease out the melodies of the different instruments.

A dragon shrieked a battle cry in the distance. It wasn't Abyss. Dionelle gasped and nearly lost the spell. She glanced at Spark, who sat alert.

Abyss was still there, less of her attention on the three humans. They'd have some warning if danger approached. They had time.

Abyss shifted and the baby lifted his head. Dionelle thought she heard shouting from somewhere below them. Maybe they should abandon purging Neesha's possession for now, restrain her, and go help.

But Abyss was calm, and Dionelle thought she was close to succeeding. It would be better to finish this sooner. She sank back into the spell, her face scrunching up as she waded through comfort and pain, pushing the light flicker of the summoning spell in between.

It came apart all at once. Dionelle opened her eyes. The demon sprang up in front of her. She gasped and fell back, her addled mind bringing her all the way back to that cabin in the woods so many years ago, when her sister's fury had nearly ended the world.

Spark caught the demon, but the way Neesha was swearing—where had she even *heard* that kind of language?—told Dionelle everything she needed to know. She pressed a hand over her mouth to catch her own strangled sob of relief.

All her limbs felt warm and loose, her body buzzing.

Spark banished the demon.

"Nanny, you did it!" Spark flung her arms around Dionelle, who patted her back and sobbed into her shoulder.

"Shit, that was tense." Neesha leaned against the two of them, her arms tight around their shoulders. Abyss must have freed her from the hatchling, but Dionelle couldn't stem the tears. She leaned against Spark and Neesha, strength flooding back into her.

Abyss growled a low rumble that made the tower tremble. Running footfalls echoed from the stairway. Spark and Neesha pulled away, and

Dionelle barely caught herself on the rough stone. Spark pulled up a small fire that Neesha quickly took control of, ready to deal with what came next.

Unari and Zev emerged from the dark stairwell. Unari carried a lantern.

"You've done it, then? Those ice dragons are gone?" Unari asked.

"Best we can tell," Neesha said. "What's going on out there?"

Dionelle noticed for the first time all the fire in the distance, back toward the textile mill.

"Most of the palace guard was sent out to deal with whatever you've stirred up at the mill," Zev said. "They didn't last long once your dragoness arrived."

"There are some stray demons to be dealt with yet as well," Unari said.

Neesha cursed and parted with Spark and Nanny.

"Show me," she said. "It's time for me to set some things right."

"But Mamma, what about the rest of the dragons?" Spark asked.

"You go. I'll meet you there." Neesha left with Zev and Unari.

Dionelle felt colder watching her go, but Spark stayed fast to her side like she hadn't since she was a little girl. And in a lot of ways she *was* still a girl, no matter how much she'd grown, how much she seemed to be a woman.

A sad and lonely girl who had been left to do far too much for far too long. Spark's lip quivered as Neesha left. Dionelle reached out and took her hand, gesturing to Abyss with her chin.

"Right," Spark said, "we need to go."

Abyss picked up both the hatchling and Dionelle. "Quickly," she said. "We've got much work left ahead of us."

Dionelle reached a hand out to Spark. The girl shook herself, clearing her expression—a smile flickered across her face, her amber eyes dancing.

"It's okay, Nanny. I'll take a fire portal and meet you there."

Dionelle watched her go as Abyss lifted off. Dionelle felt light, lighter than she had since before Neesha had even been born, and she settled in against her dear old friend as they headed into a long night's work.

CHAPTER THIRTY-ONE

As Abyss landed gently and reverently set Spark, Neesha, and Nanny down in the field of long grasses and tangled weeds, Spark looked out at the ruins of the farmhouse she'd grown up in. She'd been trembling ever since it—or what was left of it, anyway—had come into view during the short flight from Pasdale. She'd learned from Unari, after the last of the dragons were freed and the eggs carried off to safety, that neighbours had usurped the abandoned fields and orchards, but that no one came near the ruins of the buildings.

It hurt Spark's heart and made her angry. She couldn't tell what it made Nanny and Neesha feel. Both of them looked so strangely neutral in the bit of firelight from her hands.

Spark wasn't sure she wanted more light than that, but Abyss was already lighting a fire with venom, making a warm little nest for her baby to sleep in. The heat of her body was good for him, but flames would be even better for a while yet, or so she'd told them.

"I don't think I can do this," Spark whispered.

"Gods, this is awful."

Nanny squeezed Spark's hand. Then she let go and walked into the space between the buildings' ruins. Spark swallowed bile and focused on the crackle of the baby's sleeping fire to push out the sounds intruding on her thoughts. She didn't want Nanny to find anything. She braced for when she did.

Nanny gasped and sank to her knees, pulling back the tangle of overgrown weeds. She sobbed, the sound piercing the night. Spark's chest ached and her eyes prickled with tears of her own. Neesha carried over the blanket Zev had given them on parting like a peace offering. Spark stayed back, crying silently while Neesha and Nanny gathered up Pappy's bones.

No one had come out here. Nearly a year and there'd been no pyre.

It was a haunted place. No wonder the neighbours had touched only the fields. Spark wasn't sure if looters would have been worse. Then again, a lot of it had been destroyed. There were only a few charred boards left of the barn.

She went over and pulled what was left into a pile. They'd need it before long, though she guessed Abyss would volunteer a bit of venom if required.

And they might need it, if they wanted to be out of Pasdale by dawn.

The bundled blanket that Neesha carried seemed too small to hold an entire grown man. That hurt most of all. But there was plenty of hurt left to come.

Neesha used terramancy and some help from Abyss to clear away the stone debris of the old house, enough to create a path from where the porch used to be to the entrance to the cellar.

Spark came closer as Neesha lifted a charred board to reveal a jumble of bones. Bren and Uncle Breen had died huddled together.

Spark sobbed but stayed back as Nanny and Neesha carefully moved the bones onto the blanket with Pappy's. While they did, Spark gathered up more wood, occasionally kicking through the debris for any hint of her old life. But the dragonfire had left nothing recognizable. Even the bones didn't seem like the vibrant family she remembered.

When Nanny and Neesha, each with two corners of the blanket—fuller now, less of a pitiful bundle—came over, Spark had arranged everything into a makeshift pyre as best she could remember from when they'd pyred Nanny Sharice what felt like an eternity ago.

Building the pyre was to be her only contribution. Neesha had insisted before they set out that the bodies weren't to be Spark's responsibility, that she had been responsible for enough.

It felt strange not to be in the middle of it. And unfathomably relieving.

Once Nanny stood back, with everything arranged properly, Spark lit the wood and stood back with them. They huddled together, their arms around each other, watching the flames. Nanny shook with sobs and Spark held her tighter, feeling Neesha squeezing Nanny on her other side.

Spark let go only to draw the pendant out of her inner pocket. She wasn't sure why she'd brought it, but it had seemed right. She held it out to Nanny, whose mouth twisted almost into a smile before the sobbing crumpled her. But once Nanny collected herself, she took the pendant to the pyre. She grimaced against the pain of the heat as she laid it carefully among the bones, smaller now, all of it diminishing.

A rush of silver light burst forth. It was warm, like when Spark had brushed Neesha's essence while untangling it from the demon.

Nanny gasped. An overwhelming sense of Pappy's presence made Spark choke back a sob.

"I feel it too. It's him," Neesha said, the words trembling and tight through her tears.

The light faded and so did the fire, the glow of dawn gently brushing the mountains to the east. Abyss stood, having watched silently and still the whole time. She collected her baby and arranged him on her back so that the straps of the sling held him firm. Then she reached out her hand, laying it on the ground near Nanny.

"It is time, old friend."

Nanny nodded, but leaned in for another hug with Spark and Neesha. Then she climbed onto the outstretched hand to be lifted to the human-purposed part of the sling.

Nanny would not be travelling through the agony of the fire realm any more, if it could be helped. She was to travel with Abyss, first to the Wizards Guild, where the eggs would be safe, and then over land, far to the frigid north, where a vast archipelago under the ice offered them safety. It would be a long journey—two days north, five days west, and then two days south once again—before they'd reach the dragon city.

With the eggs and the wounded dragons still dealing with the trauma of their captivity, it was entirely possible that it would be even more days than that. Perhaps even double the time to safely make the journey.

"Go," Neesha said to them. "We'll have the city prepared for your return."

Abyss nuzzled the both of them before taking flight.

"Ready then?" Neesha asked, a quick glance around at the ruin of what had once been her home too.

And while this farm would never be a home again, Neesha had expressed hope that maybe one day Pasdale would be. Freeing all of the captive dragons as they had would be ruinous in the short term, but Unari and Zev were already working to blame everything on Loch's sloppy leadership—spinning the narrative that he had abandoned Pasdale to its doom. It wasn't far from the truth—Loch had taken so many of the dragons with him to build a foolish army for the king, after all. Zev was whispering in all the right ears.

Spark worried that Loch might return yet, but Unari insisted they would make sure he wouldn't have a warm reception if he did. He might take aim for the dragon city again, yes, but they had freed so many of the dragons he'd hoped to use in his machinations.

And some of those dragons had escaped into the night, offering no aid but no hindrance either. Abyss suspected some of them were bent on revenge and would seek Loch out wherever he had fled to.

Some would likely linger on the fringes of Pasdale to cause trouble. That could be a problem, but one for later. If Nandara's allies here in the city were to be believed, it would be quite some time before Loch or the tattered remains of his following would be a concern.

Spark managed a smile. "Yes, I'm ready. Let's go home."

This piece of land wasn't home anymore, but the dragon city was a place that was familiar. It was safe. Ember would be there. And maybe Jatt.

Neesha performed the summoning. Half the blaze had gone with Abyss to the Guild, but the rest were coming back with them. As they approached—dark, silent shapes against the growing light of dawn—Spark opened a fire portal big enough to accommodate them.

She stepped into the heat of it, ready for the warmth of home.

CHAPTER THIRTY-TWO

Spark hooked her new quick release for the tether onto one of the anchors in a patch of rigging to test that it worked, and set it down on the worktable. Shadow raised his head at the sound.

"What do you think? One more?"

Shadow curled up again. But only until the door creaked open and Ember came in.

"You in here talking to the dog again?" She joined Spark at the table, saw what her girlfriend was working on, and tutted. "You're supposed to be taking a break."

"I know, but I can't stop worrying." Spark sighed.

Ember gave her a sad smile and took her hand. Spark appreciated the gesture and that it didn't come with empty suggestions about just forgetting her worries. Ember *wanted* Spark to forget about it, but knew as well as Spark did that even a distant and defeated Loch was still a threat.

Raia and her blaze hadn't returned, and weren't sure when they would, as they continued the search for her brother. But they'd followed Loch as he fled and reported back. He'd rejoined a larger force on the southern shore of the ocean and they'd lost track of him after that.

Neesha was less worried. Loch didn't have the same sort of revenge complex his predecessor had had. But he was out there making the world more miserable for *someone,* even if it wasn't them. That didn't sit well. Spark wanted to be ready if he decided he *did* want vengeance, but also to be ready to fly out with the other dragon riders to stop whatever his new plot was.

But there was still the problem of crossing the oceans.

It had taken twelve days for Abyss to return with Nanny and the hatchling.

"It's your birthday, so no brooding!" Ember squeezed her hand and kissed her cheek, then pulled her out of the forge entirely.

They went to the studio, where Jatt had been agonizing over that painting again. Spark was surprised he was working on it in such a bright space, but he claimed he had the mood right and needed to see what he was doing for the final touches.

He barely acknowledged them as they came in.

Ember went to her worktable, which Stone and Jatt had put together not long after Spark had returned from Pasdale. The two of them had borrowed Hextir's mule and hauled blocks from the quarry so Spark and Neesha could finish Neesha's room, and then Spark had finished the studio. It was fully enclosed now, with a proper roof and walls, and big bright windows, and a door to the outside they could prop open on warm days to let the paint fumes out.

"What do you think?" Ember asked, picking up the expanse of lovely purple dragon skin she'd been working with. It was a flight suit, like Spark's, that Ember had made from Neesha's old wizarding robes. Robes were falling out of fashion with younger wizards, and this was more practical for Neesha to work fire in, but also for flying. Ember had stylized it with some of the straps and buckles Neesha had used to secure it in battle.

Spark wasn't entirely sure of her mother's taste—Neesha herself didn't seem entirely sure of what she liked, still growing into herself after having everything upended. But she thought Neesha would like it.

"If nothing else, it's practical. And thoughtful," Spark said. "And I like it, so if she doesn't, you can just resize it for me."

Ember swatted her. "You've got your own gift from me! You don't need to go stealing your mother's!"

While today was Spark's seventeenth birthday, they were also going to celebrate Neesha's thirty-fifth. It had been only days after her actual birthday that Spark had finally succeeded in waking her up, and Neesha insisted that was all the gift she needed, but she was getting a party anyway. And proper gifts.

Ember turned to wrap the suit in gift cloth and ribbons. Jatt called Spark over to his secret little corner, though he was less secretive today, with the easel turned toward the window.

She stopped a polite distance away, but he waved her around. "I'm ready to show you. I think."

His shoulders were bunched up like he was trying to stab himself in the head with them, and he gripped his paintbrush awfully tight. Surprisingly, he didn't back down when Spark came around to see. She stopped short.

It was a portrait of a younger Nandara, weeping at the fallen dragon city, with chunks of the city in mid-tumble and rain like demons bringing it down.

"Oh my," Spark breathed.

She looked from the painting to Jatt, but he wasn't looking at the canvas—he was looking at her. He nodded at her reaction.

"That's the look I was hoping to get with it." He pointed the brush in the general direction of her face.

"You should show it to her."

His shoulders, which had started to come down, bunched up around his ears again. And because he was distracted and his defences were down, he didn't see Ember come around the side of the easel in time to stop her. Spark tensed as well.

Ember stopped short and gasped. "Oh wow."

Jatt's shoulders managed to climb even higher, but Spark relaxed.

Ember looked at him and grinned. "Next time, paint something this good but happy, will you?"

Jatt made an exasperated sound and swiped his paint brush across the tip of Ember's nose. She shrieked with false indignation and danced away to swipe up one of his rags.

"Spark's right, though," Ember said, wiping her face. "You should show it to your gran."

"I'll think about it." He pointed his brush at Spark again. "Speaking of Gran, she'll be here any minute. You should let your ma know it's almost dinnertime."

Spark smiled, gave Ember a quick kiss, and headed up the stairs to Neesha's room, which was as fully finished as the studio. The short hallway outside her door was done, and the stairs fully enclosed as well. Spark had a makeshift door to outside just beyond the top of the stairs. There was no more need for tarps—if they didn't get the final rooms finished, Neesha's part of the building would still be cozy and safe through the winter's fury.

Spark wasn't really sure what to do with the remaining space upstairs anyway. Now that Nanny was settled with Ondias, Spark didn't need as much space as she'd envisioned. She was going to move her bedroom up here someday and leave her current room for storage, but with a cot for Jatt so he didn't have to blunder home through the dark on the nights he stayed up painting too late.

But, well, it didn't look like Ember was going to need or want a bedroom of her own. The two of them had talked about moving Jatt's studio upstairs, with skylights for even better lighting, so Ember could entirely take over the downstairs workspace.

But there was time to figure everything out, and it didn't all need to be done now.

Spark smiled and knocked on Neesha's door before letting herself in. There was a new desk that Neesha sat at, quill in hand and scribbling notes while glaring down at the book in front of her. She was studying for the Guild's full exam. Spark was too. They'd both learned remarkable things and had better control of their magic, but they had so much left to learn—Guild entrance was months, if not years, away yet. But they were studying together, with Nandara and Ondias frequently popping in to help with lessons. And sometimes Nanny helped in her own silent way.

Neesha set her pen down and smiled up at Spark as she entered. "Time already?"

"They'll be here soon."

"All right. Is Dionelle still out there?"

Spark shrugged. "I haven't seen her come down."

The two of them went out the door at the top of the stairs to the rooftop patio that Nanny had made mostly for herself, but also for all of them. There were comfortable old chairs clustered about the open space, most of them pointed toward the stunning views of the dragon city and the mountain range beyond, all of it glittering with light. There were some tables, too, and even some large containers of plants, most of them going dormant with the season.

It was a cozy, beautiful space that Spark hadn't imagined in her initial plans, but there was no way she could close in the entire roof. She hadn't spent nearly as much time up here as Nanny did, but she could envision it being her favourite spot on a warm summer day.

Nanny reclined in a chair, her gaze only half focused on the horizon, a content smile on her face. A lot of the time, Spark found her up here crying, though there'd been less of that as the days had gone on. She'd been in touch with Spark's uncles in Baymouth Shores, and there was a plan for a springtime visit that was certainly helping Nanny's spirits.

Nanny turned her head to watch them approach, her eyes glittering. She pointed to the east, to Abyss's clan tower, which was made out of a shimmering blue stone Spark could never remember the name of—something that started with an A? The inside was absolutely stunning, like a massive geode—far more opulent than she expected from Abyss, reminding her that she didn't really know her friend as well as she could.

Spark focused on the tower and grinned as a small dark shape glided in lazy circles around it. One of Abyss's hatchlings. They were just learning to fly.

"Ondias says once they're strong flyers, Abyss and her mate will take them back to the mountains near Pasdale," Neesha said. "They'll go in the spring at the latest."

"It'll be weird without them here. Is it really safe for them to be that close to Pasdale?"

"I got the impression they'll be gathering the old blaze, all of them taking up residence in those mountains again."

Nanny nodded slowly.

"I guess with that many of them, they'll be able to keep each other safe," Spark said.

"And I don't think they're going to actually go anywhere near Pasdale itself. They'll stick to themselves, or the local nomadic clans, until it's properly safe again."

"Do you think it ever will be safe?" Spark glanced at Neesha.

"I hope so. It'd be nice to be able to go back. Maybe even to stay."

Spark knew her mother was thinking of the lady friend Nandara was helping her locate. It always made her feel torn—she wanted her mother to find proper happiness, but she also didn't want her mother to leave.

The three of them watched as another little dark shape joined the first, looping around the tower. They stayed there until the clatter of a wagon signalled the arrival of the rest of the party guests. By the time Spark got back downstairs, Ondias, Nandara, and Stone were in the kitchen, making the last of the preparations while Shadow wove around their feet, trying to get one of them to trip and drop something tasty.

Nandara's birthday gift was one of food—she'd made Neesha's favourite meal and Spark's favourite dessert. Everyone crowded around the new, larger table. Enough scraps ended up in the dog that he went to lie down in the corner to nap long before they'd finished eating. Spark sank into the noise and the laughter, letting it fill her. She'd nearly forgotten this joy.

As Jatt helped his grandmother clear away dishes, gifts emerged, piled in front of Neesha and Spark. Neesha loved the flight suit from Ember, and she appreciated the thoughtfulness and skill of Jatt's gift of a portrait of her and Abyss. Spark gave her a stylized dagger that matched Spark's axe.

"Maybe I should learn how to use this," Neesha said, smirking.

Stone gifted her with a pendant made from bits of diamond, obsidian, and the red stones of the mountain, and Spark wondered what wizard he'd found to make something so intricate. Ondias had books for both of them—for Spark, she had a hand-bound copy of her latest book on dragons, and for Neesha, the books she'd been studying for her exam so many years ago.

"Found them in the back of a bookshelf while clearing some more space for Di," she said. "So now you can get back to it."

Jatt had made Spark a small sculpture of Abyss in flight to help decorate the house, and Stone had gifted a particularly generous amount of his famous wine.

With no more gifts left on the table, Nandara and Ondias left.

"They already know, but there's a whole wagon of scrap iron in the market with your name on it," Neesha said. "It'll be delivered tomorrow."

Spark tilted her head and grinned, her mind immediately making checklists of what to use it for.

Ember put a hand on Spark's wrist to get her attention. "My gift is for later." Her tone was coy and her eyes glittered.

Spark's cheeks went hot and everyone else burst out laughing.

A playful smile on her face, Ember leaned in to whisper, "I made this particular dress to be unwrapped. Slowly."

It was a good thing Spark's face was already as warm as it could get. Ember pecked a kiss on her cheek and sat back, chuckling.

"Well, I suppose it's time for me to take my leave," Stone said, looking to Nanny, who he was escorting back to Ondias's. She smiled and nodded.

Jatt stayed in the kitchen to continue cleaning up while Ember went with her father to the door to see him off.

Nanny stopped Spark and Neesha in the hallway, taking their hands and beaming at them. "I'm proud of you both. Reiser would be too."

Neesha managed to both laugh and sob at once, squeezing Nanny's hand. Spark leaned in to wrap them both up in her arms while Ember came back in, grinning at them all. Spark still felt the ache of losing Bren and Uncle Breen and Pappy—especially the way they would have loved it here and would have fit right in with all this extended family—but she also felt light and warm, like she was filled with a gentle fire. Finally, her life was full again.

Scan here or visit thodestool.ca/news to learn more about Vanessa's work or to sign up for her newsletter.

THE DRAGON NEXT DOOR: A FIREBORN SERIES SIDE QUEST

A Sneak Peek

YESTERDAY

Tollar could make water do anything she wanted, but she never expected to have to boil it under a stolen dragon egg while rafting upriver for five days straight. Her feet shifted on the water's surface as she balanced behind the egg, steam billowing warm on her face, the rapids propelling them both down the river and closer to safety. Tollar was safe enough anywhere she had a decent sized body of water to work with. But this egg? It needed fire. And it needed to stay hidden until Tollar could come to grips with the enormity of what she'd done.

She inhaled the cool night air, closed her eyes and focused on the rush of water beneath her. The roar through the canyon drowned out the sizzle around the egg, but the sound pitched to thundering fury up ahead.

"Wait, what?"

Even leaning way out, Tollar couldn't see around the enormous egg. Only the dim shape of rock walls loomed high in the darkness at her sides, so she crouched on the water, pressing her fingers down into it to extend her senses into the river.

To where it dropped.

"Shit, already?"

She kept her hand in the water, feeling the river like an extension of herself—another long, meandering limb—feeling when the water under her tipped over the edge of the rock shelf like sliding one leg over the edge of the bed. She bent her hand level with the horizon and splayed her fingers, holding the water stable under her and the egg, letting gravity do the rest.

Like she had once already. Like she'd have to do once more after this. And never mind the two sodding waterfalls she'd had to go *up*.

"Another drop," she called to the egg. "But I've got it."

While she and the egg plummeted on her little half-boiling water shelf, the rush of air lifting her long dark braid to stream above her, Tollar extended her senses to the river below. Making a fist in her mind, she held the water, stopping it from flowing away so that it piled up beneath, defying the riverbanks. Until her water shelf hit the water below and she unclenched, letting the river flow naturally.

Like that time she and her oldest brother, Jarku, had piled every last cushion against the side of the house and jumped off the roof.

A corner of Tollar's mouth curled at the memory. So few of her memories were good ones when it came to her family that she cherished them when they surfaced.

But the water under her feet lurched and sagged, like some exhausted beast collapsing. Tollar's brain buzzed behind her eyes and she closed them until it stopped. She gasped as she lost her balance and nearly tumbled into the river. Again. The water around her calmed and the egg sank.

"Gah!"

Her thoughts skipped along the surface of her mind like a stone across a pond. This was too much and it was too late. Gritting her teeth, she solidified the water under her feet, pushed more water under the egg to get it on the surface, and began the painstaking process of heating that water up through absolute stubbornness. Flapping her hands like she fanned a fire.

As the river glided around her stationary water island, Tollar scanned for a place to stop. Jumbled boulders loomed out of the dark on both banks, the silhouette of the viny jungle canopy reaching across the gap to obscure the night sky. Ahead, on the inside curve of the river, the land flattened out, looked grassy.

"It'll have to do," Tollar muttered to the egg, rubbing her hands over her face. She'd never heard a dragon talk, but she knew they listened.

The current carried her little water barge to the bend, and she stepped off the water, her boots thudding over solid ground. Dead and boring and unmoving. When she focused, the water moving between grains of sand sang out to her like her people sang on the solstice to welcome the rains and a cycle continued.

Tonight she did not have that kind of focus and was glad she wouldn't sink into the ground if she didn't think hard enough about it. Not having to think about that for the moment freed up some brain space so she could strongarm the river's current, using wide stirring gestures to guide her focus, and use it to hollow out part of the bank where she left the egg sizzling in a boiling pond.

"We're almost there, little friend." Tollar glanced at the egg and then stared downriver. "One more waterfall. A couple more hours. But not tonight."

She considered lying down with her gear and longsword strapped to her back.

"Never get any rest that way," she groaned, unbuckling everything and dropping it to the ground. She sprawled on the grass, not bothering with her sleep mat, and used her gear as a pillow.

She had to keep the water boiling to keep the egg's inhabitant warm. She'd done it for four nights. But she really didn't think she could do it for very many more. Spending two days going against the current at the start had taken far more out of her than she anticipated.

"I don't know what those raiders wanted with you, but I'll keep you safe."

In reply, the egg sat silently in its gurgling, steamy puddle. Whether the egg—more specifically the baby it contained—heard and understood her, it seemed right to reassure it the best she could. Hopefully her efforts and the boiling water were enough.

It was a far cry from where she'd found it, in a lake of fire with a half dozen other dragon eggs next to a pen of chained and captive dragons, all inside a guarded compound. Keeping dragons captive was something she hadn't thought possible, much less by the people she'd gone there to fight, the raiders who'd taken over the port and laid waste to half the harbour.

Tollar had friends in the port, ones she hadn't been able to locate. It was probably too much to hope that they were still alive.

The gurgling pond rolled to a furious boil as Tollar's pulse throbbed in her ears. She pressed her fists against her forehead and took a long, slow breath before raking her fingers down her face and exhaling in a groan.

"What a sodding mess."

She hated she hadn't been able to do more. Dragons didn't belong in chains. Port Sawulxo and her friends deserved better. She'd have taken all of the eggs and freed all the dragons if she could. Would have stolen every last grain of salt those raiders had if that would have actually done some good. Instead she'd done the only thing she could—taken this one egg and run.

There was only one safe place to go. Only one place where she could trust people until she made sense out of what she'd seen in the port four days ago. That was, if being stuck exposed on this stupid plateau didn't doom them both. Tollar was half asleep despite the cool air but watching the night sky all the same, waiting to see if any dragons would spot her with this egg she wasn't supposed to have.

So far the night was full of the usual chatter of monkeys and birds, the buzz of insects. Nothing indicated something was lurking, waiting to pounce. No mountain cat lurking nearby to make a meal of her in her sleep.

But the quiet in the skies was odd. She really had expected to encounter dragons by now. There was a whole blaze of them living in these mountains.

Sleeping in the wild again hadn't been part of her plan. She'd meant to sneak into the farm a little later in the night and be tucked away somewhere safe. Safe and next door to her best friend. Tollar smiled up at the sky.

Stars glittered overhead, sharper and clearer than she'd seen in nearly a year, and the moons either hadn't risen yet or were both set. She never paid much attention to their phases. This trip, she'd spent most of her time in damp, turbulent places where the stars were blurred if not totally obscured. And they were different stars than the last time she'd bothered looking up at the night sky. She wasn't entirely sure how long it had been since she'd crossed the equator, heading south and not far inside the borders of Upalint, her home nation, but these were the constellations of her childhood.

She tried not to think too much about that.

But Beenala would be home—she was rarely anywhere else—and that was something to look forward to. And Tollar would have somewhere quiet and out of the way to stash this egg until the right sort of dragons got her message and came for it.

Hopefully it wouldn't take long. Tollar rarely stayed home long, and Beenala wouldn't be thrilled about having a dragon egg around.

Tollar sighed. Dropping in out of nowhere like this—she always dropped in out of nowhere, but it was the part about the dragon egg that would be interesting—had all sorts of potential to go very wrong. Tollar didn't like the idea of disrupting the carefully cultivated routine of the only proper friend she had.

"Nothing for it." Couldn't go back and didn't have the energy to get much further.

She shifted closer to the riverbank, as close to the heat of the boiling water as she could—the water itself wouldn't hurt her if she fell in, it was the boiling part that worried her—and let the warmth of it lull her.

Just a bit of rest and then she'd finish the trip home.

ACKNOWLEDGEMENTS

First of all, I want to thank my burnout for finally fucking off into the sun. This is the first book I've written since the pandemic started, when I was formerly a book a year writer (at least! Sometimes I wrote more!). I'd also like to thank anyone still masking in public. This pandemic is never going to fucking end, but I appreciate the care and solidarity. It doesn't feel like we're all in this together anymore, and it just makes me so so tired. So if you're still out there rocking a mask, I see you and I appreciate you. Some of us, at least, are still in this together.

Burnout is a beast. Writing wasn't necessarily the problem, it was the world and the selfishness and the greed—all of it so much worse than I thought (and honestly I've become really pessimistic)—I was burnt out on the worst of humanity, and it sapped me of my creativity. I still had gardening, and occasionally I'd paint, but March 2020 to April 2022 were mostly filled with tears and despair.

Nothing has gotten better. Honestly, it's getting worse, but I think I've acclimatized to the new awful. Whatever the shift was, in April last year, I was finally able to start writing again. The words were often a struggle, another thing that's new for me. But the words came, usually in the right order.

I put the outline for this book together, and it was very different than what I had originally planned. I was going to kill off Neesha! I'm glad I came to my senses. This book needed to be something brighter and more hopeful—it needed to be a light shining in the dark. It needed more joy because I think we all need more of that right now, and it can be hard to find and maybe like we shouldn't be looking for joy when the world is going to hell while we helplessly stand back and watch.

I don't think we're as helpless as all that, and we need joy to fuel us if we're going to fight for a better tomorrow. I think we need the reminder of exactly what we're fighting for. In the end, that's what this book is about—coming together to make something better out of something terrible.

Anyway, I also want to thank spite. I literally would not be here without it. Especially this year, as my body rebels and my meds don't work. Spite drags me through each day, because fuck you that's why. Sometimes, that's all I've got. But if it gets me through, I'll take it.

Okay, time for some more tangible thanks. I want to thank my spouse and my kid for their support and patience as I've disappeared behind the laptop so so much this last year, struggling to hit deadlines that hadn't seemed quite so impossible when I first set them. And thanks to my dogs for always being good.

Thank you especially to my beta readers, Lisa and Nat, for reading this book without having read all of the others. It was an impossible task, but your insights helped me figure out what this book was missing. I added 16,000 words! And a lot of them are fun words. I hadn't had fun writing since the Beforetimes. Thank you for helping to make this book so much better.

Thank you to my editors, Kris and Chelle, for doing a lot of heavy lifting when I didn't get as much time to spend as I'd have liked with each draft. This year has been an eternal parade of disasters, but thanks to you both, I've been able to get this book out on time! And extra thanks to Chelle for the last-minute save and for being profoundly thorough with the copy edits.

I want to thank everyone who's given me guidance on the whole promotion thing, especially Michael and Tao. I still suck at promotion, but thanks to these two, I suck at it a little less.

Thanks to everyone who supported the Fireborn Kickstarter—this book wouldn't exist without you. And thank you, dear reader, for sticking with the series. I especially couldn't (or at least wouldn't want to) keep doing this without you.

ABOUT THE AUTHOR

photo by Mike Thode

Vanessa is a word sorceress and Nebula Award-winning fantasy author whose life seldom strays from the world of books, especially during winter hibernation. Even her volunteer work revolves around the literary world, currently as co-founder and events director of KW Writers Alliance and as coordinator for the SFWA volunteer team.

When she's not being bookish, she's into astronomy, hiking, gardening, and has a personal goal to visit all the national parks. Don't ask her about her love of trees unless you've got some time. She loves Halloween and hates to be cold. Vanessa lives in Waterloo (no, the other one) with her spouse, daughter, and dogs, where she can be found in her butterfly garden, achieving her final form as a garden witch.

To learn more, visit thodestool.ca or follow her on social media @VRicciThode

www.ingramcontent.com/pod-product-compliance
Lightning Source LLC
Chambersburg PA
CBHW061753190726
48289CB00007B/1939